BITTER THORNS

THE ENTWINED BOOK 1

CHRISSY JAYE

Cover Artist: EVE Graphic design

Content Editor: ADYTUM

Proofing: TBR Editing & Design

Format: Gina Writes Words: Author Services

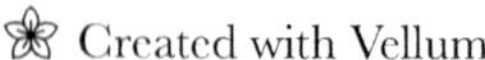

This book is dedicated to my Lehnu - the destined souls who have changed my life for the better.

WARNING

This book uses adult themes in life-like situations. If you are sensitive to emotional flashbacks, physical violence, and/or sexual abuse, you may want to abstain from reading. With that in mind, most of the events happen before the book starts and are referenced events that the main character struggles through.

CHAPTER 1

"Where are we going?" I asked Emma for the third or fourth time. She didn't answer as she threw a dark Henley tee-shirt in my direction.

"We're leaving early," my foster sister finally muttered, throwing the contents of our shared dresser onto the end of my bed.

I snagged a pair of black leggings from the pile and I rolled my eyes. I wasn't sure what the weather was like outside. August in the Pacific Northwest held no guarantees; it could be chilly, humid, foggy, or outright hot at any given moment. Mother Nature seemed to like giving us a taste of every season at least once a day.

I sat on the faded lemon-yellow bedspread and dragged the leggings on. "You said that already and totally avoided my question. *Where* are we going and why in the middle of the damn night?"

I glanced at the clock next to my twin bed. It was just after two in the morning. I'd barely been asleep before she'd rolled me out of bed. Literally rolled me. Apparently refusing her more gentle nudging had been unacceptable, no matter the time.

She tossed my sneakers at my feet with a dismissive grunt.

"Really? We're grunting now? Need I remind your grumpy butt that it was *you* who woke *me*," I quipped, hoping a bit of humor would lighten her up.

"Your brother and a friend are waiting in the car outside. I told you that," she snapped with a bit more irritation in her voice than I was used to.

She was being frustrating, but I couldn't see the point in arguing with her any further. She wanted to leave early? Fine, we'd leave early. I snatched up my bag, glaring down at her blonde head. I moved to our beat-up dresser with attached mirror and grabbed the few things I couldn't leave without. My Mother's silver bracelet was a must take and several pictures of me, Emma, and Payton as well.

"You know we can't leave without saying goodbye to her," I said, shoving one of them under her nose and pointing to Payton. It was one of my favorites from last summer. We'd gone to a party to celebrate becoming seniors. Our smiles stretched from ear to ear, arms locked around each other, running on a high after a night filled with laughter, feeling as though we didn't have a care in the world.

"We can call her when we get there," Emma said, pushing it away.

I huffed at her dismissal. Annoyance was morphing into anger really quick. She was acting ridiculous. I took a steadying breath before I said something I would regret later. "We can't just leave. We have people who will miss us. Our foster parents for one," I pointed out, trying another tactic. True, I wasn't overly fond of our foster parents, or adults in general, but I really didn't like this sudden change in our plans.

Emma sat up after zipping up her bag and pierced me with her blue eyes. "We'll call her. She knew we were leaving."

"Yeah, but—"

"For once in your stubborn life, just do as I ask. Your bullshit causes enough problems," Emma snapped.

Ouch. My mouth opened and closed as I tried thinking about what to say. We rarely, if ever, fought. I turned away from her, hoping to hide the hurt I was sure was plastered all over my face. Had I caused a few problems for us over the years? Yeah, but Emma had never called me out like that before. What hurt the most was how right she was.

A shuddering breath escaped my lips as I took a last look around the small bedroom for the last time, using it to distract myself from the tears that wanted to fall. As far as foster homes went, this was a pretty good one. Though it wasn't much of a room, it had been the safest space I'd had been in a long time. I never went to sleep on my single bed and had to worry whether someone would drag me from it in the middle of the night. But if I did, Emma was only a few feet away in a matching bed, separated by a single nightstand.

More often than not, we ended up squished together on either bed to ride out my nightmares. No one had ever run screaming into the room demanding to search our dresser, which sat across the room, just because they thought we were doing drugs. And while the cream carpet and beige walls were old and worn in places, they'd always been clean. I'd never been forced onto my hands and knees with a scrub brush, trying to get my own blood to come out of it.

"Liv—" she started, but I waved her off. It was already forgotten. Replaced with the reality that we were leaving.

"Vi's outside?" I asked quickly as I returned to packing. Mentally, I pleaded with her to let it go. I wasn't good at being vulnerable. Even if she was my best friend. At least I'd have a good excuse when we called Payton tomorrow morning. She'd understand that my brother had come to get us. I hoped she would at least. Him being here was the only reason I wasn't tucking myself back into bed. I wanted to peek out the window to get a glimpse of him, just to alleviate my guilt, but our bedroom was at the back of the house.

"Yeah. He's been driving all day just to get here

but we wanted it to be a surprise for you," Emma said with false cheer that made me snort.

"What about our fosters? You're not eighteen until next week," I said as I zipped up my small bag and heaved it onto the bed.

"I left a note. It should do," she replied vaguely. "Got everything you want?"

"Yeah," I said softly, taking in the room one last time. Was it sad that the thing I liked best about this room was that no one had ever broken down the door to beat me in the middle of the night? What a shitty thing to be grateful for.

We crept downstairs on silent feet, skipping the bottom step because it creaked like an old hag. I half expected Claire, our foster mother, to know we were sneaking out in the middle of the night, but the downstairs was dark and deserted. We tiptoed to the front door and eased it open. Guilt gnawed at me for a moment, but as soon as I stepped out, the sight of Vian leaning against the door of a shiny silver SUV stopped that feeling in its tracks.

Bag in tow, I tore across the front lawn and launched myself at him. He caught me as my arms wrapped around his neck and surprised even myself as my legs clenched around his waist. I knew in the back of my mind somewhere that we had an audience, but I didn't care. Let them think whatever they wanted. Nothing and no one was going to get between me and the best hug I'd had in months. There was nothing sexual about our reunion. Just the bitter memories of a bitch who thought to sexualize two young kids and ruin what was left of their childhood.

"Hey Olive," he said into my hair. I took in a deep breath of his spicy cologne that I absolutely loathed and relaxed into his arms.

"You're taller again," I muttered hugging him tighter, making him chuckle.

"I know. It's a product of eating. You should try it sometime," he quipped.

I leaned back and swatted at his chest, somewhat startled to realize he had bulked up some muscle in the last eight months. We talked all the time on a shitty cell-plan that he paid for, but this was the first time I'd seen him since just after Christmas.

He looked tired, but good. His shock of auburn hair was longer than I'd ever seen it. It fell in waves across his forehead and around to his ears. Green eyes, exactly like mine, twinkled at me as I noted the changes to his face. His jaw was sharper, there was less fat in his cheeks. He'd turned into a man and I'd missed it. I wondered if he saw the same thing when he looked at me.

"Speaking of eating? Are you like Popeye now?" The tension in my shoulders eased as we took stock of one another. There was so much happiness in his eyes that I was able to forget that Emma had ruined a perfectly good night of sleep. Seeing my twin, being able to hug him, to talk to him, made it all worth it.

Home. That was Octavian for me. We might not

look like twins anymore, but he was my forever person. The one who would always be there for me.

"It would be *really* awkward if I was since you're Olive," he joked.

Eww. Yeah, no more Popeye references. A horrified expression filled my features as I frowned at his humor.

"Hate to break up the reunion, but we should go," a honeyed male voice said softly.

I let my gaze drift from my brother to a guy standing a few feet away from us. I hadn't really noticed him until now. I'd been solely focused on my twin. The guy was tall with broad shoulders, but I couldn't tell what color his hair or eyes were with the dim lighting. The closest streetlamp was halfway down the block, and the moonlight tended to wash people's features out.

Sweat beaded down my forehead and I realized it was incredibly humid out. I patted Vian's arm to get him to put me down, self-conscious about our affectionate display. Neither of us really cared, but other people tended to. We'd learned that before. Once on my feet, I pulled a disgusted face, realizing I only came up to my twin's bicep. Barely. Why did he have to be so tall when I barely topped five feet?

I turned to face my brother's friend, promising myself that I'd try to be nice. Maybe. "Hi, I'm Livvy," I said, trying to keep my tone friendly and failing. My voice shook with nerves and sounded a bit hostile. Well, there went that goal. But it wasn't my fault.

Strangers always put me on edge. Yes, I knew that my brother had roommates but the reality of meeting any of them sooner rather than later was settling in and all my mental barriers were up.

"This is Liam," Emma called from the back of the vehicle. She shut the back of the SUV and stepped around it, coming to his side. They linked hands briefly and smiled warmly at each other. "He's a friend. And he's also right. We should go."

"How is it you know him already?" I asked, eyeing the two of them with suspicion.

"Later," Vian whispered in my ear.

I shook my head and rolled my eyes at Emma but took Vian's hand as I climbed into the backseat. To my annoyance, Liam climbed in after me. The overhead light gave me a chance to glimpse his more defining features and decide that he was a heartbreaker if I ever saw one. Perfectly tanned skin, with honey colored hair and brown eyes. I shot my brother a look of betrayal. The corners of Vian's mouth quirked up into a small grin before he shut the door.

Within seconds, both he and Emma climbed into the front and we were leaving. I want to say that I didn't look back, that I easily brushed off leaving the only haven I'd known for the last couple of years like it was nothing. That I didn't tear up just a bit as we turned onto another misty street. But if I did, that would make me a liar.

CHAPTER 2

Emma and my brother chatted easily in hushed tones in the front seat. However, in the backseat there was a less friendly atmosphere. Most of the problem was probably me. Every time I glanced at him out of the corner of my eye, Liam was openly staring at me with an expression I couldn't read. It started to drive me up a wall—or window in this case. I thought about pretending to sleep. Maybe the rocking of the vehicle would actually put me out, but knowing me, I'd be unable to keep my eyes closed with a stranger so close to me.

"So, where are we going? Am I allowed to know now?" I tried to be flippant, like it didn't matter, but if I was being honest, it did.

Vian glanced at me over his shoulder before focusing back on the road. "Yeah, we're go—"

"Once it's safe," Liam said smoothly. He threw me an apologetic look across the backseat that only pissed me off no matter how 'sorry' he tried to be. Seriously? Who did he think he was?

I reached for the calm place inside. "What does that mean?" I asked, completely ignoring the things his voice did to my insides. No, I wasn't going to admit how sexy it was. If anyone asked, he sounded like a frog, and fuck them for asking in the first place. He was good looking, and his voice made me want to lick syrup off the abs I was sure he was hiding under his shirt. You'd have to kill me to get me to say it out loud though.

"Liv," Emma said calmly from the front. "Please don't start."

What the fuck? I was getting tired of her attitude. First with the way she kept dismissing my concerns, especially considering she knew my history. *All* my history and hang ups. And second because she'd been blowing me off all week after a fight with Payton. I was beginning to think this abrupt change in our plans had something to do with that, but without knowing what it was, I wasn't ready call her on it.

Suddenly, all the muscles in my body went tense as a feeling of unease swept through me. My fingers flexed as it hit me and I sank back into my seat, eyes darting around to each window, trying to see where the danger would come from.

"Stop the car," I choked out.

Vian immediately let off the gas before bringing us to a slow stop, he turned in his seat to face me. "What is it?"

"Something's going to happen," I whispered, darting a look toward Liam to see how he would react. As a rule, I never told people about my knack for knowing when bad things were about to happen. Only Vian and Emma knew because I trusted them implicitly. I was already a bit of a freak as it was and had seen more shrinks than I had fingers to count on. And there was always that one thought that nagged at me in the back of my mind. That people would think *I* caused these things to happen.

I expected Liam to stare at me like I was crazy, but he didn't. If anything, he looked more alert and his eyes, that had been so unreadable moments ago, now held a glimpse of concern. His head swiveled around, looking for danger.

"Look," Emma muttered. I couldn't see her since I sat in the seat behind her, but both my brother and Liam looked out the front window. Craning my neck, I leaned around to the center console to look out the front and I sucked in a sharp breath as two people stood several feet in front of the SUV. My intuition screamed at me to run, my hand already reaching toward the door handle before I forced myself to hold still.

"I recognize Payton. Who's that with her?" Vian asked.

"Evan," Emma gritted out.

"Stay in the car," Liam barked at me, making me jump. He popped open his door and slid out before giving me a serious look that made me shiver. I found myself memorizing his features as he stared at me. I didn't know why it was important, but it somehow made me feel better to take a mental image. Like, if he died, I'd have his face committed to memory. The feeling was like a weed, wrapping itself around me until I couldn't breathe.

"Keep her in the car, Em," my brother said. He reached over the console and gripped her hand. My eyes tracked the motion, filing it away to ask about later. I followed the guys' progress through the windows before leaning forward so my head was next to Emma's.

"What's happening?" I asked, happy that my voice didn't sound as strained as I felt.

"A problem that needs to be dealt with," she answered in a clipped tone.

"Maybe now isn't the time, but I'm going to need answers sooner or later. Like about why we're leaving in the middle of the night without saying goodbye to anyone." I pointed toward Payton through the windshield. "And that's our best friend out there."

"Just because she's a friend, doesn't mean she wants what's best for you, or done a great job of protecting you. She's out there in the middle of the road right now, stopping us from leaving with a guy —" She cut off just seconds from saying something important. I could tell by the strain in her voice.

I let out a bitter laugh. "Right. And you're doing such a good job of that by keeping secrets," I mumbled to myself.

The guys had stepped in front of the vehicle and were talking to Payton and Evan. Through the glass, we couldn't hear what was said, but Payton appeared to be pleading, directing most of her attention to my brother.

I shuddered and shrank back behind the seat a bit as Evan's gray gaze slid past them and settled on me. He was gorgeous, popular, and a completely entitled asshole. I'd only dated him for a few weeks before I'd realized how much of a jerk he was. We were at a party where he slipped something in my drink and tried to screw me. I dumped him the next morning and tried my best to avoid him ever since.

It bothered me that he was with Payton. I knew she didn't care for him much, but she still hung around with him because he was a family friend. I'd never understood that. She knew that he'd tried to date rape me. If it hadn't been for Emma's intervention, he probably would have succeeded.

A slow smile spread across his lips that chilled me. While he might look like an angel, there was no doubt in my mind that he was dangerous, just another devil hiding in plain sight. The urge to run battered at me again, especially when his eyes snapped to my brother. His whole face changed, morphing into something malicious. I was up and out of the SUV before Emma even knew I was moving. All I knew was that my twin was in danger and I needed to protect him. Intuition be damned.

"—sn't matter where you take her, I'll find her," I heard Evan snarl.

"Stop, Livvy!" Emma shouted behind me, but I ignored her as I rushed between Vian and Evan.

"Leave," I shouted in his direction, unable to meet his eyes. If I did, I knew I would run. I'd turn into the coward that I was deep down. Knowing that made me sick to my stomach.

Vian grabbed me and pulled me back against him.

"Enough of this bullshit," Evan snarled. He grabbed Payton's arm, twisting it before he shoved her behind him. She fell to the asphalt with a whimper of pain. Her gray eyes filled with tears and something snapped inside me. I had to get to her, protect her.

Vian hoisted me upward and started moving toward the SUV. I immediately started screaming as Payton clutched her arm to her chest. It looked like her wrist was broken and that pissed me off even more. I didn't feel like running anymore. I wanted to rake my nails down Evan's smug face.

"Put me down, Octavian!"

As I struggled against Vian, the misty streets suddenly lit up like it was the fourth of July. Sparks flickering in the air around us. I looked to see who had thrown the pack of firecrackers but there were no sounds and it was still only Emma and Liam who stood between Evan and me. My twin carried me to the SUV as I watched Emma and Liam move. It was like they were doing karate, except it wasn't like any sort of martial arts I'd ever seen. The unease I'd felt ramped up to an excruciating level that had me screaming more than just obscenities.

The change in my screaming must have alerted Emma that something was different, that something was wrong, because it distracted her. Her focus faltered for just half a second, but it was too late. Evan tossed something to her feet. As soon as it hit the ground, it engulfed her in a blaze of white fire that flickered for just a second. When it died down, there was a swirl of ash in her place.

After that it was a blur. I went from being almost hysterical to full out hysterics. I vaguely recalled Liam sprinting toward us. Vian hadn't managed to get me into the back, despite how much he outweighed me. Liam crashed into us, and then the world went sideways, and I passed out.

CHAPTER 3

I jolted awake, heart racing, and covered in a sheen of sweat, as some animal howled in the distance. Wolves? I wasn't sure. I couldn't see much, there was the vague outline of bedroom furniture in a medium sized room. If there were windows, I couldn't see them. The only light streamed in underneath a closed door across the room. An arm flexed around my waist and I froze. *Vian,* I thought and relaxed back into the soft mattress under me as my eyes adjusted to the dark room.

He and I would always sweat when we shared a bed. There was that telltale sense of familiarity too. It happened with Emma as well, but the arm slung over my waist was too heavy to be hers. I knew I wasn't in my own bed, or even in my foster house.

I wracked my brain, trying to remember when we got here, wherever here was. All I could remember was pain and distorted voices. Something had happened, an explosion or something. And brightness. Just thinking about all that light made my stomach roll.

I gasped for breath as older memories assaulted me. A belt flashed toward my face and I flinched. A meaty fist clenched at my throat, choking me so my sobs couldn't sound. A woman screamed at me about sin and how only good girls were allowed to cry.

Another howl, much louder than before sounded, breaking the flashback and I was able to claw my way back to the here and now. It had taken a lot of time and a bunch of bullshit therapy paid for by the state to realize that flashbacks were always going to be a factor in my life. The only thing I had to be grateful for was that I could break out of my memories easier these days. No one had touched me with violence in years. Rationally, I knew that, but a single tear still slipped down my face. I swiped at it angrily and rolled into my brother. I needed him closer.

It became immediately clear I wasn't wearing a shirt or bra. I sighed and worked to tuck the sheet in between us before rolling completely into him, drawing in his familiar scent. It was there, but not enough of it. It was overpowered by the scent of cloves and cedar. The arm around me flexed, drawing me closer.

"You're awake," a husky voice said quietly into my hair.

I had no idea who this man was. My heart stuttered for a second, before I drew up my knees and pushed myself away from him. The motion pushed me straight over the side of the bed, somehow managing to bring the sheet with me. The man tried to catch me, but I fell to the hard floor with a heavy thump and hissed in pain. Ignoring it, I attempted to right myself and get as far away as possible before light bloomed in the room. One hand flew up, blocking out the sudden light as I rolled away from the stranger, clenching the sheet to my chest as I went. I didn't have time to look closely at him, but what I did see sent my mind spinning. I registered two things; one, he was a large man wearing only his boxers, and two, the light that filled the room came from a small burst of fire he appeared to be wielding in his palm. I shook my head. Obviously, I must have seen wrong, I told myself. Besides, I had bigger issues to focus on—like getting away from him.

Part of me knew it was a mistake to take my eyes off him, but I needed to see my options. I scrambled into a crouch as I scanned the room quickly, noting three doors. The one in the middle still had light coming in underneath and I hoped it was a hallway. It wouldn't be enough. I needed to stun him somehow. Keeping him in my peripheral vision I continued to scan the room, looking for anything I might be able to use as a weapon, as I tried to inch my way closer to the doors.

I'd barely climbed to my feet before he tossed his hand upward and snagged me around the waist and pulled me backward. Letting out a scream, I started clawing at his arm with my nails. He let go immediately and I fell forward, hitting my knees on the ground this time. A cry of pain escaped my lips.

As I tried to recover, he slammed into me from behind. His weight crushed me to the floor, but before my face smacked into the hardwood floor, his hand shot out and stopped us from falling. He rolled, snaking one arm around my waist as the other snagged both of my wrists. The sheet I'd been clutching fell away as he continued to roll and pinned my arms above my head. My heart pounded wildly in my chest. I tried to heave him off, but his body held the rest of me down. There was just so much of him and very little of me.

"Fucking hell, woman," he barked. I thrashed underneath him, before he gave me a rough shake. "Fucking stop!"

"Fuck you." My chest heaved against his, while my brain tried to figure out my next move. I didn't have the strength to overpower him. An idea, a very stupid one, struck me and I enacted it without a second thought, slamming my head back into the floor. Part of me hoped that if I could knock myself out, he wouldn't get any sick pleasure out of whatever he had planned for me. Either way, at least I wouldn't be around for whatever he was going to do.

He reared back in shock, his deep blue eyes widening. My wrists were released and he sat up still straddling my hips. I crossed my arms over my chest trying to keep at least some semblance of modesty. I was thankful when he kept his eyes firmly on my face and not my naked torso.

"What the fuck is wrong with you?"

"Me?" I said, trying to stall for time, hoping an escape option would appear. "You're the one attacking me!"

"No, I was sleeping next to a girl. Then she went ape shit." He sighed and then rolled his eyes as if I was being dim witted or difficult. "If I let you up, are you going to run or can we have an adult conversation?"

I sputtered. Seriously? Did he just imply that I wasn't acting normal? My eyes narrowed before I tried to smooth my expression. *Find the calm place.* I needed to find it if I was going to make it through this with as little damage as possible.

"Well? Did you stun yourself into silence or is it my pretty face?" he sneered with a lift to one heavy eyebrow.

"What the hell is wrong with you?" Apparently, my sense of self-preservation was out to lunch. I bucked my hips, hoping to catch him off guard. He barely even shifted. "Who the hell are you?"

He glared down at me. "I'm Flynn. This is my bedroom. And as for what's wrong with me? Nothing. I'm perfect." He had the audacity to smirk at me next, as if his comment were the most hilarious thing ever. Nope. Not even a little bit.

I snorted before I gave him a cursory glance, noting his broad shoulders, defined muscles, and classically handsome face. Sure, he was pretty, but I wasn't going to admit that to him or any other living being, so I stared in derision instead.

He gave a feral smile that made me bristle. "Do you make a habit of keeping half naked chicks in your bed?" Why did I let him goad me so easily? Bright side, I wasn't being punched. *Yet.*

"No," he said, still smiling. "Just the hot, bitchy ones, apparently." His voice dipped low and his eyes glittered dangerously.

Well fuck you too. Figuratively. Not literally. Nope. Definitely not the second one. What the hell, was I getting Stockholm syndrome? I needed to get out of here.

A door crashing open drew our attention. Vian and someone else barged into the room and froze. The other guy was a near replica of the man on top of me. Except his eyes were lighter in color, and he looked supremely pissed off. It took a second for me to realize it wasn't directed at me but Flynn.

"Dude," my brother shouted, already pulling off his shirt.

Flynn seemed to realize he was still on top of me and climbed off. "It's not what it looks like. She freaked out and tried to run. I just stopped her."

"By sitting on my half-naked sister," Vian clarified, his green eyes blazing, a promise of violence in them. Yay, go twin. He tossed me his shirt. I snagged it out of the air, pulling it on as I sat up. The scars on my back twinged after our struggle. I stiffened, hoping no one was going to ask about them.

"It wasn't like that and you know it," Flynn said in an overly patient voice, pointedly not looking at me. "And technically, she still has panties on so…"

I snorted, shaking my head. "Oh, gee you didn't have time to rip those off too. What a shame," I quipped, twisting with a wince as I got to my feet. I was going to pay for this evening for several days. My back hurt from irritating the scar tissue. There was a deep ache in my hip, and I was sure that my kneecaps were going to bruise too.

"You're hurt," the other guy said, marching across the room. He immediately invaded my space. I backed away until I bumped into a piece of furniture. It didn't stop him. He kept coming until his front pressed against me and started pawing at my hips for the hem of my newly acquired shirt. "Where?"

"What the—" I squealed, slapping his hand away as I slipped to the left.

"For God's sake. Can all of you be normal for two seconds and stop pawing at her!" Vian shouted, tearing across the room to push the guy away. "The next person who touches her without permission is going to lose a testicle."

"What about those of us without testicles?" a small voice asked from the door. A tall girl stood there with blue-green eyes that were rimmed in red like she had been crying. Blonde hair cascaded around her face and down her back.

"Depends," I muttered under my breath. "Are you a rapist too?" I regretted it as soon as it escaped my lips.

"I didn—"

My eyes widened, realizing Flynn heard me, and I shook my head at him, pleading for him to shut up. Surprisingly, he did. It wasn't a pretty thing to say about someone, especially when I knew that wasn't the guy's intention. I was sore, but not sore *down there,* sore. It was one of the reasons I'd stopped fighting him. At least that's what I was telling myself. The look Flynn had given me when I'd hurt myself… I gave my head a slight shake, I wasn't ready to look so closely at how that made me feel.

The girl let out a laugh, like the tinkling of bells. I grinned at her. I didn't know her, but she had a sense of humor. At least so far. "I'm Brooke. I also live here. Come on. I'll take you away from the insanity and we can get you a shower."

"And explain what's happening?" I asked hopefully, thinking about the weird fire that hung above our heads. Yeah, best not to focus on that. I skirted around Flynn and his look alike, who I didn't have a name for.

"After a shower, a snack, and a nap. You've been pretty ill," she answered as I reached her. She turned, allowing me to go in front of her.

"I'm actually not that hungry," I told her, looking away. I didn't want to go in front of her, but she wasn't leaving me much choice.

"Told you!" Vian stage whispered behind me.

At the door, I paused and looked back to face my brother. "Don't think I've missed the fact that I woke up in someone else's bed with you in the house. We're gonna need to talk about that."

"I don't doubt it," he said with a grimace. I could read the apology on his face and decided he probably had a good reason. He wouldn't knowingly hurt me.

CHAPTER 4

Brooke directed me down a hallway and then into another before opening a door. I noted that it was near a staircase that led down. Life had done a good job of teaching me that it never hurt to have an escape route in mind.

"This is my room. You can use it whenever you want," she said as she crossed the lavender carpet to her dresser. It looked exactly like the sort of space a girl like her would own. Light purple walls, with silver accents. There were pink curtains, white furniture with a large canopy bed covered in varying shades of pink and purple fabric.

Girly.

Cute.

In short, nothing I would have ever chosen for myself. "Your room isn't quite ready yet, but it shouldn't be more than a few days. Though, I'm sure you'd rather bunk with Octavian."

"So... this is my new home?" I asked, uncertainly. I had known we would have roommates, but I'd been under the impression it was one or two people. From what I'd seen so far, this place was huge. I counted at least nine doors on our way from Flynn's room to this one.

She smiled sadly and I noted how drawn she looked. Tired. But I didn't ask. It wasn't my business.

"Let's go take care of your hair," she said after a moment of me staring at her awkwardly.

The bathroom was large, and also very girly. There was a small closet that held linens, as well as another door that she quickly locked before opening up a large walk-in shower in one corner. Opposite was a sleek jacuzzi tub, complete with jets and just about every sort of bubble bath a person could dream of. I moved toward a double sink with a large mirror and gasped in shock. I looked awful. There were deep circles under my eyes, my already pale skin was devoid of any color, making the smattering of freckles I had stand out. I turned my head from side to side with a frown, taking in the clumps of hair that were matted together. How had I ended up with twigs and leaves in my hair? I picked up a chunk and pulled it in front of me. I looked like I'd fought with a bird's nest and the nest won.

"Umm." I was afraid to ask. Did I really want to know?

"Slipping," she said before smacking her head.

"Yeah, that's one of those things you won't understand. Trust me though. It can wait."

I numbly nodded before grimacing at my reflection again, hating the dark circles under my eyes. "I was sick?"

"Yeah. You were out for several days. Four, actually."

I whirled to face her. "Four days? And I had twigs in my hair?"

"I wanted to get you in a shower immediately," she rushed to say, understanding in her eyes. "But you weren't well enough to move." Only a girl would understand how bad this was. If I'd been out four days, this shit was matted in.

A guy leaned in from Brooke's room, making me jump as I let out a small shriek. He was vaguely familiar as he threw me an apologetic smile. "Liam's gonna be happy to see you're awake. Do you need help? Also, I bring food!"

Before I could get a good look at him, Brooke stepped in front of me, blocking my half-clothed body from view. I mentally gave her two points and knew she and I could be friends. Eventually. Maybe. "Could you get Octavian for now? If her hair is anything like his, it's going to be a hassle to clean, and no offense Sugar, but she doesn't know you yet."

"Yeah, no problem," he replied in a smooth voice. His head popped over Brooke's shoulder, revealing his honey blonde hair and warm brown eyes. "I'm Lucien. We'll meet properly later," he said before winking at me. He handed Brooke something before he turned and left.

"Okay," Brooke said, setting down a plate covered in crackers, meats, and cheeses. My stomach revolted at the sight. She looked at me for a second, surveying the damage to my hair before offering me a smile that didn't quite reach her eyes. "I think it's best if we get out as much as we can at the sink and then shower, yeah?"

"Yeah," I sighed. I turned on the faucet to let the water warm up in one of the sinks and felt around in my hair, pulling out dead leaves, sticks, and what appeared to be dried vines with wickedly sharp thorns on them. Brooke worked silently from the back after setting a small trash can at our feet.

"Hey," Vian called somewhat breathlessly from the doorway. Something flashed across his face as he looked at the pair of us in the mirror that made my chest tighten. As he brushed past Brooke, he leaned in to whisper something before he started the shower.

"So, about that dude," I inquired when he came back to us.

"Which one, Flynn or Kieran?" Vian asked. "Time to wash it. Duck your head under the faucet."

I did as he told me, trying to get as much of my hair wet as possible. "I don't know. Both I guess. I'm so not okay with strange dudes seeing me naked. Or chicks for that matter. Sorry Brooke."

She chuckled. "It's cool."

Vian took his time to reply. He worked shampoo

into my hair, scraping at my scalp lightly with his fingernails and I let my heart fall into happier times. He washed my hair the way Mom used to.

"Privacy isn't really a thing here," Vian finally answered. It felt evasive to me. "Time to rinse. Get in the shower. Brooke and I will find you some clothes," he said quickly, practically pushing Brooke out the door.

"Okay…."

I took my time after they left, making sure we hadn't missed any of those thorns. I didn't want to be pricked by one accidentally or have one fall out in the shower and step on it. My hair was long, and I liked to keep it that way, even if the curls were a hassle to deal with. I'd admit that some things weren't worth it though, like working out tangles or getting your hair caught on doorknobs. That sucked.

Once I was sure I wouldn't impale myself, I undressed and stepped into the shower. It was one of those nice ones that fell like rain from the ceiling. I let it rush over me, relishing in the heat. People who took cold or lukewarm showers were weird.

"Need help?" Brooke called out.

I startled and whipped my head around.

"Umm, I'm good," I called back after a second.

"We found clothes for you. Ben had errands to run and Ameris—Kieran and Flynn's mother—gave him some clothes that would work for you." Her voice echoed throughout the room as I rinsed soap from my body. "No one wanted to go through Emma's things just yet."

Emma.

Emma.

Emma.

Her name echoed through my head. By the time it processed through my brain a third time, Brooke's voice had morphed into my own, sounding like a panicked scream. My whole body sagged toward the floor as hot tears filled my eyes.

I forgot? How could I forget? Who does that? What sort of friend did that make me? My last memory of her flashed through my head over and over. I could almost feel the heat of that white fire blazing up around her as I stared down at the tiled shower floor. Her blonde hair hung like a curtain around her head as she turned, her devastated blue eyes on me just before she disintegrated into ash. It was too much. I didn't want to see it, but I couldn't stop myself from reliving it. I could live for a thousand years and I would never forget that moment. How was this ever going to be okay?

I was dimly aware that people were speaking to me. The shower had shut off, a towel was thrown over me, and two sets of arms wrapped around me. My body shook so hard as I cried that I was certain if they let go of me, I would shatter apart.

The pain was like crushing waves. One would ebb before another crashed down. The sounds of my crying were so loud that it echoed. Either that, or someone must have been crying with me. Somehow that made it worse. Whoever said shared pain was better was a fucking liar.

My mind was a hazy mess of chaotic thoughts and feelings as I was led from the bathroom. I all but collapsed once we reached Brooke's bed. She crawled in behind me as Vian covered us both up. He left for a few minutes and I ended up with my head nestled in Brooke's lap while she stroked my hair. The action reminded me so much of Emma that I ended up crying harder. I wanted her to stop, feeling as though I didn't deserve it, but I was too selfish to tell her. I both wanted and loathed the comfort she offered.

Maybe I slept at some point after Vian came back and wrapped himself around both of us. The next thing I knew, Brooke was speaking to someone at the door.

"She's not hungry, Honey."

I opened my groggy eyes to find someone standing in the doorway. He looked vaguely familiar. What was his name again? Logan? No… Fuck, I was too exhausted for this. I'd ask Vian later.

"Neither of you have eaten all day and everyone is restless. You don't have to eat, but it would go a long way in settling things if everyone were together." He gave me a weak smile, but I could see the exhaustion on his face.

"We'll come down in a bit," Brooke replied, pushing a stray curl off my face.

I sat up, expecting to see Vian but he was gone. I

didn't remember when he left again. "Where's my brother?" I asked in a hoarse voice.

Liam. That was his name, I remembered.

"Downstairs," he answered immediately. "I'm glad you're better."

I stared at him blankly, unsure of how to respond to that. As a rule, I was distant with most people. Brooke was an exception I'd made in the face of so much testosterone last night. "Umm, thanks," I finally said. I didn't like how his eyes warmed over when I spoke to him, as if I were someone he had the right to have warm feelings for.

"I'll let them know," he said before closing the door.

"How many people live here?" I asked. I really wanted to be prepared if I was going to meet more people.

Her eyes were tired and bloodshot, but she threw her head back and laughed. "Having you here is going to make this so much better. The answer is six others, including my own brother and yours. Lots of testosterone around here."

I groaned and sank back into the bed. Brooke started playing with my hair again, combing her fingers through some of the tangles after such a restless night. "Don't worry, they're not a bad group of guys, you just have to get to know them."

Great. Just. Great.

CHAPTER 5

I took a deep breath as I took in the room, noting the light gray walls, stone fireplace, and simple furniture spattered around. The only thing that gave it any personality at all were the five guys spread out amongst the room, eyes fixated on a large screen. There was no art on the walls, no artistic flare. It looked exactly like a bachelor pad, except there weren't beer cans littering every available surface.

I snorted at my wardrobe as I stood at the bottom of the steps. The noise brought everyone's attention to me in my pink pajama pants that said, 'Boys are stupid, throw rocks at them.' I had no doubt that Brooke had picked these for me.

Vian started laughing. Of course, he would find this funny. I shook my head with a sigh and looked at Brooke, who beamed at my brother. She was going to be trouble. Not that I was against taking digs at people, but only if I knew about it beforehand.

"Hey guys, this is Olivia," Brooke said, stepping forward to introduce me. She pointed at a guy sitting in a brown recliner. He had the same blonde hair and blue-green eyes, as well as her high cheekbones. While he was thin, he was all corded muscles. "That's Ben, my twin brother." He looked me up and down, not in a predatory way, but more assessing, like I was an interesting puzzle. "Those two idiots are Lucien and Liam," she continued. Both had honey blonde hair, warm amber colored eyes, but where Liam was built, Lucien was slim, like a swimmer, though they looked about the same height. Without waiting, she waved an arm toward Flynn and his twin. "And that's Kieran. You've met Flynn already."

I nodded, unsure of what to say. How the hell were there so many twins in one room? Attractive ones at that. "Did your mothers all form a club and insist on having designer babies or something?" I blurted into the silent room. Seriously, that had to be the answer. There was no way three sets of twins won the genetic lottery like they had. It just didn't happen.

Lucien and Liam ducked their heads together, but their shoulders shook with silent laughter, while Ben looked like he was trying to decide if I was serious or not. Asshole and his twin shared a look between them, having one of those private twin conversations I was well acquainted with. And speaking of mine, he looked like he wanted to sink into the couch and never resurface, which was just fine with me since he'd laughed at me before.

"Well?" I asked turning to Brooke who leaned against the wall with a huge smile on her face as she watched things unfold. I shrugged my shoulders and crossed the room to Vian and worked out a plan so I could tell Asshole and Wandering Hands apart. I smacked my twin's leg, urging him to scoot over, and plopped down next to him.

I already knew that one of them had lighter colored eyes, but as I continued to watch them, it became clear who was whom. Asshole was slightly smaller than his brother and lacked a pair of piercings in one ear. Plus, Flynn seemed to naturally brood. As if he sensed me staring at him, his gaze whipped in my direction and settled into an intense glare. Before I could do something childish, Lucien sat forward and cleared his throat to get my attention.

"So, I'll start," Lucien said before glancing at Flynn. "Unless you'd rather?"

"By all means," Flynn said, flashing him a genuine smile before focusing back on me. It was unnerving. I glanced at my twin, wondering if it was because we were cuddling, but quickly decided I didn't care. At least the others were trying to be sneaky about looking at me. Even Liam didn't openly stare this time. I would just have to deal with Flynn looking at me as if I was some sort of plague.

"Right. So, Livvy, would you rather ask your questions first and we can fill in anything you might not have thought to ask, or do you just want me to lay it out for you and answer any remaining questions?" Lucien ask, focusing back on me.

I offered him a smile, but I doubt it looked genuine. "Actually, I'd rather just ask questions, if that's okay?"

"Of course." He sat back, relaxing and waited patiently.

I took a shaky breath, working past the lump that had formed in my throat. I knew what I wanted to ask but was I really ready for the answer? Fuck it. I had to know. "What happened to Emma?" Everyone, and I mean everyone, sucked in a breath. And just like that, my bravery ran out.

I swallowed, growing nervous as my thoughts spiraled. I clutched Vian's hand in mine, giving it a squeeze. I didn't even have to look at him for him to know I was freaking out a bit. I watched as shock, anger, and grief played out in varying degrees across everyone's faces. I shouldn't have started with Emma, but it was already done. "How many of you knew her? Was she how you met Vian? Why was I unconscious for four whole days, and why didn't you take me to a doctor? Come to think of it why did I wake up mostly naked next to that guy?" I motioned to Flynn with my head as Vian squeezed my hand again. Yeah, I was freaking out alright. I made a point to take a deep breath and try to calm down. Everyone was staring at me, half of them with their mouths hanging open.

"We're Entwined," Ben stated matter of fact. Out of everyone in the room, he was the least ruffled. "We're humans, but also not. And before you ask, by 'we' I'm talking about you and your brother as well..."

"What does that mean?" I asked, focusing on keeping it to one question this time. Anything to not break down in tears again. That was a one-time thing. I didn't know these people and I hated that I'd already shown my vulnerable side.

"It means that we have access to a science the rest of humanity doesn't. Well, most of it," Ben continued. "To really understand, we would have to delve into thousands of years of history and theory."

I nodded, accepting his answer even though I had no clue what that really meant. Entwined? Was it a race? He made it sound that way. There'd always been something different about me. Something that set me apart from my peers. My heart was beating in my chest, and I knew I probably looked a bit wild. Once upon a time, I hadn't been so good at hiding my emotions. I was often described as reactive, impulsive, and destructive. But after years of being in the system, I'd mastered my brash nature. Except I felt far too readable to these people, especially with Flynn studying me so intently.

"Okay, let's say I believe all of this so far. How did we get here? I don't really remember anything beyond..." *Emma dying in front of me.* I couldn't say it out loud.

Lucien sat forward again, piercing me with a look. "All of us have natural abilities, instinctive ones. We know that you and Vian are Precogs. As in you know things about the future before they happen. Well, you do at least. Vian's works differently. He dreams the future."

I knew that, but Vian never liked talking about his dreams. They weren't reliable and tended to be metaphoric, open to interpretation. We'd learned that lesson the hard way after our parents died. He'd admitted sometime after it happened that he'd dreamed them as birds falling from the sky.

"Well, Liam and I are Benders," Lucien said, breaking into my thoughts.

I stared at him for a beat. "Like Airbenders?" I couldn't help it when a small laugh escaped me.

Vian snorted next to me. I elbowed him. I wasn't trying to be funny. I was being serious. Sort of. Hitting him only made it worse though. He broke into laughter that he tried to hide by pressing his face into my hair. Lucien ducked his head as I turned bewildered eyes on him, but I caught the amusement in his gaze and gave up. Whatever.

"No," Liam responded with a smirk. "More like we can bend reality and step through it from one place to another. And we can take people with us. All Entwined can do it, but most need a separate conductor. I believe Brooke mentioned Slipping to you earlier. But if you want some elemental shit, Ben and

Brooke are your twins. Just don't ask them to fuck with the weather. It always ends badly."

"Noted," I said, bothered when my voice shook a little bit. Who could blame me though? I was in a room full of people who could bend space and control the weather. My free hand clenched into a fist, using the pain of my nails to center myself before speaking again. "Does this 'ability' stuff have anything to do with why I was out cold for four days?"

"Yes and no," Liam answered. "When we travel, you have to be hyper aware, but you…" He looked around, as though he were struggling with what to say. His eyes landed on Flynn who gave him a meaningful look. "You completely drained yourself when Emma—"

"What he's trying to say is you expelled all your energy. A perfectly natural reaction to what you witnessed," Ben said. "Then, during the travel, Liam had to fight off the beings that live between reality."

"You almost died," Vian added. His voice was strangled. I clutched at his hand when he looked away from me. Unshed tears clung to the corner of his eyes as he refused to look at me.

"I can't say I totally understand…" I shook my head, trying to clear the image of Emma that rushed forward. "What about my bag?" I asked quickly. "Mom's bracelet was in it. It's all I had left of her."

Lucien cleared his throat, scooting to the edge of his seat. "We went back but everything was destroyed.

We're not sure if it was because of your reaction or if the witches did a poor job trying to cover it up."

"So, it's gone?" I said quietly. He nodded and my eyes closed automatically. Grief crashed over me as I leaned into my twin, trying to suck it all back into the darkness of my heart. I could cry about it later when there were fewer eyes on me.

Vian's lips mumbled into my hair, "I'm sorry, Olive." I drew in one ragged breath, the only indicator of just how big a loss this was for me, and let it out slowly. Breathe. Just breathe. This wasn't as bad as losing our parents. It's just a bit of metal she used to wear.

"Okay." My voice shook, but it wasn't as bad as I had feared. "If I was so sick, why didn't you take me to a doctor or something?" My eyes opened slowly to look around at their faces.

Asshole's twin leaned forward, a twinkle in his eye. I really wished I could remember his name. "You didn't need a human doctor. You needed us," he said, waving his hand around the room. "But our natural Art isn't just healing, it's pain too. Sometimes you need both in order to heal."

Note to self, do not piss off Asshole. Maybe just a bit, but yikes… pain? Not my thing. "I can't keep calling you Asshole's twin, but I've forgotten your name," I blurted. Oh, for fucks sake, Livvy. You are the dumbest chick sometimes…

"Name's Kieran, but I'm okay with Asshole's twin as long as you don't switch me out with him." He jerked his thumb in the direction of Flynn and I almost laughed. The man in question was back to glaring at me. Or maybe he'd been doing it the whole time and I'd managed to block it out.

"No promises," I quipped, meeting Flynn's stare. Silently, I counted backwards from fifty. For whatever reason, Vian trusted these people. I was determined to behave, not for them, but for him. "Right. Okay. Hard stuff now." I turned to my twin. Part of me wanted to have this conversation in private, but the nastier side of me wanted to make him squirm. Just a bit. "You knew about all of this. Obviously. But you didn't feel the need to tell me." I stated it plainly, trying to keep any inflection from my tone.

His green eyes were guarded as he stared back at me. "I did keep secrets, yes. But not because I didn't want to tell you," he stated hastily. "I couldn't. Not with the situation you were in."

"And what situation was that?"

"When Kieran and Brooke approached me, I was already trying to get myself emancipated. This was just before I tracked you down two years ago." I nodded, remembering the few years the state had kept us separate, to *help us flourish* without a crutch or so they claimed. "You'd been placed in a foster home near a coven of witches."

I smirked, wondering how that was different than *Entwined* but I said nothing. They'd all but admitted that we were magical beings. "Why does that warrant you keeping secrets?"

"Because," Flynn's voice cut across us. "Witches are selfish bastards who collect our kind to use as batteries." I could feel him glaring at me again, but I refused to look at him or even acknowledge the shitty tone of voice he used. He and I were going to have issues if he didn't let me and my brother talk.

"He's right," Vian said softly. "By the time we got Emma into that home with you—"

"Wait." I threw a hand up to cover his mouth. "You placed Emma with me?" I could feel the blood draining from my face. My breathing sped up as my mind raced through what that meant. My hand fell limply into my lap.

"Olive, no," Vian whispered. "She loved you. It wasn't—"

"You don't know that. How could you?" I whispered, feeling a pressure build in my chest.

"Know what?" Flynn asked sharply.

Vian sighed. "She thinks it wasn't real. Her relationship with Emma."

I hated him for knowing that. In that moment, for probably the first time ever in my life, I hated him. My lip trembled. "Just finish," I whispered. "Just spit it out. Please."

"Right, so Payton was already setting up to recruit you."

"Payton?" I scoffed. "She never mentioned anything about becoming a witch or Entwined to me." And she hadn't. Not even once. And Emma had never mentioned this Entwined bullshit either. I had always known Vian and I were different, it was almost a relief to find out that I had been right all this time, but it was still confusing. They were talking about magic for Christ's sake, which shouldn't exist. Then again, Vian shouldn't have prophetic dreams and I shouldn't be able to sense danger.

"Because she was gaining your trust. Maybe even used witchcraft to influence you. Emma never found any proof of tampering from her," Lucien offered.

"Payton would never…" I gritted my teeth, glancing at him out of the corner of my eye and saw he wore a very serious expression. I scanned the rest of them. It hurt, realizing I didn't know my best friends in the world as much as I thought I had. "So, you're saying that you planted one of my best friends to live with me, and that another was manipulating me." By the time I finished saying it, my heart was racing again. I looked around the room finding nothing but looks of sorrow and pity. The room suddenly felt too cramped and crowded. I bolted from my seat and charged out before I did something stupid, like start screaming, or worse, cry.

I paused just outside the door, trying to figure out where to go. No one called after me or tried to follow. I didn't know if they were giving me space or just waiting until I was out of earshot before talking about me behind my back. A numbness settled into my limbs as I struggled to breathe. I was on the jagged edges of a panic attack.

Where the hell was the way out of this place?

To my right through one doorway was a kitchen with a combined dining room. I could just see the edges of a heavy looking table. In front of me were the stairs that would lead me upstairs to the bedrooms. I didn't feel like trapping myself up there, so I veered around the stairs and followed a hallway that thankfully led me to a large dark wooden door. I tore it open, relieved to find it let out to the front of the house. I pulled it closed behind me as I stepped onto a wide wrap around porch.

I leaned against a railing, working hard to catch my breath as I worked through all the new information in my head. I could handle being different. That was nothing new for me. I could even forgive Vian for keeping things from me. Holding a grudge against him would be too hard. What I couldn't deal with was questioning the few friendships I had. They were everything to me. I'd clung to them, used them to beat back the pain. For fuck's sake, how many times had I cried in the middle of the night while Emma held me? And Payton… she was rough around the edges, crass, utterly beautiful, but fiercely loyal. Always able to make me laugh. It had to be real. It had to.

Slowly, the yard in front of me came into focus and my breathing evened out. The feel of aged wood under my fingertips helped to calm me. It was something solid I could ground myself with. I took several deep breaths and let the scent of pine fill my lungs.

Looking around, I noted two SUVs parked on a dirt road that led right up to the house. In the opposite direction was a forest. It brought me completely back to myself as I stared into the trees. There were small flickering lights that I couldn't make sense of. It reminded me of fireflies I'd seen on television, but we didn't have any of those in the Pacific Northwest.

Something brushed the back of my legs and I screamed as I whirled around.

CHAPTER 6

I whirled around and looked down, but there was nothing there. At least not in front of me. Flynn however, sat in a chair a few feet away from me. His large frame was relaxed, legs stretched out in front of him as he stared at me, a small tingle ran up my spine.

"Wha…"

"Guardian," he said simply.

"What?" I asked again. How the hell had he slipped out here without me noticing? My eyes were still wide as I tried to make sense of everything.

"You have a guardian. A rather large one in fact. I can see his energy. He sensed you were upset and was offering his comfort," Flynn said, as if it were the most natural thing in the world.

"What are you talking about?" I asked in exasperation.

"Never mind. You'll learn more about him once

you start training. We all have one," he said dismissively.

Whatever. Why did he bother bringing something up if he wasn't going to fully explain things? I leaned back against the rail while he continued to stare at me.

"Why do you goad me so much?" And why did I let him?

"I dunno, maybe it's another natural affinity I have," he said, shrugging. "But let me ask you this, are you always this selfish?"

My eyes narrowed and my shoulders tensed. A belt flashed through the air between us and I fought not to flinch. My palms grew sweaty while I focused on pushing the flashback away. I was too ramped up emotionally, which always made the flashbacks worse.

"Fuck you," I gritted out. Self-preservation be damned.

"You said that before, yet we're still clothed, and your body language says you have no intention of following your crude remark." He smirked, obviously finding himself far more amusing than he actually was.

"What the fuck is your deal?" I snapped, already tired of his shit.

"Me, nothing. I just don't like your behavior."

"My behavior?" My voice went up an octave, completely shocked and annoyed. I stepped forward, holding up a hand. "Let's count this out shall we. One, I woke up naked in your bed. Without my permission, I might add. Two, you attacked me when I didn't want to be there. Three, you've glared at me since you laid eyes on me. Four, you're an asshole," I said ticking each point off on my fingers as I went. The last one was just to make it clear that I didn't like him. Childish? Yes. Had I somehow managed to already forget that his 'abilities' included giving pain? Yep, but I honestly dared anyone else in my position to just magically be okay with his actions.

He snorted. "Listen up, Princess," he said leaning forward, placing his elbows on his knees. "You arrived here so ill that if it weren't for me, you'd be dead. That whole permission thing goes out the window when one of my family members is dying, not to mention your brother consented for you. Next, you completely freaked out, you didn't let anyone explain the situation. You just assumed that I'd taken advantage of you, and trust me, I wouldn't have. You're not my type. Also, you're a bitch. The rest of them probably can't see that, but I do. Sure, you probably cared about Emma, but you didn't love her like we did. We lost our sister. Gave her up to protect you. She died for you. Think about that."

He stood abruptly and stormed off, leaving me stunned and speechless. The front door slammed, making me flinch. I stumbled toward the chair he'd vacated and toppled into it, pressing my face into my hands. Why couldn't everything just…slow down. No sooner had I collected myself before something else would crash into me to knock me over again.

It hurt because it was true, though.

Not the first part, because fuck no. I had too much baggage and a long history with people thinking they could do whatever they wanted to me. I had no way of knowing that Vian was around, let alone consenting to their brand of healing, so fuck him for not giving me a pass on that.

I didn't even want to touch the whole 'not his type' thing. It wasn't relevant. I didn't want or need to be anyone's type, especially his. No matter how aware of him my body seemed to be in his presence.

But the rest of it? It ate at me. I had loved Emma in my own way. It may not have been the way I blindly loved my brother, but it was as much as someone as broken as I was could offer. And it hurt to know that. To be reminded that I wasn't capable of more than a great fondness for others. It didn't change that I would have protected her like my own family. I'd tried, I remembered trying to get to her. Vian hadn't let me. That made a difference didn't it?

My thoughts spiraled again as tears dripped down my nose to stain the wooden deck. My chest ached, my skin felt tight, and I was so tired. I wished my mom were still around. She had died when Vian and I were only eight. I didn't remember much of her, but I remembered that when I was upset, she had always known what to do or say to make things easier or feel better.

"Hey."

I jerked upright and met Liam's warm gaze. He'd

appeared silently, crouched in front of me while I was lost in my own head. He smiled sadly, but there was a warmth still in his eyes. "Flynn, huh?"

I swiped at the tears on my face. "Yeah."

"He's… complicated," he offered. "Don't let it get to you. Everyone is dealing with--"

I waved him away. "I get it. I really do." I took a shuddering breath and sat back. "Did you need something?" I asked.

"Dinner's ready. Lucien will pitch a fit if you don't eat."

"Right..." I said. I wasn't hungry, but I had no idea when I'd last eaten. Looking back out on the yard I noticed I'd sat here for much longer than I'd realized. When I'd first come outside, it was turning twilight. Now it was fully dark. Long shadows caused by the moon stretched across the porch.

Liam stood and offered me his hand. I looked between it and his brown eyes before standing on my own. It was sweet that he offered, but that's how people fooled you. They acted kind at first. And then they ripped it all away from you. At least he didn't look offended when I didn't accept it.

I followed him inside, through the kitchen which I had to admit was sort of stunning. I slowed for a minute to take it all in. Dual ovens, a large silver refrigerator, white cabinets, with cherry wood butcher block counters.

Just how much money did these people have? And where were their parents? I hadn't seen a proper adult yet. A pit of dread built inside me as I neared the open doorway, my head bent to watch my bare feet as they shuffled against the ash wood flooring.

I shouldn't have worried though. I caught up just as Liam entered the dining room. The table I glimpsed earlier was large and could easily seat a dozen people, though there were only eight chairs around it presently. All the seats were covered in leather, matching the dark wood of the table. There were more dishes here than I think I had ever seen for just one meal, and that included Thanksgiving. All the serving platters and bowls seemed to be piping hot and ready to eat, but no one had touched anything yet.

"Finally," Flynn muttered as Liam pulled out a chair next to my brother for me to sit in. I slid into it quickly, glancing around.

"Sorry, I didn't know you were waiting," I mumbled as I dropped my gaze to my lap.

"It's fine," Vian said, leaning into me. I looked over at him. His eyes were searching. No doubt he could tell I'd been crying again. With my pale skin and the bright lighting from a chandelier that hung over the table, everyone could probably see the redness around my eyes. "You okay?" he whispered.

"Yeah," I whispered back, even if I wanted to talk about this, I was done having private conversations in front of these people.

Everyone started digging in. Brooke smiled at me

from her seat across the way as she pushed a platter of meatloaf in my direction.

"We usually eat dinner together," she explained. "Well most meals, but dinners are about as formal as we get around here. Help yourself to whatever you want."

I took a small portion of meatloaf and scanned the table. There were several dishes of mashed potatoes, rolls, asparagus smothered in some sort of creamy sauce, and a bowl of yellow-orange fruit that might have been mango, but it had a weird star shape to it.

"Who cooks?" I asked.

"Normally Flynn or I do," Lucien answered. "However tonight we both pitched in."

I side-eyed Flynn down the table but quickly looked away. I had taken a small portion of everything. The meatloaf was good. Someone had put cheese in the center, and the whole bite melted in my mouth. I quickly got more, which caused some of them to chuckle, but I didn't care.

So good. The fact that it was homemade made it better somehow. I wasn't a huge eater, something almost everyone I knew hated. They couldn't ever understand that I just didn't get hungry. When I did, I ate but even then, it was hardly ever much. It wasn't my fault that I filled up quickly. This food though? I could see how people could eat just to eat if it tasted like this.

"It's good," I said around a bite of potatoes, realizing a few of the others were watching me. I flicked my gaze down the table at Asshole, hoping he hadn't made much of it.

"Thanks," Lucien said, beaming in my direction.

I'd expected dinner to be awkward. Thankfully, it wasn't. Everyone was engaged in conversations while they ate. I sat back listening as they made plans for the next day. Apparently, I needed to be presented for some testing with their council. The thought of meeting more people made me nervous, but from the sounds of it, it was required and Vian had promised he would be there with me. With that settled, I decided I'd deal with feeling nervous tomorrow when I had to and not a minute before.

I started to flag about half an hour into the meal, but I wasn't sure where I should go lay down. Brooke had offered her room, but I didn't feel comfortable taking it. I'd just slept for over four days straight, yet my eyelids were beginning to droop, and I wasn't sure how much longer I would remain upright.

"Are we not engaging enough for you down there, Princess?" Flynn sneered, jerking me out of my stupor.

I sat up straighter, my blood already coming to a boil as it flooded my face. Why couldn't he just leave me alone?

"For fuck's sake," Liam spat. "She's exhausted. Let her be."

"So are the rest of us. We've all been waiting hand and foot on her for the last four days. She can stand another hour," Flynn snapped. "Just because she's pretty and not related to you doesn't mean she gets special treatment."

"Why do her looks factor into things?" Ben asked quietly. "Everyone can tell she's more depleted than the rest of us. She used more of her own energy to heal than you did to help her."

Flynn raised an eyebrow at Ben. His face contorted for a second as something familiar flashed across his features before settling into a scowl. "Wow," he said quietly.

"What?" Ben asked. "It's a valid question." He skirted a look in my direction with a flash of empathy.

"He's trying to imply that none of you can think without your dicks," Brooke mumbled to her brother.

Lucien pinched the bridge of his nose between two fingers. "What are you playing at, Flynn?"

"You know exact—" Flynn started.

Dishes clattered on the table as Vian stood abruptly, causing me to flinch slightly; every line in his body was tense as he put a hand on my shoulder and stared at Flynn. "I told you already to give her a break. Three times now, I've said it. She's been through a lot. A hell of a lot more than you ever have." I stiffened under his hand and started shaking my head back and forth, silently begging him to stop. It wasn't their business. My brother's green gaze caught mine, but he plowed on and I held my breath. My hands clutched at the table in front of me. "She just found out I had to lie to her for years. Her best friend died, one of the few people in her life that she trusted. And the other was a liar too. And some of that lying is your fault. All our faults. So whatever fucking problem you have, you better fix it and leave her alone."

I was relieved for a moment before I sat back in my chair stunned and a tiny bit sad. The boy I'd grown up with had been shy, reserved. It had been up to me to defend both of us. It made me sad to see how much he'd changed without me. It wasn't a bad change, but it was one that showed me how far apart we'd grown.

It was clear now. He had transformed into this confident man that I knew, but at the same time didn't. I wanted to be proud of him, and I was, but the gnawing and broken part of me hated that he didn't seem to need me anymore.

The table was silent. Not a single person spoke or touched their food. Everyone watched as Vian and Flynn stared at one another. I waited to see what Flynn would do. Part of me wanted him to say something to my brother, but another part of me hated that I was obviously causing a rift in the family dynamic.

He didn't. After a few seconds, Flynn sat back, ran his fingers through his hair, then grinned at me, like he'd won something important. Except I had no clue what it was.

I stood, shoving my chair back and left the room without a word. I didn't have it in me to go another round with him right now. I was tired and so close to my breaking point; I feared what I might do. Then whatever friendships my brother had here would be ruined. I would be okay with that, but something told me Octavian wouldn't.

CHAPTER 7

After leaving the table, I'd gone up the stairs and opened every door until I found Vian's room, grateful I hadn't been followed by Flynn or the sounds of people shouting. It made for a nice change. I knew I found the right room when I smelled his shitty comforting cologne. A mixture of Old Spice and his natural scent. If that hadn't given it away, the room also screamed Vian. It was painted in his favorite color, sunburst orange, with posters of bands I knew he liked.

Brooke came in and sat down next to me, Liam quickly followed, sprawling out next to me on my other side. He laced one of his hands with mine which drew my attention away from an *Arctic Monkeys* poster I'd been boring holes in for the past five minutes. My eyes widened, completely put off by how touchy-feely he was, but he just smirked at me with a *deal with it* look that made me roll my eyes. I'd talk to Vian later about his roommates and my need for personal space. If I was being honest with myself—and I rarely was—I could feel the spark between our clasped hands. I was energized just having him close to me. At least he wasn't playing with my fingers, because I didn't know what I would do if there was any more friction between us.

"You alright?" Brooke asked.

"I'm good. Just tired," I answered, surprised that it was actually the truth. I was good.

"Vian will be up in a few, it's his night to help with the dishes," she sighed down at me. "So, you have probably about ten minutes to tell me some silly stories about you guys growing up."

I giggled—probably because I was mentally exhausted—and tried to think of something good, but not too personal. "Hmmm…. First tooth or swiss cheese?" I asked them thoughtfully. Both stories were equally hilarious.

Brooke's eyes lit up as a smile took over her face. She was already pretty, but when she smiled, she was stunning. A twinge of jealousy shot through me, but I pushed it away. I didn't like being a vain person.

"I'm gonna go with first tooth," Liam decided, smirking at me. Butterflies erupted in my stomach and I forgot what I was thinking about. His lips completely fascinated me. My gaze flickered up to his eyes and I saw the heat in them. Oh my god… I'd been openly staring at his mouth.

"Don't listen to her," Vian said from the door. "She lies." He glared at me, but I welcomed his attention. A distraction from my traitorous thoughts about Liam was more than welcome. I giggled again, unable to keep it in and mentally kicked myself. I couldn't remember another time where I'd giggled like a fool.

"That's not fair!" Brooke laughed. "You've heard all sorts of stories about us. Now that Liv is here, I want to hear all about young Octavian." She smacked my thigh with the back of her hand. "Let's hear it."

I grinned as Vian marched towards us. There was a dark twinkle in his eyes that told me he was enjoying the teasing, but he was going to fully retaliate against it.

"So, it all started when Dad let us watch some movie about the tooth fairy. If you woke up and saw her when she collected your teeth—"

Vian launched himself at me and attempted to cover my mouth without crushing me which only made me laugh harder.

"I will tickle the shit out of you if you don't stop!" he promised.

Someone grabbed him from behind and hauled him off me. Shouting ensued as Liam wrestled my brother to the bed. Rolling away from them, I continued, "If you saw her, she would murder you. It completely freaked us both out. Then a few weeks later, he lost his first tooth, so he tried to super glue it back in. Instead, he managed to glue half his mouth shut and Mom had to use nail polish remover to get him unstuck."

Liam and Brooke dissolved into a fit of laughter. I was nearly crying by that time, gasping for breath. Liam let go of Vian and he launched himself at me again, this time pinning my arms down as he tickled my sides.

"You. Are. The. Worst. Twin. Ever." He panted each word as I struggled to get away from him.

"Help," I gasped. "Can't breathe."

"You're heartless, Olive." I giggled some more before he leaned down into my face. "I'll tell them about your first period."

"No!" I bucked trying to displace him.

"Oh, that's just mean, Vi," Brooke said with mock horror. She'd finally recovered enough and was tugging at his arms.

"What's going on here?" Lucien asked, striding into the room and surveyed us on the bed.

Ben walked in behind him, seeing us all tangled together and sprinted toward the bed before jumping into the air and landing on top of us. A play fight ensued. Someone grabbed pillows as Lucien joined us and we spent a good fifteen minutes trying to knock each other off the bed. I landed a really good hit to the back of Liam's head as he took aim at his brother. He turned toward me with a wide grin.

"You're dead, Kitten," he said before he shoved me down into the mattress. I waited for the panic to spring forward as his body crushed me, but it didn't come. The whole situation felt unnatural to me but at the same time, it wasn't. I wanted these people to include me and be comfortable with me as much as I hated myself for wanting it. With a nervous laugh, I shoved at his face, the only part of him I could reach. My palm covered his mouth as I tried to push him, but he just licked my palm.

"Eww!" I shouted, wiping my palm on his shirt. "You can't just lick people."

He sat back and smiled, victorious. "What's the matter, Kitten? Scared of boy germs?"

I scoffed at him and his stupid nickname for me, shoving him the rest of the way off me. I took the chance to get my breath back and grinned as everyone else continued to play fight. It was the first time in days, hell months really, that I'd enjoyed myself, I realized. Like we were all normal teenagers. Like I'd never suffered. Like I hadn't just lost my best friend.

My mood shifted and a deep throb of pain settled in my chest. Tears stung my eyes and fell before I could get a handle on myself. Liam noticed first, but within seconds, Vian was gathering me up in his arms and held me against his chest as grief rocked through me.

That was the thing about grief. One moment, you could be fine. And in the next, all the ugliness poured out of you. I'd gone through all of this before. First with losing my parents and then when Octavian and I were separated.

The atmosphere around us grew quiet. I ended up with my head in Brooke's lap again with Vian rubbing my back. No one said anything as I cried silently. I was too exhausted to do much else. Everyone spread around us on the bed. A large hand stroked my arm. Someone else had my feet in their lap and kneaded them gently.

I wanted everyone to stop touching me, but at the same time, I didn't. It was a comfort I didn't feel I deserved. Instead, I just closed my eyes and tried to block their presence from my mind as I dealt with the pain of being alive when my friend wasn't, and I realized that it didn't matter that she hadn't come into my life on accident because I knew that no matter what, Emma had been my best friend through and through.

I wasn't just grieving for her either. There were years of grief and pain that poured from me in that moment. My ruined childhood. The loss of time with my twin. And the absence of companionship. The fact that for the first time, I could see how I was supposed to be. I'd always ignored it before. I saw the kids in school who laughed easily, free to make friends, to trust completely and told myself that it just wasn't who I was meant to be, but here with these people, I could see just how much I had been lying to myself.

"What happens tomorrow?" I finally managed to ask, working to distract myself. Anything to try and claw my way back out of that dismal pit again.

"Tomorrow, we'll visit the council physician to get

a physical and to get you into the network," Ben answered smoothly.

"Don't get him started," Flynn groaned.

My eyes popped open at the sound of his voice to find him lying on the end of the bed. I hadn't heard him come in and I was shocked to see him. He smiled at me with an unreadable look in his eye. I almost —*almost*—drew my feet away from him, but just bit my lip instead.

"He's not wrong," Brooke said with a small giggle. "Ben can talk your ear off about science."

"So, if I want to fall asleep, just ask him to talk. Got it," I quipped.

"I'm hurt. She's wounded me," Ben said seriously.

I lifted my head to find him sitting against the wall with Kieran. Looked like we were all piled into Vian's bed. Not that it was hard. All the beds I'd seen were huge. Still, we were tightly packed together.

"I was kidding," I told him. "I'm sorry for wounding you."

"Oh," he replied, a ghost of a smile on his lips. "I do like science though."

"And Disney," Lucien supplied, giving Ben a fond look as his blonde hair fell forward into his face. He raked his fingers through it before smiling in my direction. "He's strange, but we keep him anyway."

I laughed as the last of my tension left me and found myself staring at the long line of his neck and how it moved when he talked as he relaxed back against his brother. "That is a bit weird but meh, if he's happy, I say let him be."

Flynn snorted and we shared a grin before I caught myself.

Fuck. No. I didn't like him. Why was I smiling at him? I closed my eyes again and lay my head back in Brooke's lap. She resumed combing my hair with her fingers.

"Lucien, I've decided to ban you from her hair. I'm claiming it," Brooke announced.

I flew into a sitting position. "What?" I squeaked. Since when was my hair claimable? No one was claiming it. I could take care of my own hair just fine.

"That's not fair. She should get to decide which of us has rights. Not you," Lucien exclaimed.

What the hell? My eyebrows shot up as I looked between them with horror. "No one is claiming my hair. And no one is cutting it except a professional. Just going to state that right now."

Several of the guys snickered and I glared at them. Lucien smiled and pulled a wallet from his back pocket. He opened it and dug around for a second before handing me a card.

It was a beautician's license. *Fuck me.*

"No," I said firmly, handing it back. His smile fell, making me feel terrible. He was really beautiful when he smiled. My stomach clenched and instinctively, I reached forward to touch his arm. I pulled myself back at the last second, surprised by the action. "I… I'll think about it, but I get final say on what happens to it." I pointed a finger between them, making it plain that I was not joking on this matter.

"Good luck with that," Vian said quietly. I grimaced at him as I propped myself up, not liking how quiet the room had grown. Lucien was looking away from me, but I saw a tightness in his eyes. At the end of the bed, Flynn looked like he was ready to murder me but that wasn't anything new. Even Ben's jaw was tight and clenched. I couldn't see the others faces since most of them were laying down or turned away from my position, but the tension of their bodies made it clear something was wrong. What had I done?

"I'm going to sleep," I hedged, feeling like I should apologize but not knowing what to say sorry for. I somehow maneuvered myself out of the bed and was halfway across the room before someone caught my arm. I turned to see Flynn's hand on my forearm.

"Where?" he asked calmly, his blue eyes staring into mine.

"Umm, Brooke's room?" I asked, uncertain by the sudden change in his demeanor. His mood shifts were unnerving.

He nodded and let go. "We should have your room ready in a few days. We weren't prepared yet," he said, matter of fact, though he shrugged his shoulders. My arm felt cold without his hand on it anymore and I trembled with the effort not to grab him to bring his warmth back. Then his words registered, and I was blinking.

For some reason, I really hadn't thought about having my own space here. I knew before the beginning of summer that I was going to live with my brother. Living here with seven other people was staring me in the face and I was completely unprepared.

I nodded after a deep sigh. "Alright. Thanks."

CHAPTER 8

"Ugg, Luc—Sugar, it's too early," Brooke's voice woke me as light from the hallway streamed through the open door. "Seriously, Lucien. Scram. We'll be out in a bit."

"She barely ate and we're going to be busy most of the day," he called softly from across the room.

I hit the pillow next to me with a moan of frustration. Sleep was the only thing I cared about in that moment and Lucien was ruining it.

"Good job," Brooke sighed. "You woke her."

Lucien scoffed at her and the bed shifted under me before her lap jerked. Something thudded on the other side of the room.

"Wench. You hit me in the face," he snapped followed by the door closing.

"Okay, now that Sugs is gone, we need to get you up. You do need to eat," she told me with a pat. I grunted at her, not confirming or denying what she said. She could try to boss me around but there were only a few things that could have gotten me out of the bed. When I didn't move, she smacked me on the ass. "Up, woman. We have a council to please and shopping to do."

"I'm up," I groaned as the light clicked on, making me wince, but also trying not to laugh. It would only encourage her. Make it easier for her to hurt me later when she lost interest in being my friend.

That's what usually happened with people. With the exception of Payton and Emma. Thinking about them made me a bit bitter though, knowing what I did now. At some point, I wanted to call Payton, even though she'd lied to me. I'd have to borrow a phone though. None of my belongings seemed to make the trip.

"Good. You can use my bathroom again. Just knock first if you don't want to catch Ben in the nude. We share," she said, breaking into my thoughts, already hurrying around her room like a tornado.

I sneered at her in disgust. "How are you so awake, it's unnatural."

"It's a gift. Not a morning person, I take it?"

"I don't really sleep well most nights," I replied quietly as I rolled out of the bed and looked around. "I have to say, I'm surprised the rest of the brood isn't in here," I remarked. Brooke had warned me before we fell asleep that I should not be surprised if we had extra company in the morning. Apparently sharing beds was not an issue around here, even though everyone had their own room.

"We're called a Circle," Brooke said absently as she stripped out of her pajamas. I admired her figure, still not moving from the bed. It made me even more self-conscious about my own body. I was small, barely above five feet tall and thin as a rail with barely anything resembling curves to speak of. Paired with my scars, I was like teen Skipper after one of my younger foster sisters had mutilated her. With a sigh at my dark thoughts, I heaved myself up from the bed.

"Why not a coven?" I asked, going back to our conversation.

"Because we're not magic. And they're actually sort of gross."

"What?" I asked. "How are they gross?"

"They're all into using body fluids and animal parts." She paused, scrunching up her nose. "I mean, we use herbs and such for tinctures and whatnot, but everything else we do is science. Perfectly natural. What they do is perverse. Not that all witches are bad. Just…gross." She paused again to smear clear gloss across her lips. "Plus, all their witchcraft comes with nasty costs for using what doesn't belong to them."

"None of that makes sense. Except for the animal parts stuff. That does sound gross," I replied. I shuddered just thinking about all that implied. I decided to change the subject. "So, how much of a fool did I make out of myself, you know, with the random breakdown and all?"

"Oh, that's nothing. There were way worse meltdowns when we lost Emma's sister."

I stopped short. "I didn't know she…" My throat grew tight again.

"It was a long time ago," Brooke replied, not meeting my eyes. "Let's go eat before the nag is back. The guys will want to drive into town. I mean, I could drive us myself, but without you having any training, everyone has gone into protective mode. I know you value your independence and I want to encourage that, but until things settle, the guys and I want to operate as a unit." I met her eyes nodding that I understood her reasons.

"Plus, if it was just the two of us walking in, it would be like inviting people to talk to us. Everyone in town is going to be insanely curious about you." She sat on the end of her bed and pulled on a pair of flats before throwing her head back to laugh. "So Vian said you'd be crazy about privacy and while the guys and I are trying to respect that, I can promise you, the rest of the community is not going to abide by it. You'll learn pretty quickly that touching strangers here isn't uncommon. Everyone likes to let the energy flow. Plus, horrible gossips."

"So, I shouldn't punch some old man in the face if he grabs my ass?" I quipped.

"I mean, you can, but it won't just be old men. We've got biddies like the rest of the world," she fired back. "Oh, and I should tell you, most of them hit back," she tacked on with a small laugh.

I sighed. Great.

Pausing at the bathroom door, I debated whether I should knock or not. It didn't sound like anyone was in there, but I wasn't sure. I started thinking about how I would feel if someone walked in on me and knocked on the door. No one answered and I breathed a sigh of relief before pushing it open.

I rushed through getting ready, using my finger to brush my teeth and borrowing a comb from Brooke to tame my wild hair before braiding it. She waited calmly for me as I grimaced over my wardrobe choices. All of them were extremely girly. There was a disturbing amount of pink and purple in the bag of leftovers Brooke had given me. I finally decided on a dress, only because it was green, and because it looked sturdy. It fell just below my knees, but it had sleeves and covered my nonexistent cleavage.

"We're definitely going shopping?" I asked as we headed downstairs, fingering the hem of my sleeves.

"Yes. Afterward. Lucien is going to insist on it," she replied.

"Is he gay?" I asked. I was starting to get the impression he might be, by the way Brooke seemed to mention him when it came to fashion and whatnot.

She laughed and shook her head. "Definitely not."

Well okay then. He was just weird. Like everyone else, apparently.

We headed toward the kitchen. Vian sat at the bar, his head tucked down over a steaming cup of coffee. I settled into the seat beside him and regarded him with a look.

"I can practically feel you judging me from here," he muttered into his cup.

"I just don't understand the obsession," I said simply, eyeing the mug of black coffee he seemed to be inhaling instead of drinking, as if the fumes alone where fuel.

He groaned and turned a bleary eye in my direction. "Don't start. I'm not awake yet."

"And what would Princess like to drink with her breakfast?" Kieran asked, coming up behind me. His large hand pressed against the small of my back and I shifted in my seat, trying to dislodge it. Instead, he shifted his hand to rest against my hip and ran his thumb over it. My entire body came alive, thrumming with excitement, something I was not even close to being ready to acknowledge.

"This," I said, motioning toward his hand on me, "is how you go from being 'Asshole's Twin' to 'Other Asshole,'" I said, pushing his hand away. He grimaced as I turned to face him. Brooke could talk all day about how touching was perfectly normal. Didn't mean I had to go along with it just because they wanted that. "And please don't call me Princess." His palms came up as he backed away. I turned and looked at the others in the kitchen. "That goes for everyone else. Ask first," I finished sweetly.

Lucien breezed by us, throwing Brooke a dirty look and rounded the counter, heading toward the stove. She snorted a laugh at him as he pulled the oven open and waved an arm. I could hear him muttering under his breath about pillows and messing up his hair as a tray of muffins floated out, making me lose my train of thought.

"So weird," I mumbled, all my previous irritation gone in the blink of an eye.

"You'll get used to it," Vian replied, following my line of sight. "Though most of us don't really use it for mundane shit. He's just showing off."

"Him muttering under his breath?" I asked, not really having listened to the rest of what he said. I was focused on the way Lucien moved around the kitchen. Graceful and light on his feet.

"Earth to Olive?" Vian said, waving a hand in front of my face. I jerked and stared in his direction. Vian's line of sight shifted to the right over my shoulder. I turned, realizing I'd forgotten about Kieran and raised an eyebrow at him because he was staring at me.

"What?" I asked, bewildered by his expression. He looked so perplexed and lost. Something told me I'd put the look there.

His mouth opened and closed for a second before he gathered himself. "I was wondering if you'd mind…that is…"

"Just spit it out, Kier," Brooke said. She'd sat on the other side of my brother but was now leaning around him with an exasperated look.

"Your hip is still bruised. I'd rather you didn't go

to the council with injuries. It would look bad for us. Can I heal it?" he asked.

I thought about it for a second. "Do I have to take my clothes off for that? Because the answer would be no."

"It would work better if we had direct contact with the injury, but not necessary," he replied. For a moment, his eyes hooded. I knew what that look meant and it was so not going to happen. He was cute and all, but this was not only not the time, it was certainly not the place for me to toss my virginity out the window.

"It doesn't hurt," Brooke interjected. "The healing. If that's what you were worried about."

"Fine," I said, giving him a long look. "Just no funny business like before." I pointed a finger at him, showing him I meant business, but I forced myself to smile to soften the reprimand. He visibly relaxed, not at all bothered by my threat.

I turned in my seat as Kieran brought a hand up and placed it on the back of my neck. It brought his body almost flush with mine. Close enough that I had to spread my knees so I didn't hit him in the dick.

No. No thinking about dicks, I chided myself. No matter how yummy said owner of the dick was. He smelled like cedar and something flowery. It was similar, yet different from Flynn. For fuck's sake. Now I was thinking about Flynn with his brother between my thighs.

"Did she just say something about dicks," Lucien asked.

I went to jerk away from Kieran, but he pulled me in tighter and my neck grew cool under his palm, almost to the point that it stung. I sucked in a breath, and with it his scent. It seriously made my insides flutter. My head leaned forward to rest on his chest without me even thinking about. Something foreign coiled around me, bringing goosebumps to my skin before it rippled inward. I groaned as my hip flared up with heat. It burned in a flash and then soothed away. I shivered as the sensation ebbed.

"All done," he said softly into my hair. He let go of me slowly, making sure I was upright before stepping back. I stared up at him in a daze before my brain reconnected with the rest of me.

I let out a shuddering breath. "I…"

He smiled. "Just an after effect. It'll pass in a second."

I nodded as something thudded onto the counter behind me. I turned slowly and blinked at a cup of coffee, heavy with cream, and a blueberry muffin.

"Eat up," Lucien said with a wide knowing grin.

"This sucks," I whispered under my breath as I tentatively poked my hip to see if it was still bruised. He smiled even wider, flashing me all of his teeth.

"Just eat, Beautiful," he said with a chuckle.

CHAPTER 9

The sun beat down on us as everyone piled into a single SUV. I wondered briefly why there were two but decided to file that question away for another time.

I leaned into my twin who sat next to the window in the middle row beside me. "How come there aren't any adults living with us?"

He smirked. "Entwined are considered adults at fourteen but have to wait to start living with their circle till they are sixteen," he answered. "Flynn and Kieran's parents live just down the road from us though."

"Oh," I said, surprised.

"Not to mention, we're technically all adults now. Time to start thinking like one," he said briskly.

"Is that a dig?" I asked, slightly put out.

"No," he answered with a sigh. "Not at you." He

nodded toward the front passenger seat where Flynn sat watching us.

Seriously? Why was he watching me again? Didn't he have better things to do? I wasn't going to rise to the bait. This time. I hoped...

The SUV started moving, with Kieran in the driver's seat. I glanced back at the house, finally getting my first look at it from the outside. Just as I had thought, it was a large house. What I hadn't expected was how quaint it looked. The bottom floor was made of stone but had stripped wooden siding about halfway up the wall where the windows started. It seemed that the porch only wrapped around one side, disappearing toward the back. The stripped siding continued up to the second story and then a third. I silently vowed to explore the rest of the house soon. I wouldn't be surprised if there was a basement. I knew there was a backyard, but I'd only gotten a glimpse of it through the sliding glass door last night at dinner.

The place disappeared as we headed down the dirt road, the sunlight suddenly blocked out by the thick canopy overhead. The woods were thick and stunning. We drove for a few miles as I stared out my brother's window, tuning out the chatter of the others as we went. Every now and then, the road forked, and I caught sight of other cottages through the trees. Most didn't look nearly as large as ours, but I couldn't say for sure.

"I'm surprised you haven't tried to head out into all this yet," Vian said, leaning into my side.

I glanced at him and shrugged. "Where would I go?" I loved the outdoors, something that Vian knew all too well. But it was also dangerous to go out into unfamiliar woods by yourself. "I'd probably get lost."

Flynn let out a derisive laugh. "I'd rather not have to form a search party for our resident princess."

Vian cut a glare in his direction. "Our dad taught us how to read the land. We used to go on weekend orienteering trips. She's actually pretty good at woodcraft. We used to spend hours outside as kids. She never gets lost." My heart swelled at my brother's praise, even if it was a bit of an exaggeration. I hadn't been orienteering since before our parents died and that was a long time ago.

"Well, she shouldn't go out by herself just now," Brooke piped up behind us.

"No one's saying she should," Kieran said from the driver's seat. "But we should make an effort to do things she likes. Besides, Flynn and I spend a lot of time in the woods. There's nothing dangerous around here."

"I'd be down to do some hiking," Lucien murmured, drawing my attention to him on my other side.

"You?" I asked, a bit astounded. "You don't seem the type who likes to get sweaty."

He tilted his head toward me and lowered his voice so only I could hear. "I love to get sweaty." His brown eyes dug into mine with a smirk that told me he wasn't talking about a hike in the woods. I looked away quickly.

"Jesus, Luc. Why don't you just throw her down and rip her clothes off already?" Liam quipped behind us. Several people chuckled, making me wish I could melt into the seat and pretend I didn't exist.

"There's a fine line between flirting and being a pig," Lucien snapped over his shoulder. Then to me, "Sorry, I didn't mean to embarrass you."

"It's fine," I said quietly, unable to meet his eyes. Was it fine? No. Okay, maybe a little bit, but also no. Just no.

"Livvy," Kieran called, grabbing my attention just as the SUV filled with sunlight. Out the front window, I could see a valley spreading out before us. We rolled down a hill that overlooked a small town, connected by a few paved roads. At the center of it all was a gothic monstrosity that looked like one of those abandoned hospitals from a horror flick.

"What is that?" I asked.

"Well, that's the town, but I assume you mean the building at the center," Lucien said next to me. I'd largely been ignoring how close he sat to me after his earlier comment but once my attention shifted to him, I caught his scent and leaned in. It was a cross between citrus and cotton. An odd combination, but I liked it. It was better than Vian who I swear had bathed in his cologne this morning. I was going to have a come-to-Jesus talk with him about it soon.

Sure, it was comforting because I associated it with him, but damn son, he didn't need to use the whole fucking bottle.

"Yeah, I'm not going in that. Not happening. Just the sight of it makes my skin crawl." It really did too.

"Not an option," Flynn remarked, throwing a wolfish smile at me from the front seat.

Bristling with irritation, I closed my eyes and willed myself to calm down. "You can't force me," I tried to reason.

He snorted a laugh and turned back around to point at it through the window. "That's where the council is. Pretty much every job associated with our kind happens in that building. It's not as creepy as it seems. I promise."

I shook my head even though he couldn't see me and changed the subject. Avoidance. Always the best option. "Where is this town anyway?"

"An island just off the coast of Oregon called Vol. It's hidden though," Ben said behind me. "It's actually rather large, but completely cloaked to any kind of radar detection and there's some Arts in place that keep it that way."

"That's not weird at all," I whispered. Lucien chuckled beside me. His shoulder brushed against mine as he covered his mouth to hide a smile. A small grin bloomed on my face, unbidden but his reaction was sort of infectious.

Ben continued as if he hadn't heard us. Maybe he hadn't, but it only made Lucien struggle not to laugh more. "There's also a specific Art that has to be used every day to keep the place clear of military drones. I have a book—"

His voice cut off as a hand reached over the back of the seat and hit Lucien in the back of the head. I burst out laughing as Brooke's hand disappeared and she said something quietly to her twin in the backseat. I twisted in my seat to get a look at her. She glared at the back of Lucien's head while Ben sat beside her blushing furiously. It sobered me up quick.

I mouthed an apology to them. Brooke gave me a small tight smile in acknowledgement, but Ben just ducked his head.

Shit. I got the feeling that it happened a lot. It made sense that he tended to be quiet. I wouldn't talk much either if people made fun of me for being passionate about something. And it was obvious that Ben was passionate about this stuff. I didn't really want to get involved in their drama, but I also didn't want to add to it.

We pulled to a stop in front of the monstrosity and it immediately called for my attention. Everyone started to pile out of the car, but I sat frozen in my seat as I stared at the building up close.

The creep factor had ramped up from a five to an eleven. Overtly, it wasn't that bad. Just a huge structure that looked completely out of place. There were at least four stories, all with beautiful sweeping lines that I could appreciate. There weren't any broken windows and the gray stonework was actually sort of nice, but something about it didn't sit right with me at all.

"You coming, Olive?" Vian asked. He held his hand out to me to help me out of the back, but I still couldn't move. Someone brushed up against my other side and I jumped, but when I turned my head, the door was closed, and Lucien wasn't in his seat anymore. My twin reached into the car and took my hand, grabbing my attention. "What's wrong?"

"I don't know," I answered honestly.

"What's the problem?" Flynn barked, coming up behind my brother. I looked at him for a second before my gaze slipped past him to the building they wanted me to enter. I shook my head. I was being stupid. It was just a building. Nothing creepy. Just old.

I slid across the seat and accepted Vian's help getting down. Sometimes, being short really sucked. Like climbing into SUVs with high seats. Flynn shut the door as my twin tucked me into his side and moved toward the front of the car. I felt Flynn's eyes on me, assessing as we moved but I didn't look back. My gaze kept going back to the building before I would realize it and I'd try to focus on something else.

"She's as white as a sheet," Liam said with concern. He moved toward us and cupped one of my cheeks.

Normally I would have swatted him away, but I couldn't stop looking at the damn building. The urge to run, to move away from it grew inside me. I shuddered, realizing what was happening.

"We can't go in there," I found myself pleading. "Something is going to happen if we do." My hands trembled as I stood there facing it.

"Shit," Flynn muttered, brushing Liam aside. Flynn clutched at my forearms. Cedar and cloves wrapped around me as he stepped into my personal space. He glanced down. A small smile formed on his lips, but he erased it with a shake of his head. "Kier, she needs a boost."

He pulled me around to the other side of the hood and spun me away from the building before grasping at my waist and lifting me to sit on it. Kieran placed his hand on the back of my neck before that crisp sting took hold and I sighed into it.

I immediately started to feel better. A few seconds later and I was warm all over and his hand dropped from my neck to my back.

"That's incredible," Flynn said to himself. I had no idea what he meant.

"Hey guys," Ben yelled. We all turned to see him at the top of the steps holding something in his hand. Brooke was halfway up the steps behind him.

A strange mix of fear and rage swept over me at the sight of them there. I roughly shoved Flynn backward. I was surprised to see him stumble back, but I didn't pause as I hopped off the hood and marched toward them. When someone moved to follow, I rounded on my feet, glaring at the others trailing behind me.

"No," I said firmly. Octavian pulled to a stop that

halted everyone else. I turned again and stomped up the steps toward Brooke. Did I barely know these people? Yes. Did that matter in this moment? Not even a little. When I reached her, I grabbed her by both shoulders shaking her. "You don't ever do that again. Ever! When I say we can't do something, I fucking mean it!" I was shouting, beyond angry and terrified. My whole body vibrated with the warring emotions. I pulled her into a rough hug before pushing back and away. She opened her mouth to say something.

I brushed by her and glared daggers at Ben. He stared at me, confusion clear on his face. In his hand, he held a small bone that looked like it had a bundle of dried flowers tied to it with a silver ribbon. I had no idea where he'd found it, and I didn't care. I was in front of him within seconds.

Reaching up, I snagged his ear, pulling him down so his eyes were just inches from mine.

"Ow, fuck!" he cried out.

"Shut it, you idiot. The same goes for you." Without letting go of his ear, I dragged him down the steps. "Never again will you ignore me when I say something is wrong. I've lost too many fucking people and sacrificed enough of myself to this stupid power or whatever you people call it." When we reached the bottom, I let him go and rounded to face him. "Do you understand me?"

"Yes," he breathed, already rubbing at his ear.

I stepped back, bringing my hands up to cover my

mouth, slightly horrified by my reaction. Violence had never been my thing and of all people, I'd used it on Ben. "I'm so sorry," I whispered.

"Don't be sorry," Kieran said, stepping up next to me. "If you hadn't done it, I would have. Part of being in a Circle is communication." His words did nothing to alleviate the guilt churning in my chest after putting my hands on someone who had never been anything but kind to me.

I swallowed and looked down, shuffling my feet. "It does matter," I whispered bitterly. "No one should put their hands on someone like that."

Ben's feet entered my vision just before he tucked a finger under my chin and forced me to look up at him. "You didn't hurt me." I scoffed, darting a glance at his red ear. "No, you didn't. You were frightened and I didn't think. We're both in the wrong."

I could accept both of us being wrong. Nodding, I let out a slow breath and focused on the thing in his other hand. "What is that?"

"Looks like a witch hex. What the fuck is it doing here?" Liam said. He stepped up next to Ben and plucked it from his hand. "Oh hell," he said, letting it drop to the ground. "It's got her resonance all over it." He pointed toward me.

"What does that mean?"

"It means someone wants to hex you," Flynn said quietly. He muttered a curse behind a clenched fist. I watched as he began to pace back and forth. "We're going to need to have someone look at that. See what it does."

"Liam and I can do that," Kieran offered. "We can keep it quiet while you guys go to her appointment." He looked at me. "Feeling's gone, right?"

I nodded.

"Good. I think Ben picking it up probably canceled it out. If it was keyed to you, it probably detonated, but you weren't close enough for it to take effect. I wouldn't be surprised if we found a bit of your hair in that bundle." My eyes widened at his words. "We'll find out for sure. Let's go in."

CHAPTER 10

I gaped as we entered a long room. There were several crystal chandeliers that lit up the space. The floors were a rich dark mahogany, polished to a shine. I could literally see my reflection in it. Walls were painted in warm neutral colors and the entire room was richly decorated in plush furniture and expensive vases. And the plants. They were everywhere. The whole room seemed to overflow with them. It was almost too much, but it all seemed so natural. Unlike the grey impersonable exterior of the building, the reception area felt like I was walking into a high-end hotel.

"Whoa, this is so impressive," I breathed, my eyes looking everywhere, trying to take it all in. A few people sat in chairs scattered around, but I ignored their curious expressions.

"Really? This is the big shocker?" Flynn quipped.

"Not the impressive fires or our abilities to heal the human body?"

"Shut up," I muttered, though I did grin at him. Catching myself, I smothered it quickly. He was still an asshole and someone I couldn't let myself get too close to. As soon as I covered my smile, his open and friendly gaze shuttered.

"Yeah, keep lying to yourself, Princess," he said quickly before turning away from me.

I hated the guilt that tried to creep up inside of me. And I hated his nickname for me too. Somehow, I didn't think he would change it even if I asked. The others, probably, but not him. Because he was an asshole.

I followed as he approached a large desk, almost overlooking the old lady behind it. I stopped a few feet away, but Flynn reached back and snagged my hand, dragging me toward him.

"Hey Melina, we're here for a registration appointment," he said smoothly, almost with charm. I had to crane my head around to be sure it was him speaking. His tone was so similar to Kieran's I had to double check who was talking, but to my complete shock, it was in fact, Asshole speaking.

Out of the corner of his eye, he caught me staring and smirked. I quickly looked away and focused on the small woman in front of me.

The little biddy smiled up at us as she tidied her silvered hair, blushing at him. She looked between us and then down at our joined hands with a knowing look. "Well," she said smiling up at me. "Ya've been a long time comin', haven't ya?" she drawled. My eyes widen as she stood up and puttered around the side of the desk. "Look just like yer momma when she was yar age. Bit of ya Father in there too, I spose. Got his cheeks."

I looked over my shoulder, searching for Vian. When I spotted him, I gave him the *help me* look. He smiled at me and shook his head. Damned traitor. I turned back as the woman stepped right in front of me and grabbed my free hand in her old wrinkled ones.

"Umm..." What was I supposed to say to some sweet old lady who just dropped the fact that she knew my parents on me like a bomb? Okay so it might not seem like a bomb in her eyes. She probably thought she was being nice. To me though, it was a shock.

"Never ya mind. Ya wouldn't remember little ole me." She patted my hand and addressed Flynn. "They're waitin' on ya upstairs, I 'spect." Her gray eyes twinkled as she patted his cheek before throwing an exaggerated wink my direction. "Bet they're all in a tizzy. Nobody knew ya'd fetched her. Probably get a talkin' to," she warned.

"Don't worry about us, Mels. We always skate by," Flynn said, his voice practically dripping with charm. It made me want to smack him upside the head. Either for leading the poor lady along or out of jealousy that he was never this nice to me.

I let go of his fingers like they'd burned me. This was heading into dangerous territory I didn't want to explore. *Do not go and develop feelings for another asshole. That didn't work out so well last time.* Boys did not make the world go 'round. I had bigger problems anyway. Like getting hexed by a witch spell. Figuring out what being Entwined meant. Rebuilding my relationship with my brother. Confronting Payton about her role in all of this. Making Evan pay for what he'd done to Emma.

Flynn grabbed my arm and led me back to the others while I made a mental list of all the things on my mind. The last one surprised me, even though it shouldn't have. Did I really want revenge? I examined the thought while the others talked. My wants and needs were a tangled mess. The truth was that I did want Evan to suffer for what he'd done. I cared about the lies between me and my friends. But Emma hadn't deserved to die for it. And something nagged at me about Payton. The look in her eye in those few seconds after Evan pushed her. She'd been afraid more than anything else.

"—Valek should know what it does," Kieran said as I clued back into the conversation.

"Alright, you guys take care of that. We'll meet you back here," Flynn agreed.

Liam and Kieran nodded before taking off across the room. Liam paused long enough to brush my arm as he passed and offered me a small smile that I didn't return. My mood was completely soured from the day's events.

"Why not the elevator?" I asked when we started up a flight of stairs. I gave the elevator bank across the reception area a look of longing. I didn't dislike exercise, but come on, why take the stairs if you didn't have to?

"Less people," Flynn said, dropping my arm.

"What he means is we're trying to keep the hyenas at bay," Brooke quipped, turning to give me a small wink. I smirked back at her, remembering our earlier conversation.

Vian fell back to walk beside me. I linked arms with him, trying to hide my nervousness as we spilled out of the stairwell into a long, carpeted hallway. Ben took the lead, leaving the rest of us to trail after him as we passed white doors on either side. Something about them bothered me but I couldn't say what until we paused in front of one.

Where were the doorknobs?

Ben pressed his palm flat against the door and waited a second before there was a humming noise.

"Is it going to explode?" I stage-whispered to Vian. He snorted and shook his head.

"Biometrics," he answered, as if I knew what the hell that was.

"Bio-what-ics?"

"He means it reads our biology and resonance," Ben said absently.

"Science is my all-time worst subject." It always

had been. I had a hard time retaining all those facts, which was weird because it was the only subject I struggled with.

"Never mind," Brooke said in a placating voice. "It's not that important." I smiled at her gratefully. More and more, I was starting to feel stupid when it came to this world. I wasn't dumb before this, but something in my brain refused to cooperate with the rest of me.

The door opened and Ben dropped his hand, stepping back. He motioned for me to go first. How chivalrous of him.

I paused halfway through the door. Having already let go of Vian, I reached out to snag Brooke. No way in hell was I going in there alone. This was the sort of thing I always did with Emma. But she wasn't here anymore. My lip trembled as I took in the room beyond. It looked like a lab, complete with all sorts of scientific gizmos I couldn't name. Like ordered chaos and my own personal hell. I'd never liked doctors, but I understood the need for them.

The last time I'd seen one was just before being placed in my last foster home. I'd spent two days in the hospital after one of my foster family's real children had smacked me around for having a smart mouth. He liked to use his hands and had left me with a broken jaw, a fractured wrist, some severe bruising, and possible internal bleeding. No one had operated on me, so I wasn't sure how true that last one was. It'd only felt like it.

"You're shaking," Brooke whispered to me. I nodded, acknowledging her, but didn't say anything. I was too busy staring at the three lab techs, wondering which one would examine me.

"She doesn't like doctors," Vian answered as he wrapped an arm around me. "It's fine, Olive. They'll do a quick physical and some readings. Very standard."

"Right," I said, trying to trust his words. It was hard though. "Just no needles."

The only man in the room had noticed us finally and put down whatever he was doing. He looked to be in his early thirties, with dark hair and hazel eyes. He smiled as he approached us, and I forced myself to relax.

"Renee," he called over his shoulder. "Can you assist?"

I looked past him to see a woman stand up slowly and waddle toward us. She was very, *very* pregnant with light brown hair and warm blue eyes.

The man waited for her to join him before he continued toward us, assisting her as she moved. I wondered if it hurt to be that pregnant. She looked ready to pop. How the hell did her back support all that extra weight? I decided right then and there that I never wanted kids. I couldn't imagine my small body contorted like that. Just…no.

I looked back to the man. I watched as the friendly smiles and nods he gave to the others melted away as his gaze came to rest on me, frowning as he looked down at me. I instinctively took a step back and bumped into someone, letting out a squeak of surprise.

Lucien's arms came up around me to keep me steady.

"I'm so sorry," the man said. "I didn't mean to frighten you. It's just a shock," he said before looking over my head. "Hi Flynn, how are you?"

"Good, sir. We're here to get Olivia registered and have her testing done," Flynn said quickly, skirting a look in my direction.

"Yes, of course. I've been expecting you." He helped Renee into a nearby chair and started going through the equipment on the desk. "Though I can tell you now, this is going to take a bit longer than expected."

"Why is that?" Brooke asked, concern was clear in her voice and written all over her face.

"Well, she's not quite right, is she? Surely, you've noticed her stunted growth," he said, slightly exasperated. I flinched as if he'd struck me. Being small wasn't new to me, but having it stated so bluntly, as if something were wrong with me, hurt. Fucking doctors.

"Demaric," Ben said sharply. "She's right there. You're scaring her."

"Right, sorry," he said, offering me an apology with his eyes. "I didn't mean it in a bad way. It's just not natural is all. But I'm sure we'll get it sorted out."

I wasn't sure how to feel. Nothing he said was

comforting in any way. In fact, I wanted nothing more than to walk right out the door and pretend he didn't exist.

Vian leaned into me. "You know I love you, right?" he asked, chucking me under the chin. I recognized what he was doing. Distracting me. I rolled my eyes and leaned back into Lucien. His arms tightened around me.

"Whatever, can we just get this over with?" I'd never been good with verbal communication, especially when feelings were involved. It was comforting, having all these people around me, even if I didn't quite trust them yet. Lucien in particular seemed to know that words wouldn't help right now. His chest pressed into my back and I felt his steady heartbeat beating between my shoulder blades. I wouldn't be able to stay there, but for now, it helped.

Demaric smiled at me and motioned for me to move closer. I took a fortifying breath and left the safety of Lucien's arms. The man held out a small silver device in his hands. There were several leads attached to one end. I eyed it warily, wondering what I was supposed to do with it.

"I need to attach these to your stomach," he explained.

"Why?"

"It's an electromagnetic machine that works best if placed over a major artery," Ben supplied. "The best place is the abdominal aorta." I looked at him like he had two heads. Seeming to realize what he'd done, he smiled at me. "Sorry. It, uhh, measures certain things in your body through the bloodstream. Like sugars. It can also test your resonance, see how powerful you are. Whether you're blocked, or scarred, that sort of thing."

"I get everything but the bit about being blocked or scarred," I said. I knew what blood sugar was but the rest of it was sort of gibberish. "Give me a book later?" I added with raised eyebrows.

His small smile morphed into a beautiful smile that lit up his face, just like his sister's. The ice in my heart melted just a fraction, and I blinked at him.

"Exactly right, though. Good job, Ben," Demaric said. "Just lift your…." He trailed off, realizing I was in a dress at the same time that I did.

Fuck. I turned and glared at Brooke. The chick had watched me get dressed this morning and hadn't said a damn word.

"Sorry!" she rushed to say. "I didn't think about it. Plus, you look so cute in it."

Kill me now… cute? Ugg. My face heated and a shudder rippled down my spine. She and I were going to have a talk later.

"Actually," Renee said, "this is perfect. I have to do a full physical on you, including a pap, so you'd have to change anyway." She smiled at me with sympathy as my expression fell into a grimace.

Double fuck.

CHAPTER 11

The room Demaric left me in was cold. It looked like a typical exam room, complete with a sink along one wall, one of those small spinney stools, and a table for patients to sit on. I was staring up into a blue cupboard above the sink, cursing my own height. The gowns were on the top shelf and I could either ask someone for help or climb for it.

Nervous, I looked between the door and the black countertop before muttering a curse. Just before I put my hand on the door to open it, I heard voices from the other side and paused. It sounded like Flynn and one of the doctors were having an argument and all my resolve to ask for help flew out the window. I turned back toward the counter and started to hoist myself up. I had just put one knee on it when the door opened.

"—not mention our dynamic in the report?" Flynn was asking someone.

"You know I have to," Demaric's voice answered. "The council is already up in arms about the stunt that you all pulled. It would just cause more issues if I left something out and they take notice of the problem."

Flynn sighed and backed into the room. "What are you doing?" he barked when he caught sight of me frozen halfway up the counter.

"Umm." I slowly slid back down until my feet touched the floor. "I can't reach."

His eyes drifted from me to the gowns on the top shelf before he smirked and turned back. "She's not dressed yet. Give us a moment." He shut the door and strode across the small room and snatched one down for me. "Here. Get changed."

"Where is everyone else?" I asked.

"Brooke and Lucien left to get you some clothes since we don't know how long this will take. We have dinner tonight with my parents. Vian and Ben got called away by Liam. It's just you and me."

I blinked at him as he explained. The others leaving I could sort of understand, but not my brother. I worked to keep my breathing even, but I could tell by the way Flynn was looking at me that he could see the struggle.

"I asked them to leave," he admitted quietly.

"Why would you do that?"

"Because, we need to have a discussion. Get

changed." He pointed to the gown I was worrying in my hands.

"I'm not going to change in front of you," I snapped.

He rolled his eyes as he turned around and showed me his back. "Better?"

I eyed him as I pulled up the hem of my dress. *No more dresses. Period.*

The gown was thin, but thankfully, not white. It didn't take me long to pull it over my underwear before shucking those too, rolling my clothes into a ball and set it all next to the table. I wasn't wearing a bra, mostly because there wasn't one that could fit me, and I didn't know what happened to the one I'd been wearing when I'd arrived. The back of the gown was open, so I had to hold it shut as I climbed onto the examination table.

"Done," I said, somewhat bitterly. I still couldn't believe Vian had left me here, or even Brooke for that matter. All that talk about being a unit and doing things together felt like a lie. "What do we need to talk about?"

He turned, giving me a once over from head to foot and smiled warmly. "I'm not the best with words so I'm just going to say it. The bullshit needs to stop."

"What bullshit?" I asked, feeling my hackles start to rise again.

"The evading, standoffs, the lack of trust in our family. Just all of it." He walked closer to me and tipped his head down so that I couldn't see his eyes anymore, just the tops of his lashes which were dark and impossibly long. "If you want to be like that at home, that's fine. I'll accept that. But not while we're in public where people are watching. Not everyone around here is a friend."

This was probably the most candid conversation we'd ever had. Even so, it still pissed me off. He threw out the word trust like I should be blind with it. It felt more like he was trying to manipulate me into doing whatever he wanted and not what was best for me. I didn't even really know *what* he wanted from me. Do we become friends? Family? Why was it so important that I had to immediately be everyone's best friend?

Tears burned at the corners of my eyes. My breathing grew ragged. I had to look away from him. At the wall. My feet. Anything but him. My fingers clenched into fists in my lap and it was with effort that I made them relax.

I jumped when his fingers ghosted along my back, skimming over the raised skin there, but I still couldn't look at him. "Where did you get these?" he asked softly. I didn't have to ask what he meant. His quiet tone and his touch were obvious. He wanted to know about the scars on my back. They weren't pretty. Angry, puckered red lines that could almost be mistaken for blisters. They stood out against my pale skin.

A finger drew my chin upward. "This is what I'm talking about," Flynn said when his eyes met mine.

He didn't say it in a mean or accusing way, it was just a fact.

"I don't like talking about them," I answered, not at all surprised by the devoid tone in my voice. "Why do you care?"

His mouth turned into a grim line, but he was saved from answering when the door opened, and Renee waddled inside followed by Demaric who carried two folding chairs.

"Hi, Olivia. We haven't met properly," Renee said as she sat down and wheeled toward me. "I'm Renee, one of the council lab technicians. I took the chance to go over your file quickly while you changed and I just wanted to reassure you that aside from what needs to be reported," her blue eyes cut to Flynn and then back to me, "everything else will remain private."

Flynn's fingers ran up and down my back over my scars. Demaric unfolded one of the chairs while Renee spoke. Without removing his hand from me, Flynn dragged the chair right up next to the table and made himself comfortable. Had I not been so petrified of what was to come, I would have swatted his hand away, but right then, I need it, his warmth and presence to anchor myself. I refused to admit what that might mean in the future, still not ready to count him as an ally. As much as he pissed me off, I think I preferred his brooding and hostility. Or maybe that was just me trying to keep him and the others at arm's length.

Fuck, my mind was in shambles. How had my life grown so complicated? Life hadn't been easy, but it had been simple. Survive, that was all I had to worry about. But now… now things were not simple.

I was staring at Flynn as I tried to wrap my head around everything. He turned to me with a raised eyebrow and nodded toward Renee. Shit. She'd been speaking to me and I'd completely ignored her.

"Sorry," I muttered, giving her my attention.

"That's okay." She smiled and patted my knee. "Just go ahead and lie back. I'm going to get the medical tests out of the way and then we can talk about the results."

What followed was a complete exam of my body, which thankfully both Flynn and Demaric turned away from me without me having to ask. However, Flynn clung to one of my hands at all times, which I was annoyed to find were trembling. I was blaming that on how cold the room was.

She checked every inch of my body, even going through my hair, which she rebraided when she finished. My reflexes were tested, eyesight. Endless medical questions about my health. I sat through it all, answered what I could, and only blushed a little bit when asked about my sexual experiences. Go me!

When Renee had me sit up to check my spine, I was thankful I couldn't see her face. There was no gasp of surprise, so I assumed they were mentioned in the file she'd read. She traced the line of my spine with her fingers and announced that I had excellent posture before having me lay back again. As I complied with her request, I noticed that her face was guarded. I had to admire her ability to control her emotions. When I was sixteen there'd been a nurse who'd burst into tears at the sight of my back. I'd hated her for showing such weakness. They weren't hers to bear so why cry about them?

"Okay, all that's left is the electrometer and the pap. You ready?" Her voice was light as she took her seat.

"Sure," I deadpanned. Out of the corner of my eye I saw Flynn smiling at me. He'd been surprisingly silent throughout the whole thing, something I hadn't thought he was capable of.

Demaric put a sheet across my legs and asked me to pull up my gown so he could put the leads on my stomach.

"We're going to do both at once and try to get you out of here quicker. Scoot down just a bit and put your feet against your butt and spread your legs," Renee requested. I did as she asked, trying not glare at Flynn like this was his fault. It wasn't, but I wanted to, if only to feel like I had control somehow. It was either glare at him or start crying and I was getting so sick of that. I didn't want to be this bitter person who hated everyone and everything.

The sheet was pushed down low on my hips as Demaric loomed over me and attached a few sticky pads to my stomach.

"Try to relax, Olivia," Renee asked gently.

Honestly? That's really the last thing someone should ask you to do. My body tense all over as she turned on a light and dragged it closer. I could feel its heat as it beat down on my inner thighs and wished I could be anywhere else.

"What's your favorite ice-cream?" Flynn asked suddenly, squeezing my hand.

"Uhh, mint double chocolate chip," I answered. I felt Renee down below and stiffened. "All of you suck. This was not what I expected my day to turn into." The words blurted out of me before I could stop them.

Flynn smirked at me. I turned my head to stare at him, trying not to wince at the uncomfortable pressure. Demaric stood back, writing down whatever readings he was getting from his little machine.

"Almost done," Renee commented. My hand clamped down on Flynn's when I felt a sharp pain.

"Fuck, that hurts," I hissed. I blinked back a few tears as the pressure disappeared and Renee sat back. Something plunked into a metal dish and my head popped up, but I couldn't see over the sheet.

"Good job, Olivia. You can relax now." She patted my legs and I put them down. "I'm going to have my sister Jenee rush the results and we'll be back in a few minutes. Sit tight."

"So, I don't need these wires on me anymore?" I asked, nodding toward the leads suck to my skin.

"Nope. I've got everything I need," Demaric smiled, taking the leads off before he turned and helped Renee stand. She waddled out of the room with her clipboard and a dish in her hands.

Flynn finally let go of my hand and collected my dress from the floor. "Here. You're probably freezing."

I mumbled a thanks and waited for him to turn before shedding the gown and pulling the dress over my head. "All good," I mumbled once I had my underwear back on.

I felt awkward as he reclaimed his seat. Had he just sat through that whole thing with me, for me? I blinked at him, overcome by a swirl of unfamiliar emotions. The words bubbled up out of my throat before I could collect myself, but surprisingly, there was no panic. "We were thirteen," I started. "After our parents died, we bounced from home to home." Images I could never forget leapt to the forefront of my mind. Two caskets side by side. Small hands linked together as a social worker walked us into our new home. It was always the same. Vian and I had clung to each other even harder after they died. "We'd always been close, but it became more after that. Neither of us could sleep alone. Families would take us in, but we never stayed for more than a few months. I was always the problem. I had—have—a lot of anger."

I pursed my mouth for a second, questioning whether I really wanted to tell him all of this. Flynn didn't say a word. My hands ended up linked with his at some point, but I finally looked at him and found no judgement in his eyes. If anything, I think he looked relieved. That wasn't going to last.

"We ended up in the home of this very religious woman. A widow. All her kids were grown, and she liked to foster—doing God's work, I suppose. Anyway, our bodies were starting to change, and I don't know if she just woke up one day and realized I had boobs or what. She came to check on us one night. We woke up to her screaming at us. Me, really. She dragged me from the bed, yelling about sin and how I was a temptress." A lone tear streaked down my face as a belt that wasn't there flashed before my eyes. I didn't flinch like normal. I just shut my eyes and shook my head to clear it. Taking a shuddering breath, I continued. "She beat me severely with a belt. I don't think she meant to make me bleed, but by the time she came to her senses…" I watched his eyes for a few seconds, trying to gauge what he was thinking or feeling, but he gave me nothing. Just an open expression that wanted me to continue.

"A teacher noticed the next day at school when I bled through the bandages and my shirt. That same night, Vian and I were taken from her custody, but she must have told them she caught us doing something wrong. Some therapist talked to me and the State decided we were too reliant on one another. We were placed in separate homes and I didn't get to see him again for two years." I sniffed and wiped at my face with my shoulder. "I know I started this, but I don't want to talk about it anymore," I whispered.

"You didn't start it. I asked," he said softly, placing a kiss on my forehead. I barely reacted, only quirking my lips up in a half-hearted smile. Telling him had been both a relief and a curse. Just one of the many demons I carried around with me. He didn't need to know that one event was only the beginning to a cycle of abuse or how I still struggled to recognize that it wasn't my fault.

I needed to forget again, I thought, as I squeezed my eyes shut.

CHAPTER 12

It took Renee almost forty-five minutes before she came back with my results. Flynn and I had lapsed into a comfortable silence, him on his phone while he checked in with the others, and me to my own thoughts. When she entered the room, I knew something was wrong by the pinched look on her face and braced myself for the worst.

Demaric followed her in and shut the door tightly before turning to face us. "I'm sure you've noticed that she's a bit underdeveloped," he stated.

"How can you tell that? Maybe I'm just destined to be short," I quipped, trying to cover the rise of panic stirring in my gut. "Also, right here!" I tacked on, realizing he'd once again talked about me and not *to* me.

Flynn tried, and failed, to hide a grin behind his hand. Demaric looked a bit shocked. "Yes, of course. I apologize."

"Why don't we start with the easy stuff first," Renee suggested.

"Right. Well, your resonance looks great. You're a bit low on your energy flow, but Ben mentioned that you don't have any control yet, so that's to be expected."

I put a hand up, stopping him. "I have no idea what you're talking about."

"It's fine," Flynn said quickly. "I do. We can explain it all later."

I sighed. "I really hate not knowing things, just so you're aware."

"I am aware. But we're just going to have to go over it with everyone else, so it makes sense to wait."

I took a breath trying, and mostly failing, to find my patience. "I know I'm not the best with all this scientific magical stuff, but I really do want to learn more about it." My gaze darted between Flynn and Demaric for a second. "Besides, I'm not sure I'm comfortable with everyone knowing more about me when I don't. And they sort of ditched me." I went for honest. I wasn't happy with how everyone had run out of here.

"You're the most frustrating woman," he barked.

I released his hand, practically flinging it away from me. This was better. Angry Flynn I could handle with ease. The sweet guy he'd been for the last couple of hours had messed with my head

I met his heated stare and narrowed my eyes. "You're not going to budge on this, are you?" I huffed, crossing my arms. "Fine, "I conceded. "I don't see how they wouldn't find out anyway so it's a moot point."

He closed his eyes, as if pained and sat back before answering. "Just get on with it, Dem."

Asshole.

To his credit, Demaric looked slightly uncomfortable as he glanced between us, trying to decide whether he should listen to me or Flynn. Renee on the other hand was trying to hide a smile behind her hands.

I finally relented and motioned for Demaric to continue. I'd deal with this later. They wanted me to trust them, I could try, but they were going to have to stop brushing my questions off for later.

"I think it's important that she understands as much as she can now. Some of what we found won't be easy to deal with," Demaric started. A small part of me wanted to grin or stick out my tongue at Flynn but I couldn't. The look Demaric and Renee shared had me more worried about what they thought was wrong with me.

"Fine," Flynn muttered, turning his head to glare at the wall above my head.

"Resonance is basically a frequency in which your body conducts energy. Our people are able to use that energy. Yours is perfectly in tune with the rest of your circle, so there are no problems there." He paused, giving me time to absorb what he had said. It wasn't much better than before, but I thought I understood. I nodded, telling him to continue. "Your chakras are completely open, which are sort of like ports in the body that help you channel the energy. I'm quite surprised by that since you didn't know about any of this before you arrived. The problem that we're seeing is actually witchcraft. Your growth, or the lack of growth, is due to a hex."

"What does that mean?" I blurted.

Renee leaned forward, at least as much as she could, putting a hand on my knee. "What he means is that I found something during my exam, specifically attached to your body. You wouldn't have been able to find it because of the intimate place it was put. Unfortunately, it's a common practice in witch communities."

I was sure the blood drained from my face and my head swam. Flynn put a steadying hand on my shoulder when I listed to one side.

"You mean someone…" I couldn't finish the sentence. "Am I still a virgin?" I asked instead.

"Yes. And I want you to know it was removed. That was the pain you felt during your exam. We've concluded that the spell was almost completely drained. Someone had been regularly keeping it charged. Which is the main problem."

"Someone tried to hex me," I admitted quietly. "Just before we got here. How did I not notice?" My thoughts moved swiftly. It didn't make sense. I'd felt that hex outside the building before we were even in town properly. How could someone have gotten it on

—*in*—my body without me noticing or sensing it? "I don't understand…"

I took a deep breath, but it didn't help. Black spots bloomed in front of my eyes and I knew I was going to faint soon. I felt disgusting all over. Violated. In the back of my mind, I realized there were two people who could have done it. One was unlikely, given she'd been—was—my friend but the other… My stomach churned and I bent over the side of the table, vomiting up bile.

"—anything else?" Flynn asked in a tone colored with concern. "I want to take her home."

The door opened as I lifted my head. Flynn smoothed some hair out of my face that had fallen out of its braid. Vian strode into the room, lifted me bodily from the table. Liam and Kieran stood in the door.

"Are you okay? I could feel…" Vian crushed me to him.

"Get me out of here," I begged quietly, closing my eyes.

We moved across the room. Words I ignored were exchanged. Someone grabbed at my hands, and the world turned sideways. It was like I was being torn in several directions at once. Not in a painful way. It was like something or several things were plucking at my skin, whispering at me to let go. It only made me cling tighter and squeeze my eyes shut. The sensation died away and I opened my eyes to see the living room in our house.

I stared around for one bizarre second. "What the fuck?" I whispered.

"Liam Slipped to bring us here," Vian answered. I shook my head, not understanding before letting it go. Did it really matter? Did anything matter right now? I pressed my face against his chest and focused on trying to calm down. It didn't help. All I could smell was his stupid cologne.

"I hate how you smell," I muttered.

"I know."

"You should change it," I suggested.

"Brooke likes it," he replied. Then after a beat said, "Want to tell me what has you freaked out?"

With a groan, I shook my head. I wanted to forget. Flynn wouldn't let me though. I heard him behind me, explaining things.

"I'll get the others back here," Kieran said quickly once his brother was done. Part of me wanted to be mad that he told them, but it saved me from having to do it later.

"She's shivering," Vian added. "I'm gonna get her into a shower."

"I'll help," Liam said.

"No, let me." Flynn said quickly. I lifted my head to look at him before I realized the favor he was for doing me. Ugg, couldn't he just be a dick? "I'll explain later. Call my parents, tell them we won't make dinner. Any excuse. I'll call them later." He handed a folder to Liam. "Give this to Ben when he gets here. And keep everyone calm."

Instead of a shower, Vian helped draw me a bath and then asked if I wanted him to stay or go. I'd opted for him to go and to take Flynn with him. I needed a minute, or thirty.

I wasn't sure whose bathroom this was, but it was nice. It had the same layout as Brooke's, but instead of purple walls, they were light grey. A two-sink counter ran along one wall until it hugged a walk-in shower. On the other end were two doors. One went to the room we'd entered through. The other probably led to someone else's bedroom. The tub could easily hold three large people comfortably, which had me questioning again just how much money these people had.

I sat back on a grooved seat, water up to my chin with bubbles that were starting to thin out. While I soaked, I could hear Vian and who I thought might be Flynn talking in low voices through the door. I was surprised they'd allowed me this much privacy, but I guess I'd earned it somehow.

Yay. Get violated and earn some freedom. I snorted at the absurdity of my own thoughts. After my initial reaction though, I found myself angrier than anything else I was feeling. The real problem was that I couldn't remember. Something like that? There's no way I would have forgotten.

I was so deep in thought, trying to sort through

the probabilities, that when the door banged open, I screamed. A nice high girly scream that echoed. Ick.

Brooke stood in the doorway looking like a wild ball of rage. Her eyes settled on me and softened just a fraction. "Sorry," she muttered before shutting the door behind her. She started stripping as she headed toward the tub. Then she climbed in and claimed one of the other reclining spots.

Seriously, the tub was like a mini hot tub, complete with jets.

"Whose bathroom is this?" I asked. I wasn't going to ask her why she was in here. It was obvious she needed to relax. That was, assuming she was up to speed on the new developments regarding me. Also, she was the only other chick in the house. The guys had probably sent her in to check on me.

"Lucien and Kieran's." She waved a hand around the room. "They have the best tub because this room sits in a corner of the house. I mean, my tub's okay, but it only fits two people." She paused to grab a rolled-up towel that sat on a shelf just within reach and put it behind her neck. "You know, we didn't know why Emma wanted to leave early. When she called me with the change, I didn't think… Now I know I shouldn't be mad at her for throwing her life away."

I stared at her, stunned by her confession. "You think she knew what had been done to me?"

"Probably." She sniffed and I could see her struggling to control herself. I totally got that. "I won't tell you I'm sorry. Or make it anything more or less than it is. Bad shit happens to good people all the time. Look at your parents. Your past. Even Liam and Lucien. Two of the sweetest people I've ever met. You have to take that and make it yours. Make yourself stronger. That's how you survive. But I think you know that. You're just going about it the wrong way."

"What do you mean by that?" I asked. My breathing sped up as her small speech marinated in my head.

"I mean that you bottle it all up. I know you think it's for the best and I don't blame you at all, all things considered, but I think if you owned your past and funneled all that anger in the right place, nothing in the world would ever topple you again. People are always going to hurt you, Olivia. It's up to you to decide how much."

Unbidden, tears surged forward and slipped down my cheeks. Who knew I was such a crier? I swallowed past the lump of emotion in my throat. "You're sort of smart, you know that?" I choked out. She opened her eyes and winked at me. Now if only I could figure out how to do what she said…

CHAPTER 13

I shifted uncomfortably on the couch and looked around the room. Every eye was on me. No one had spoken since I entered the room. We sat in this uncomfortable silence, where I sort of felt like they were waiting for me to crack apart. They could wait for it, but it wasn't going to happen.

I refused to be a victim. I still had the words of Brooke's speech fresh in my thoughts and wanted to be what she described. Someone who took control of how they felt and gave it direction. I don't know when I'd stopped fighting for myself, but I missed that girl who was full of fire. Not this broken shell I'd been functioning as for the past few years.

"Olive," Vian started but I waved him away.

"I want to start learning magic. Now. Today," I stated.

Brooke snickered. "It's not magic. We don't break

the fundamentals of nature, we evolved into this. Witches use magic. Steal it actually."

"I agree you should start learning Arts," Ben stated, "but there's something more pressing that we need to deal with." He eyed Flynn across the room and raised an eyebrow. When he nodded, Ben continued. "According to the report Renee gave us, the spells placed on you were done by a medical professional and you're going to have to purge a spell or two. The one stunting your growth is almost completely faded, but there's a tracking spell in your bloodstream and another that's in place to make you forget things when it's triggered."

My head spun as I tried to wrap my mind around what he told me. "What do you mean a medical professional?"

"Only that they implanted you with a spelled object." His ears turned bright red as he talked, clearly uncomfortable even thinking about it. "There was minimal scarring. Anyone with the know-how could have done it, but it wasn't sloppy like we normally see with captives in the witch community.

"So, it couldn't have been Evan?" I asked quietly. "It doesn't make sense. It had to be him. I've only seen a doctor twice in the last two years." My hands trembled as I struggled to focus my mind. Whether it was Evan or some nameless doctor, it was still an invasion.

Ben paused and scrutinized my face. "You've seen one every three months since you were sixteen."

"I think we can figure out what the memory spell was for," Kieran said dryly.

I closed my eyes briefly, questions flying through my head. "How is that possible?" I breathed before waving my hand, staving off any possible answers. Speculating didn't help me right now. If I wanted the truth, I'd have to go hunting for it. When my eyes opened, I pushed it all aside and focused on the rest of what Ben had said. "Okay. What about this purging thing you mentioned? Cause I'm pretty sure I've puked enough today." I shook my head in disgust. Puking was seriously not my thing. I was tiny enough. No reason to get rid of what little nutrition I needed to stay alive.

"It's not that sort of purging," Brooke rushed to answer. I noticed how she scooted closer to my brother and narrowed my eyes. A small smile crossed her lips that didn't quite reach her eyes.

"Yes, it's more like a detox through water purification and sweat," Lucien continued to explain. "Basically, you get to drink about a gallon of saltwater and a few herbs and then sit in the sauna."

That didn't sound too bad. Well, the saltwater didn't sound fun, but I could sit in a sauna for a couple of minutes. No sweat… or lots of sweat? So not the time to be witty. "The one stunting my growth, does that mean I'm finally going to grow into a real woman?"

No one laughed at my vague Pinocchio joke. Not even Ben.

"Unfortunately, some of it isn't reversible. You'll probably start aging, but you won't grow taller," Ben said quietly, looking down at his hands. "We're just lucky they got it wrong. I'm pretty sure it was meant to stunt your resonance growth which would have rendered your place in our Circle useless."

"What does that mean? Everyone keeps mentioning resonance. Demaric kind of explained things but I still really don't have a clue what it all means!" I really wanted to understand all of this. I'd never been good at science. I was more of a literature nerd than anything else.

"The human body is made up of electromagnetic pulses. Think of a computer, except organic. Everything that makes you, you, is determined by these waves of electricity," Ben explained. I was with him so far. Electricity, human computer. Easy. Out of the corner of my eye, I watched Lucien giggle quietly behind his hand and glared at him quickly. "With Entwined, our bodies can absorb outside energy, which everything is made of. Over time, we developed the ability to use it. Because of that, all of us have a specific energy signature. Circles are made up of people who resonate together, at the same frequency."

I shook my head and blew out a breath. "So, in short, we're energy conductors and we're a Circle because we have similar signatures?" I tried to summarize, unsure if I had it correct or not.

Kieran sat forward. "Basically—"

"Hold on, Sweet," Brooke said sharply. She sat

forward and pointed a finger at Lucien. "Sugar, if you don't stop that, I'm gonna ask Olivia to smack the shit out of you."

"What?" he exclaimed with wide eyes.

"I would happily," I deadpanned. "I don't know why you think it's funny to laugh at Ben, but it's kinda dickish."

"I'm not laughing at him. I'm laughing at the look you get on your face whenever you're confused. You sort of look like a fish, a cute fish, but still. Your mouth gets all round and your eyes go wide."

I pulled a face at him. "I do not do that."

"Actually…" Flynn said.

"You do," Vian piped up. "Always have."

I blinked several times and sat back and frowned. "Fine. Whatever, but stop laughing. Ben thinks you're laughing at him."

"Not anymore I don't," Ben interjected.

I gave him a look that said, '*really dude?*'

"I give up," I muttered. Then an idea struck me. "You know what, no. Fuck all of you. Stop calling me cute. Quit looking at me at all. Seriously." I crossed my arms over my chest and glared at them before dropping my eyes to my lap. "It confuses me," I tacked on in a whisper, feeling my cheeks heat but I didn't think anyone heard me.

"Come on," Flynn said, standing up and motioning to Lucien. "Help me get things set up for a family purge." Several people sat back groaning. Only Brooke didn't. She smirked.

"Usually when we have to purge, only your sibling has to do it with you. Four hours is a long time to sit by yourself."

I choked on whatever I was going to say. "Four hours?" I squeaked. How was I going to survive four hours in a sweat box? "Isn't that dangerous?"

"Not if we hydrate well," Ben answered.

"Is there anything else I need to know?" I asked, changing the subject. Yep, that was me. Ms. Avoidance.

"Other than the fact that you're extremely powerful and that you might never grow up, you mean?" Brooke quipped. I beamed at her. She knew exactly what I'd been asking for. She was growing on me so quick it wasn't even funny. Or maybe it was.

"Great. Okay. I want to call Payton. I think it's time I talked to her. Vian, can I borrow your phone?" I asked. He got up and handed it to me. Before he could move away, I grabbed his wrist and pulled him down. I pierced him with a meaningful look. "You are so going to explain about you and Brooke later."

"Noticed that, huh?" he asked with a small grin.

"Duh. I'm not blind." I rolled my eyes and let him go. He stayed where he was for a few seconds, giving me a look. "What?" I finally asked.

"It's just good to see more spirit," he said with a small smile. "I was worried for a bit that the girl I grew up with was gone and I'd missed the important changes."

I was struck dumb for a second. It hadn't occurred

to me that I might have changed just as much as him or that it would affect him in the same way. "Well, even if we're both different, we have plenty of time to get to know each other now," I stated firmly. "I'm gonna go make that call."

I got up and headed out of the room. When I passed by the kitchen, I spied Lucien and Flynn at the island with several large bottles of water. They were adding salt and dried flowers to each. Flynn spotted me before I could pass.

"Where are you going, Princess?" he asked, making me pause.

"To make a call. I'll be right out front. And cut out the princess shit."

He threw me a roguish smile. "Nah. But please stay on the porch?"

I waved, not saying whether I would or wouldn't and headed outside and collapsed into a chair. I saw Flynn at the window with a stupid smirk on his face, so I flipped him off before searching for Payton's number in Vian's phone.

I snorted when I found it. It was under Wicked Witch of the West. Seriously? I mean, I'd known he'd saved that for her, but now it had a whole new meaning. Let's hope he was wrong. I hit call and waited as it rang. If I couldn't get ahold of her, I'd leave a message. I wasn't sure if I could trust her anymore, but I needed to know what she knew.

It rang five times before someone picked up.

"Well, well, well. What did you do with my prize,

Octavian?" Evan's voice rang out loud and clear over the speaker and my blood turned to ice in my veins.

I sat in shock for a moment before a blinding rage took over. "Guess again, fucker," I said sharply. Emma flashed in front of my eyes and I almost regretted not hanging up as she burst into ashes.

"Oh good. No middleman. Not sure I like your tone though. You've only been gone a few days and they've already ruined all the work we put into you. Such a fucking waste. Though, I'm definitely going to enjoy breaking you again," Evan said, his voice morphing into something coiling and sweet. Like he was talking to a lover and not someone he wanted to dominate.

I repressed a shudder, before steeling myself. I needed to be stronger, like Brooke said. "Where's Payton?" I demanded.

"Busy fixing the mess you left her in. You're a terrible friend, you know. Just left her here to deal with your foster parents. They reported you two missing, did you know that?"

My rage sputtered out for a second at the mention of my foster parents and I had to push it aside with effort. "Fuck you," I snarled. I refused to give him power over me.

"Oh, most definitely babe. You can count on that once I find you. I'm getting pretty close. Somewhere out at sea. Won't be much longer and you can fulfil that promise."

The phone was snatched out of my hand before I

could answer. I looked up in shock to find Lucien looming over me as he pressed it to his ear.

"Who is this?" he demanded. His brown eyes practically glowed as he inspected my face. After a few seconds, he pulled the phone away from his face and then leaned down until our noses were only inches apart. "They hung up. Who was it, Dollface?" His voice was hard, angry, completely unlike the guy I'd been slowly getting to know. He seemed to realize it at the same time I did, his stare softened. He closed his eyes and pressed his forehead against mine. "Sorry. Please tell me?"

"It was Evan," I whispered. "I was calling Payton, but he answered. I wanted to ask her what she knew. You scared the shit out of me."

"I'm sorry, Doll. I really am. You just looked so…I don't even know, and I freaked out." He pulled back enough so he could look me in the eye.

"It's okay. I wasn't prepared for him and…"

"What did he say to you?" he asked, collecting my hands in his and kneading my fingers with his own.

"That he was looking for me and I'd see him soon." My skin crawled just saying it and I cringed.

"Well don't worry about that. We've got your detox ready. Better start it now rather than wait," he said quickly.

"He knows we're on an island, I think."

"There's no way he'll find us here. Our people have been here a long time. Only a few witches have ever been allowed here, and that was only because they promised to share their knowledge with us. You are perfectly safe with us, I promise." He stood abruptly and helped pull me to a stand before tucking me into a hug.

"Didn't stop someone from trying to hex me earlier," I said, testing his statement.

He pinched the bridge of his nose for a second. "We're working on that. Kieran knows more but I don't want you to worry about it," he promised.

So many things were happening at once and it was hard to prioritize where my focus should be. My thoughts strayed back to Evan and grief took me. "He killed her," I whispered, staring up into Lucien's brown eyes. I don't know why I felt the need to remind him or any of them that Evan had taken Emma away from us. I doubted they had forgotten so quickly.

"We'll deal with that once we're all stronger. But come on, one problem at a time. Let's go get naked and sweaty."

Unbidden, I let out a silly laugh and I put my worries in the back of my mind. It was hard to stay troubled when Lucien was determined to keep me steady. Plus, there was no way any of them were getting me naked. I'd wear my dress in. Let them try and stop me.

CHAPTER 14

I wavered from side to side, feeling a bit full after chugging down a gallon of saltwater. Well, chugging might be a bit of an overstatement. There was a lot of gagging involved, no actual vomiting thankfully. Apparently, that's what the dried jasmine and violets were for. Lucien had patiently explained what was in it when I'd stared at the jug with distrust. It was only after he finished that I had grudgingly started to drink it.

"Why do I feel so weird?" I asked Brooke. I felt buzzed, fuzzy, and not entirely all there. I kept dazing out, only to jerk back into full alert. This feeling, it was similar to being drunk and I didn't like it. There was no way I could protect myself if something happened while I was like this.

She giggled, stumbling as she threw on a long white robe. I had one of those too, in green, but she still insisted I needed to undress. I was… procrastinating on that.

"Probably the Morning Glory." She giggled again. "It's to help us relax. Doesn't seem to be working on you though."

"Is that why you're like that?" I waved an arm in her general direction. I'd never seen her so giddy before and it was weird. Not in a bad way, just… not herself. Or maybe she was? Didn't drugs bring out a person's nature?

She walked over to me, a smile on her face. "Probably. Now strip woman or I'll have to call the boys."

I snorted at her commanding tone. She wouldn't really call them if I refused, would she? Taking a moment to examine that thought, I considered her with a frown. She was all smiles and sunshine but behind all that, there was a seriousness in her eyes.

"You really would, wouldn't you?"

She nodded enthusiastically. "Yep. Your safety is more important than your modesty."

I sighed and started pulling off my dress. "So, do I have clothes for later?" I staggered, feeling a bit dizzy with my arms over my head. Someone grabbed my waist to keep me from falling over. Once I got the dress over my head, I looked around to see Brooke, but she wasn't looking at me. She was staring at my back with a dark look in her jewel colored eyes.

Her gaze flicked up to meet mine for half a second before she threw her arms around me, hugging me from behind. It was almost funny since she could easily tuck my head under hers. Almost. She wasn't really hugging me for me, but for herself. I knew how ugly my scars were and most people couldn't hold themselves together when they saw them. She'd seen me naked before, but I think this was the first time she allowed herself to see them. I closed my eyes and leaned into her and patted her arms awkwardly. Brooke just seemed to know what she could and couldn't do with me.

"Okay. Naked hugging is done," I cried out, forcing a laugh when she held on a second longer than I wanted her too.

"Right, sorry!" Her voice was stiff, like she was still struggling with whatever she was feeling. When she spoke again, her voice was back to normal. "Get out of those panties. There's a towel on the bed and I brought your robe up earlier. It's on the back of the door."

"Thanks, Brooke," I said, trying to put as much feeling and meaning into it as I could so she'd know it wasn't just for the clothes. It was the best I could do to let her know I appreciated her.

I really did like her, the realization made me sad. I mean, I'd known that I was warming up to her. The curvy blonde was easy to be around. Did she know how broken I was? That I would never love her half as much as she would try to love me? I peeked at her as I wrapped a white towel around myself.

Fuck! I took several fortifying breaths, trying to keep the tears at bay. I definitely did not like this feeling. I wanted to be in control. I'd done enough crying to last me several months. Crossing the room with more confidence than I felt, I snagged the hunter green robe from the back of the door.

"Let's go get sweaty," I called, eliciting another giggle from her.

Fuck. My. Life.

That's all I could think as I stared around the sauna, still wrapped up tightly in my robe. I was squished between Ben and Vian on one of the benches that ran along three walls. The guys must have been in here for a good fifteen minutes before Brooke and I got there. Each of them had a towel wrapped around their waist, leaving their chests exposed, their skin already slick with sweat. I was doing my best to ignore it, but I dared anyone else not to look in my position. Not my brother, obviously, because eww, but yeah. Admiring people's bodies wasn't the same as touching them.

"You know, most of us have seen you naked," Liam remarked, a lazy grin stretching across his bow shaped lips.

"When?" I squeaked, tearing my eyes away from a bead of sweat that rolled down Flynn's stomach. If I wasn't already flushed from the heat, I might have blushed.

"Well, I mean..." Liam looked away, uncomfortable.

"He means while you were sick. Everyone took a turn taking care of you," Flynn said from his spot across from me. His legs were kicked out toward the middle of the room, completely relaxed. "But not as much as I did. Still waiting on you to thank me for that."

"What a pity that you're going to have to wait so long then. You don't seem like the overly patient type," I teased. My head fell back as I squeezed my eyes shut. Everyone else chuckled.

"Shall I go into detail about how you kept pressing your—" One of my eyes popped open at the sound of something being hit. Flynn glared at his twin as he clutched the back of his head. I shut my eyes again and smiled to myself.

Ben leaned into my side. "I know you want to be modest, but the robe is really dangerous to wear in a sauna, especially for how long we have to sit in here."

"He's right," Lucien said. "I didn't bring enough water to keep you hydrated and wear that thing."

"Yes, please strip," Flynn said loudly.

My eyes flew open again as I glared at him. He just smiled back, acting completely innocent.

"What happened to me not being your type?" I snapped. The words left my mouth before I even thought about them and I internally kicked myself. Why does it matter? It shouldn't. I don't care about whether Flynn or any of them find me attractive. So why did I even bring that up?

"When did he say that?" Ben asked. He sat forward slightly to look at me before turning to Flynn. "Please tell me you didn't." Flynn shrugged and rolled his eyes.

"Umm…" I was suddenly more uncomfortable.

"Olive, just take off the robe. I will personally kick the shit out of anyone here who bothers you," Vian said. His voice held an edge of dark promise.

"Here, I'll help you," Ben offered.

I side-eyed him. "I know how to undress myself," I replied, trying to keep the bite out of my voice. I stood quickly and shed the robe, making sure my towel was still wrapped tightly under my arms. I folded the robe in half and placed it on the bench. As I sat back down, I noticed everyone except my brother and Brooke were staring at me. Swallowing, I forced myself to relax back in my seat.

After a few moments of awkward silence, everyone started chatting and the tension slowly leeched from my body. Lucien placed a jug of water at my feet. Right. I'm supposed to drink from that every fifteen minutes. Thankfully, the saltwater was done. This was just regular water with a hint of lemon in it.

"Drink up, Clones," Lucien said. Both Flynn and Kieran glared at him.

"Don't call us that," they said in perfect unison, causing everyone else to erupt in laughter. My cheeks hurt by the time I was able to catch my breath.

"Why do you call them that?" I asked, catching Lucien's eye.

He stretched back, folding his hands behind his head and giving me a full view of his chest and abs. "They're the only set of identical twins in our Circle, and it annoys both of them."

Flynn grabbed a towel and threw it, but his aim was off and didn't hit his intended target. It hit Brooke full in the face which started a mini war as towels flew through the air.

I let the heat sweep over me as I started to notice the others. I mean, I'd seen them, but it was almost like I was seeing them for real. As if everything from before had been a show and they were finally being themselves.

Liam was the center of attention, constantly up out of his seat as he talked. He had a habit of touching everyone, whether to brush their legs with his hand, to steady himself on someone's shoulder, or to lace his fingers with someone to get their attention. I found myself fascinated with the way his muscles bunched and uncoiled underneath his tan skin. His honey blonde hair was damp with sweat and slicked back away from his face, so I could easily see his dilated pupils. So unlike how he normally carried himself. Not so much serious, but sad, like he carried a heavy burden.

My eyes were often drawn toward Flynn and

Kieran as they talked back and forth, laughing. Both of them had a smattering of hair on their chests, though I noticed that Kieran seemed to be a bit bulkier than his twin. Their muscled chests gave way to flat, hard abs. A warmth that had nothing to do with the sauna filled me, and I had to force myself to look away.

Ben was a great source of distraction. He'd collected one of my hands in his, rubbing his thumb in a delicious circle against my skin. Whenever he did it, a shiver would run up my arm and coil in my chest, making it hard to breathe. I think he did it on purpose. Every time I broke out in goosebumps, I'd catch him with a secret smile on his lips and his eyes would sparkle like two-toned jewels. At one point, his eyes dipped to my lips and something akin to terror tore through me as I ripped my gaze away from his.

Lucien was content to sit back with a delirious grin on his face as he watched us all. He kept checking in with everyone, lazily pointing to our jugs of water, reminding us to drink. He winked at me several times when he caught me looking at him around Vian and Brooke. He spent a fair amount of time observing the two of them which made me want to see what was so special about them too.

The pair of them were close together on the bench, their heads tipped toward each other as they talked softly every so often. Brooke's eyes met mine a few times, shining with a happiness I vaguely recalled from my childhood. My brain became so muddled, I struggled to bring the memory to the front of my mind, but once it was there, I saw it for what it was. Love. They were in love. My parents used to look at each other that way. I searched within myself, looking for the jealousy I thought I'd always feel if Vian ever found someone he loved, but I couldn't find it. In the back of my mind though, I'd always thought he and Emma were secretly a thing, maybe I'd been wrong about that.

"How much longer?" I blurted out, interrupting Liam who was in the middle of an impression of Flynn.

"Not much," Lucien answered, eyeing his watch. I wondered how it was still working with so much steam. Probably money. "About ten minutes. How are you feeling?"

"Umm, okay?" I wasn't sure if I was supposed to feel different. I was still sort of dizzy from the heat. Or the dried flowers.

"You'll probably see a difference when we get out," Kieran supplied, leaning forward to stare at me. I sucked in a breath as his blue eyes searched my face. Out of everyone, I think we'd interacted the least.

"What did you guys find out about that hex?" I blurted. Seriously? A hot guy stares at you and you want to know about witchcraft? I mentally kicked myself.

Wait… No. He's not hot. Wait. Shit. He is but I'm not… What the fuck was wrong with me?

"It was a renewal," he answered honestly. If he

saw the war of my thoughts, he didn't react to it. "Of the growth blocker. That's what Valek told us, at least. We're not entirely sure how it got there, but someone will be looking into it."

I cut a glance in Lucien's direction. He'd told me not to worry about it, but if someone knew about the spells they found on me, how had someone set up a renewal? He frowned slightly but I looked away quickly.

"Oh." I didn't really know what else to say. Thanks? It was a bit disconcerting how nonchalant they were about it. I thought back to my conversation with Evan, however brief it was, and I had to suppress a shudder. He was looking for me. But, if that hex was any indication, it seemed someone else had already found me.

CHAPTER 15

Everyone except for Brooke and Vian got out of the sauna. I gave them a lingering look as I left but decided now was not the time to question them about their relationship. No matter how much my curiosity burned. The way they were looking at each other suggested they had something else in mind entirely.

"Let them be," Kieran said quietly after I stood in the door a second too long. The cool air hit my skin like a soothing balm as he dragged me away. My fingers were pruney and I wondered if I'd ever properly dry out. Lucien and Flynn disappeared into the house through the sliding glass doors, while Liam and Ben collapsed into sunning chairs next to a pool that looked more like a pond. The water had a slight teal color to it, suggesting that was what it was. It was surrounded by a small patio of white cut stone with a few chairs dotted around it and a natural looking waterfall that bubbled softly on the other side. As with the front yard, the back was also lined with trees and plant life. The whole setup had a very chic natural resort vibe going for it.

"We're gonna need more chairs out here," Kieran remarked. "The ones that we broke haven't been replaced yet." He moved to one of the remaining sun chairs and sat, pulling me to sit down with him. Because of his large frame, we just barely fit with his arm tucked over my shoulders.

"Put it on the list. Brooke planned to do it, but we got distracted," Ben answered tiredly. His head rolled in my direction. "Notice a difference yet?"

I thought about it for a second and realized he was referring to my body. Kieran had been right. Out of the sauna, I felt different. Better. Less tense, but there was something else too. I was lighter; my mind clearer. "I feel surprisingly good," I finally answered.

He nodded. "Good. Tomorrow I want to look at your levels. Dem sent over some equipment so we could do it at home."

"More tests?" I groaned. "No. Just no. I've had enough of those."

Ben looked at me with sympathy. "I understand but I have to insist. We need to be sure you're in the clear. I promise I know what I'm doing. I've been volunteering in my spare time at the lab."

"Plus, you want to get your hands on her again," Liam quipped from where he was stretched out on his own lounger. I glanced over and then quickly averted my eyes. His towel sat low on his hips, revealing the vee of his abs more and a small bit of his pubic bone. I felt my skin heat.

"Dude, don't embarrass her," Kieran barked, making me jump. His hand smoothed up and down my arm.

Shit, what were we talking about? I searched frantically for a safe topic. My eyes latched onto Ben. "You really like that sort of stuff, don't you? Science, I mean."

His face lit up. "Yes. We've been holding off on careers until our Circle was completely trained. Family will always be our priority. But, yes, I want to go into the research department. There's still so much we don't know about what we can do." The longer he talked, the more animated he became. I couldn't help but grin at him. Aside from Kieran—who barely talked at all—Ben was the quietest. Well, okay so I couldn't be completely certain of that. Maybe Kieran was a chatterbox and I just hadn't seen that side of him yet. Either way, I liked how Ben talked when he was passionate about a subject.

"You're doing that thing again with your face," Kieran whispered in my ear. I clamped my mouth shut quickly and internally cringed. I needed a picture of this look so I could work on not making it. Especially if it was going to garner so much attention.

"Speaking of training," Liam said, completely oblivious to what Kieran had just said. "You'll start yours in the morning. I'm sure we'll all vote at dinner, but I think defense should be a priority. What happened to you shouldn't have been possible."

"I'm sure Emma did her best with the constraints she had," Kieran remarked.

"No, I know that. But she should have had more support. Why the council decided a fifteen-year-old girl in the middle of a coven of undeclared witches was the best idea, I'll never understand." Liam sounded angry, but his face was clear. If anything, he looked thoughtful.

"Why did they then? Send her I mean," I asked. "Why not just do what they did with Vian?"

Kieran smoothed my hair down on the side of my head and pressed his cheek against my forehead. I was so interested in getting answers to my questions, I didn't even bother to swat away Kieran's affections.

"They couldn't," Liam stated. "Your file—Look, it's clear you've had a much harder life than any of us imagined. But you were under observation by people who would have fought tooth and nail to keep you. Witches are much more integrated into Human society than we are. They would have locked you up and—" He stopped abruptly, a haunted look bleeding into his eyes. My heart sped up as I recognized what was happening. He was reliving something, and I hated myself for doing that to him.

"I understand," I rushed to say. "I get it." He didn't have to say anything else. The details weren't important, especially if they caused him pain.

Liam stood up and stretched before flashing me a

mischievous grin. The look from before was completely gone and I sighed in relief, returning his smile. "I'd cover your eyes, Ms. Modest," he said throwing his head back to whip his blonde hair out of his face.

"What?" I asked but it was too late.

His towel dropped, flashing me with his impressively toned ass before he jumped into the pool, splashing us all in the process.

"You asshole," Ben shouted, jumping up. His towel fell to the ground before he launched himself into the pool on top of Liam.

Holy fuck. How was I going to survive living here if they insisted on flashing me?

Kieran chuckled behind me as I stared with wide eyes. "You'll get used to that," he said, adjusting his arm around me. "Circles are not modest. Or secretive," he added.

"Yeah, I think I'm starting to get that," I muttered still a bit stunned.

"So, these scars," he said, making me tense and forget about the two naked men wrestling in the water.

"I don't want to talk about it," I said quietly and cringed. "But if you have to know, ask Flynn or Vian. You have my permission," I added quickly. Ugg.

He tucked a finger under my chin and turned my head toward his. His blue eyes were like deep pools, full of concern. "You're not the only one who's suffered here. I'm not trying to undermine your pain and I won't go into details, but you should ask Lucien about his past. Liam doesn't like to talk about it, but Luc will. You're not as alone here as you think." When I didn't speak, he pulled my head forward between two hands and kissed my forehead before cradling me against his body.

He was being sweet, really. I logically recognized that, but emotionally it wasn't that easy for me. I couldn't just magically change how I was and open up to them. I'd admit to trying. Part of me wanted them to like me. And I wanted to like them too. But I could never be what they wanted me to be. Trusting. Easy. Open.

"Is it always like this?" I asked. I wanted to understand what *this* was, to see how this worked in their family.

"You mean, does trust come easy or this between you and me?"

I paused to think about what he was saying. Was there something between he and I? I didn't think so. Then again, I was plastered to his side, despite my aversion to romance or relationships. I knew it sent the wrong kind of message to not push him away. My gaze drifted toward the door to the sauna. Brooke and Vian were still inside.

"I feel out of place here but not at the same time," I finally admitted quietly. He shifted beside me. Liam and Ben were still rough housing in the pool, and I returned to watching them absently, waiting for his response.

"We fight," he said. "Of course, we do, but we love each other." Kieran nodded to the sauna. "Vian had some trouble at first too when we found him. I know you're probably still mad at him for hiding it. How could you not be? But he adjusted eventually. So will you. Knowing about all of this wouldn't have helped you. I can see it in your eyes sometimes, how you watch us, waiting for someone to light a match and burn it all down. That won't happen. Not with us." The breeze from earlier picked back up causing me to tremble as I leaned into Kieran more. I heard his words but couldn't imagine what it would be like to trust that things weren't constantly on the edge of falling apart. He sighed. "Some things have to be learned over time, despite what Flynn thinks. Realistically, we all expect a much longer adjustment period for you."

"And this whole touching and affection thing you guys do, I should just let that happen?" I don't know how our conversation turned to this. I'd barely spoken ten words to the guy directly, but it felt like gliding through water. There was some resistance, but I wasn't afraid of him.

"I wouldn't go that far," he said, laughing softly. "Anything you aren't comfortable with, you should just tell us. Like the other day when I tried to heal you. If we get hurt by it, that's on us. Not you."

"Supper's ready. Should I leave the lovebirds to it?" Lucien called out from the back door, breaking the moment Kieran and I had been in before we could say anymore.

"There's the confirmation I needed," I said, swinging my legs off the chair and crossing the patio. "Great way to out him before he told me." I threw Lucien a wink and sauntered over to the sauna door. I banged my fist against the frosted glass door. "Dinner!" I shouted and chuckled when I heard startled movement inside.

I walked back between Kieran and Lucien, heading towards the stairs to go get changed for dinner. Brooke met me a few minutes later, her skin flushed, but there was a sparkle in her eyes that made me laugh as she smoothed her hair.

"Just so we're clear. You are *never* allowed to talk to me about your sex life with my brother," I stated firmly.

"Noted," she said with a laugh. "As long as I get to dress you, we're good." I snorted in response. If that's what she needed to believe, I wasn't going to burst her bubble just yet.

Dinner was much of the same from the night before, except with less yelling. Everyone ate, including me this time. No one glared at me or made snide comments. When everyone was finished eating, I decided to turn in while they went to watch a movie.

"I'm gonna crash," I told my brother. "Can I sleep in your room?"

"Sure, Olive," he said. "You okay? It's fine if you aren't. I'll come hang out with you instead."

"I'm good," I said, and I meant it. "Just a long day, plus Liam said I start training tomorrow so probably best to get some sleep."

I turned toward the stairs, but he stopped me before I could leave. "Luc said you spoke to Evan." I nodded, glancing away from his face.

"I did," I answered honestly. "He said he's going to find me."

"I'll kill him before he gets the chance to put his hands on you," he promised. He grabbed my face between his hands and forced me to look at him. "I will. I'm so sorry, Olive."

My chest tightened at the look in his eye. I didn't want to see so much anger on his face. "Not before I do. And no, don't be sorry. This wasn't your fault." When he still didn't let go, I grabbed his wrists and pulled his hands away. "I want to sleep. I'll see you later, okay?"

CHAPTER 16

After a long shower to wash away the sweat, I found the clothes Brooke had gotten me. I barely got them on before my head hit the pillow and I was out. My eyes didn't open again until someone wafted a cup of coffee under my nose. My eyes opened instantly and chased after it. I wasn't a coffee person, but it smelled good. I pushed up on whoever's chest I had been laying on only to come face to face with Liam, who was sipping from a mug.

"That's unfair," I growled, narrowing my eyes on his lips. They split into a grin behind the mug.

"You're crushing me, woman," Flynn muttered from under me. "How can someone so small make me feel like I'm suffocating?"

I laughed as I moved over him, making sure to press my full weight into his chest as I climbed off the bed.

"Fucking evil too," he grunted. He rolled over and

snuggled into Ben who'd been on my other side. I looked back at them for a moment, confused. I wasn't really sure when they'd climbed into bed with me, but I wasn't going to complain about the company, I had one of the best nights of sleep ever.

Once I had two feet on the floor, I grabbed at the mug in Liam's hands, but before I could reach it he moved it out of my grasp and backed up toward the door. "Here, sleepy kitty. Come get it!" he taunted.

I huffed and followed after him, but he kept backing up. "Stop that," I grumbled. He stopped immediately but I bypassed him, not in the mood to be teased so early in the day. "Worst wake up ever. You're down five points."

"When did we start a point system?" Flynn called from the bed.

"I just started it," I called over my shoulder and headed down the hallway. Then for good measure, I stuck my tongue out at Liam who just laughed. "Blame Liam," I shouted. My remark was met with several groans from Vian's open doorway.

Downstairs, I found Vian and Lucien. The latter was at the stove, cooking something or other while my brother looked ready to fall into his own mug of coffee.

"You're a traitor," I said without preamble, climbing up onto the stool next to him. "I demand coffee."

"Why am I a traitor?" Vian asked.

"What did I do?" Lucien said at the same time,

spinning to face me.

"Guilty much?" I deadpanned to Lucien before turning to Vian. "And you," I said pointing a finger at my brother. "I woke up sandwiched between two dudes."

He made a derisive sound into his cup and peeked at me from the corner of his eye. "Oh no, I'm not taking the blame for that one. They were already there by the time I went to bed."

Lucien set a fresh cup of coffee in front of me with plenty of cream so it wouldn't taste gross. "You get five points." I beamed at him over the counter, earning me a toothy grin in return.

"Points?" he asked.

"Oh yeah, she's started a point system," Liam answered. He'd claimed the stool beside mine, but I was ignoring him. "Apparently, that's my fault. But if you get five points, and I lost five, that makes us even out."

"That's not how points work," I said with indignation. "Your twin can't earn you points. Everyone has their own points. Why do I keep saying points? Seriously, someone shut me up." I slapped a hand over my mouth so I couldn't ramble anymore. I couldn't remember the last time I'd felt so playful; it was a bit weird for me. Maybe it was the talk I had with Kieran. Or the detox they put me through last night. I was lighter, freer than I had in a long time. Sitting back in my chair, I pondered what had changed so quickly.

"Since when do you demand coffee," Vian asked, changing the subject.

"Dunno," I said, taking a sip. "That's how Liam woke me up. It smelled good. I wanted it. It's that simple."

"It did get her out of bed," Liam offered, ruffling his hair. "Sort of regretting it now," he added, bumping my shoulder with his arm.

"So, what's the plan for today?" I asked, giving him the evil eye because he almost made me spill coffee all over myself.

"Is she still drugged?" Vian asked over me. "She's far too happy. Maybe it's body snatchers."

I smacked at his arm. "Shut up, grump." The real reason I woke up in such a great mood was that I was finally going to learn something. This was my life now and I was ready to start taking control of it.

"You and I will be out back," Liam answered after chuckling at our exchange. "Everyone else is working on a surprise. I'm sure the others will join us later. For now, we'll talk about theory and experiment with some cards."

I nodded, acting like I understood what he meant. "Okay, someone feed me so I can learn magic."

Lucien winked at me, but Liam sputtered. "It's not magic, Kitten! It's technically called Mystic Arts."

I snorted and drank more coffee. "Yeah because calling it mystical is any different than magic."

"Eat your breakfast and meet me in the backyard," he snapped before leaving the kitchen muttering under his breath.

My breakfast consisted of fried eggs and some toast. I wasn't a big eater and almost complained. The only reason I didn't was because Lucien probably knew something I didn't. By the time I took the last bite of my toast, I was bouncing in my seat with excitement. I pushed my plate away and ran up to Brooke's room to get dressed.

I threw my messy hair into a loose braid and dressed in a pair of leggings and a long-sleeved boyfriend shirt before bounding back downstairs and outside.

At the backdoor, I paused, sucking in a breath when I caught sight of Liam. He was further away from the house in a section where the patio gave way to grass. I watched as he went through several movements with his body. It was almost like martial arts, except there didn't seem to be any part of it where you made bodily contact. Instead, it was more like ballet. Every line of his body flowed like a piece of art as he brought his arms up in sweeping arcs, only to spin in place and have one leg sweep out. Something about it nagged at the back of my mind, but I couldn't pull it forward. I was too focused on how beautiful he looked in that moment.

"What'cha staring at?" Lucien asked behind me, making me jump.

My hand flew up to my chest as I spun to face him. "Nothing, I just..."

He smirked. "Go. Have fun. Learn some stuff. That way the rest of us can relax a bit."

My eyebrows drew together, trying to figure out whether he meant because I made them all tense or something else? I put my hands behind me, slid the door open, and backed out. Only when the glass was between us did I turn and walk toward Liam.

"Bout time, Kitten," he called when he saw me approaching.

"Why do you call me that?" I asked. "So far, I've been called Kitten, Doll, and Princess. What's next? Baby? 'Cause I'm certain to get violent about that."

"You let Vian call you Olive," he pointed out.

"Yeah, but we shared a womb. He's allowed. I just don't see what's wrong with Liv or Livvy. Perfectly good nicknames." We were only a few feet away from each other now so I could see the twinkle in his eye clearly.

"Is it that important? Or did you want to learn?"

I huffed. "Fine. Teach me, Yoda."

He snorted and sat cross-legged, patting the grass in front of him. From a pocket, he pulled out a deck of cards. He waited until I sat down before speaking. "So, these are Tarot cards. A popular belief is that witches and psychics use these. They don't. We do. Each deck is charged, and we can use them to answer questions."

"And that's not magic, how?"

He rolled his eyes at me hard. "You've got to stop thinking about it as that. Magic is where you pay a price in exchange for something. What we do has no price. We evolved to use the fabric of reality. Everything is made up of energy, and we can use it."

"Why is that?"

He groaned and ducked his head. "Okay, I'll concede that we don't really know why we can do what we do, but that doesn't make it magic. And before you argue, can I just explain things and then you can ask Ben all sorts of questions that will drive him nuts?"

I nodded, that was fair. Not the driving Ben nuts part, but he'd probably be better for discussing magic versus science.

He set the deck in front of me and motioned toward them. "Pick one up."

I eyed the cards in front of me while he waited. Gingerly, I stretched a hand out and picked up the first card, turning it over. A sense of complete wrongness coiled inside me as I stared down at it. On the front was a fairy, her wings splayed out behind her, with a crown of white flowers. Her breasts were bare, and her exposed nipples were erect. The urge to drop it rippled through me and I shuddered.

"Sorry, I…" I felt like I'd invaded his privacy. When I looked up at him, he was studying my face, his mouth set into a grim line. He leaned forward after a moment, catching my wrist in his hand and tilted the card so he could see.

"No, you're supposed to feel that way. The deck is tuned to me. Can you tell what it means?" he asked. I shook my head and released the card. Whatever it meant I didn't want to know. He watched it flutter to the grass before speaking again. "It's the Lady of Song." His thumb stroked the inside of my wrist. "She wants me to listen."

"Listen to what?" I asked softly, still staring at the card.

"Just to listen." He sighed, dropping my wrist and pointed at the cards again. "Okay, pick up the whole deck and shuffle. But while you do, I want you to focus on your desire to read the cards."

Warily, I eyed the deck. I didn't want to feel what I felt before, but after another round of coaxing, I picked the stack up and sighed in relief when nothing happened.

"How's the lesson going?"

I whipped my head around to see Ben loping across the grass toward us.

"Good. Just started. She's a natural, actually. I've never seen anyone pick up the cards and freak out so quickly," Liam answered with a smile in my direction.

I wasn't so sure being a natural was a good thing. Or did he mean that because they thought I had precognitive abilities?

Ben settled into the grass beside us and sat back on his hands, regarding me. I scrunched up my nose and looked at the cards in my hands again. "So, I just shuffle these?" I was nervous now that Ben was here. He'd already proved he was pretty smart, and I was worried about looking like a fool in front of him.

"Yeah. Ignore Ben. He's just curious," Liam answered, giving Ben a pointed look that he pretended not to see. "Stalling won't help, Kitten."

I moved my hands absently, shuffling the cards. A daze swept over me and it took effort to remember I needed to focus on… What was it again? Desire? To read the cards. Not desire for the guys in front of me. I blinked and shuffled faster until a feeling told me to stop. I didn't know how I knew, I just did. I set the deck in the grass again and pulled up the first card.

The card had a total of three faces on it, two were women and the other a man. My eyes locked onto the face at the top. The woman was gazing off into the distance. Her hair was long, flowing with flowers that ran down the length 'til they morphed into the eyes of the man. His gaze was unnerving, as if he could actually see into the heart of me. A horn was attached to his head jutting up through the first woman's throat, as if it held her gaze in place, looking back in time. The third face showed a woman staring off in the distance in the opposite direction of the first. Her hair flowed in the wind as she looked on, her eyes full of wonder and hope. Out of the three of them, I liked her the best.

As I stared at it, a lump formed in my throat and I placed the card on the grass. Someone touched my knee and I glanced up. Ben was leaning forward, questioning me with his eyes.

"Shadows of the Past," Liam said softly. "What does it tell you?"

"That I should let go, move forward. Looking back only brings pain," I answered immediately. Ben's hand squeezed down and I took in a shuddering breath.

"Draw another."

My hand shook as I reached out for the next card. Liam's hand shot out, grasping my wrist before directing me to place the card in the grass next to the first one. On it was an old man with timeless eyes. A single braid of hair hung over one shoulder, drawing my gaze to his collarbone and down his chest. The man was all sharp angles, like a knife, made to cut through a harsh world.

"What card is it?" Liam asked me.

It was only a heartbeat later that I answered even though I'd never touched a tarot card before. I just knew the answer, as if I'd always known. "Speaker of Truth. But I don't know what truth he wants to tell me. It's a mess," I mumbled.

Liam nodded. "That's okay. Not all the meanings are immediately clear. Sometimes you have to relax more. Especially if one of the other cards upsets you. Close your eyes and try to relax."

I did as he said, closing my eyes and breathing evenly. Thoughts swirled around in my head as I kept the image of the man in the forefront of my mind. I sat there for at least five minutes, trying to separate them, but they wouldn't settle.

"Relax," Ben whispered in my ear.

CHAPTER 17

Relax.

The word rolled around in my mind while the rest of me floated. The grass brushed against my thighs, the sun beamed down on my head and shoulders, but the sensations were muted. Peace coiled inside my chest, filling me with a lightness I'd never felt before. It was freeing, unhurried, and full of endless potential.

Something coarse brushed my shoulder and I popped my eyes open, coming face to face with a very large cat. It had a wide head with a short snout, ears pointed forward with thick tufts of fur sprouting from the corners. The fur was a silvery brown that matched its eyes.

"Umm…"

Shush, girl. The words echoed in my mind, sounding distinctly male. I let out a small squeak and pulled my head back in fear.

The rest of the world bloomed behind him, as if coming into focus for the first time. Several yards away, I saw Ben and Liam chatting quietly as they stared down at my prone body, which lay in the grass. What the fuck? I looked down at my arms, trying to make sense of how I could be in two places at once.

Shaking my head, I looked back beyond them. Where there should have been a forest was a thicket of twisting thorns. In places, they glowed with a silvered purple sheen. In fact, almost everything had a shimmering quality to it.

"Am I dreaming?" I asked aloud.

The cat chuffed, grabbing my attention again. *No, you're not dreaming. This is the Thorns.*

"The Thorns? What is that exactly and what are you?" I pinched myself, trying to see if I could wake up. There was a dull pain in my arm but nothing like a normal pinch. And I certainly didn't wake up.

You're not usually this stupid. I'm a Lynx. What does it look like? And this is the place between the worlds.

"I am not stupid!"

Exactly. So, stop acting like it. The cat yawned and started to circle me, sniffing me from head to toe. I was so short, he barely had to stretch out his neck to snuffle at my hair before dipping down to my torso. He paused briefly between my legs and I had to fight the urge to clamp my legs together. "*Your flow is good. I was worried.*"

"What?" I stammered, looking down. Had I started my period?

I mean your energy. Not that other thing.

"This is some Narnia shit, isn't it?" I tried to reason. What else had it said? The place between worlds. I hadn't meant to do that. Maybe I did need to understand some theory before I started practicing magic.

We're about to have company, the cat told me, tipping its head to my left.

I glanced over to see Vian and Flynn striding across the lawn toward Ben and Liam. Flynn's gazed darted in our direction for a moment before taking a seat, he leaned into Liam's side to whisper something. I moved closer to see if I could hear what they were talking about, but it just sounded like white noise.

I know they're all very interesting, but I only have a few minutes before something finds you, or I'm needed elsewhere.

"They're not that interesting," I said quickly, turning to face the cat. "Wait, what do you mean?"

It purred and brushed against my side before sitting back on its haunches again. A wave of peace swept over me. It felt so familiar and yet foreign.

Why don't you have the girl with you? he said, leveling me with his gaze.

"What girl?" I asked dazed, trying to figure out why I wasn't freaking out more. I was outside of my body, yet not, talking to a cat who could talk in my head. Surely that should merit freaking out a bit.

The one sent to protect you. She's supposed to be here.

Did he mean Emma? I looked down at my hands,

wringing them. "If… I… shit. She's dead," I managed to get out at last.

I know but, where is she? The cat licked its chops, revealing large wicked teeth. *The Thorns aren't as safe as they should be. We need to hurry.*

"I…" I stammered. "I don't know where she is now. She died. Turned to ash."

Not her body, her essence. This is bad. She should have come to you.

There was a crashing sound in the distance, like something was breaking through the thicket. I jumped, startled by how loud it was. The lynx sprang to his feet and prowled in front of me, pinning me with his eyes every so often before he would stare at the twisted vines.

We're out of time sooner than I expected. Listen to me. Bond with your Circle. Go nowhere without them unless you have me with you. I'll find the girl and be back for you.

"What are you?"

I'm your guardian. Ask your Circle. They'll explain. You have to go. The lynx stopped pacing and nuzzled into my stomach. The world lurched underneath my feet and a harsh wind ripped at my skin.

I sat up, gasping for breath, back in my body. My wide eyes met Liam's brown ones. "I have a cat," I breathed, frantically looking around, waiting for something to jump out of the woods.

Flynn chuckled. "I told you that," he said, his voice bringing me back from the edge of hysteria.

"No… I mean, I met him. I think. Why is my head spinning?"

"Umm, guys, should that be happening," my twin asked, pointing down to my hands. The grass under my palms was dying quickly, spreading out in a dark circle. My palms tingled, and a rush of *something* swept through me. The dizziness abated. I shrieked and pulled my hands up, staring at them and then back at the ground.

"Wow," Ben breathed. I lifted my eyes to meet his. He stared at me with a reverence I found unsettling. "I can barely believe it and I watched it happen. No wonder you barely eat. You've been living off the earth."

"What's happening to me?" I squeaked.

His eyes softened. "You pulled energy from the ground to save yourself from burn-out on instinct. Most people wouldn't think to do that." I turned to Liam and Flynn. Liam just gaped at me, but Flynn… he was unreadable.

"Family meeting," Flynn barked out, standing abruptly. He reached down and grasped my hands and jerked me upright before leading me into the house.

"TELL ME AGAIN WHAT HE SAID," Ben asked again.

I sighed in exasperation and explained it all again. Everyone stared at me with varying degrees of disbelief. All except Flynn who seemed to be getting frustrated with everyone else.

"He said that we needed to bond, well specifically me. And that I couldn't be alone. That Emma was important somehow and..." I clutched my head between my hands. "I'm trying not to freak out here. I just had a full-blown conversation with a cat."

"About that," Ben said. I looked up to see that look in his eyes again and cringed.

"We all have guardians to an extent," Kieran cut across him with a look. "I think Ben is just surprised by yours."

"How do you even get a guardian?" I asked.

"They're asked when we're born. There's a ceremony immediately after birth. The first being you bond with is your guardian. Then your parents," Ben explained.

"So, I've always had this...cat guardian, thing," I was going around in circles.

"I admit, I haven't read up much on them so I can't say for sure," Ben said, chagrined.

"How is that not magic!?" I blinked rapidly before slamming my eyes shut. Everything I learned just brought more questions and it frustrated the hell out of me.

I opened my eyes again when I heard someone get up. Brooke moved from her seat and crouched in front of me. "Take a deep breath, babe." I did as she said. I hadn't realized how close I was getting to hysteria. My pulse thrummed in my fingertips. My breathing was erratic. I was hot all over.

"It's not magic. Or maybe it is," Kieran finally conceded. Liam sneered at him but didn't say anything. "We've been raised on this as a science. What I do know about guardians is that the stronger ones have a physical body somewhere. But they can be away from it for long periods of time."

Ben's eyebrows raised in surprise. "I didn't know that. Where did you learn that?"

Kieran smirked, clearly happy to know something Ben didn't. "Mom has several books about them in her library. I'm sure she'll let you borrow them."

"I think Livvy needs a break," Lucien said behind his hands. He was leaning forward, his eyes on me with his fingers steepled in front of his mouth. "Why don't we get some lunch and then we can all practice Arts together. We're all supposed to bond with her, according to her guardian. We haven't been doing enough." He stood, pulling Liam up with him.

"What does that entail?" I asked, focusing on my hands, trying not to clench them into fists.

"It means," Lucien said over his shoulder as he dragged his brother behind him, "that you're going to have to get comfortable with being touched a lot more." Tossing a wink at me as he went.

Fuck me…wait, no. Don't fuck me.

I groaned as they left the room, watching Liam's back disappear through the doorway. It was Liam who was freaking me out the most. He'd been quiet throughout the whole meeting. Barely even looked at me. Like he was almost afraid of me or something. It bothered me, if that was the case.

"It's fine. He'll snap out of it," Vian whispered to me. I shook my head. It wasn't fine at all. I was usually the one afraid of people. Not the other way around.

Everyone left except Flynn. I was waiting for him to leave. I just wanted a moment alone. Time to digest what had happened.

The couch dipped next to me and I startled, looking up to the bluest eyes I'd ever seen. Heat rolled off him like a wave as his gaze bore into my own. He had an intense way of looking at people. I wanted to smooth it away, get him to relax. He was intense by nature, but I had seen a different side to him too. The side that had allowed me to open up and didn't push for more than I'd been ready to give.

For the first time—possibly ever—I reached up and touched him first. If I had to bond with them, might as well start now. My palm cradled his face and I could feel my own expression soften. I had no idea what I was doing. Internally, I was on the verge of another freak out, but I forced myself to remain calm.

His eyes morphed from intense to something else as a shadow passed through them. Like he was uncertain. If he rejected me right now, I'd lose whatever courage I had managed to work up. My heart beat heavily while I waited for him to say something scathing or to shove my hand away. The seconds ticked by, long enough for me to start trembling and consider dropping my hand.

"I hate the walls you have up," he finally admitted, leaning into my palm. I held my breath, afraid that if I said something, whatever was happening between us would break. I was so out of my depth here. I didn't do feelings well. Didn't get attached to people. I'd lost the luxury to care about them long ago. If I cared, then they could hurt me. Brooke's words came back to me, bad shit happened to good people and I had to stop running from my hurt.

"I'll try harder," I whispered, dropping my palm, as I swallowed around the dryness in my throat.

"No. That's not…" His eyes closed and he turned his head away. "Never mind."

"Lunch!" Lucien shouted from the kitchen.

I stood and grabbed Flynn's arm, giving it a tug. "Come on. You're not you when you're hungry," I quipped, trying to lighten the mood. He smiled at my joke and I had to fight my own smile in return.

Finding a stool in the kitchen was easy as only Ben and Lucien were there. Flynn trailed in behind me and leaned back against the counter next to me.

"Where is everyone?" I asked.

"Remember that surprise I mentioned this morning? You'll find out tonight," Lucien said with a smile. He brought me a cup of juice and set a monstrous sandwich in front of me, loaded down with turkey, tomato, and romaine lettuce.

I eyed it warily. There was no way I'd finish it.

"We really need to talk about wasting food," I remarked, picking it up gingerly.

"No, what we need to talk about is eating right," Lucien said neutrally. "You don't eat enough. And that changes. Today." He tapped the counter with a long finger and pierced me with a stare, one eyebrow cocked upward, daring me to challenge him. He turned his head to the other two. "Give us a minute."

"Right, lecture her about eating but deny us the pleasure," Flynn muttered as he strode from the room.

Ben shook his head at Flynn's retreating back. "He knows they took food up. I swear…" He offered me a smile before leaving.

I turned my head in Lucien's direction. "I don't eat a lot. I'm tiny. It's not a crime," I said defensively. Then for good measure, because he was still staring at me, I took a bite of my food.

"Look, technically it's Brooke's job to make sure everyone is eating right, but for some reason she doesn't like pushing you. The rest of us don't give a fuck. Well, we do, but fuck, Doll. Just eat. It makes me happy."

"You know those points you earned earlier?" I asked around another bite.

Lucien snorted and shook his head. "I don't give a fuck about points. You like me so you'll eat."

I huffed. He wasn't exactly wrong. I did like him and the others. Maybe too much.

"What exactly is bonding?" I asked, changing the subject.

Lucien leaned on the counter, a crooked smile on his face. "Every time people touch, they exchange energy, even humans. There's a percentage of people who get goosebumps from it. They're most likely descended from Entwined and have no idea. With a circle, because we resonate at the same frequency, our energy moves through each other, almost completely unnoticeable." He reached forward and grabbed one of my hands in his. "Right now, you feel nothing. But if I were to…" My hand started to feel warm and my core clenched against my will. I gasped and jerked my fingers from his grasp. He smiled wider at me and I wondered if he knew what he'd done. "In time, we'll develop unique skills as our natural Arts blend. We have a while for that yet. But I'd prepare yourself for the exchanges.

Fuck, I groaned internally. If all exchanges felt like that, I was in serious trouble.

CHAPTER 18

The only reason I emerged from the house in a skimpy tank top and tight yoga pants after lunch was because I promised Flynn that I'd try harder. Brooke had insisted I change as practicing Arts was hard work and I'd hate how sweaty I was afterward.

Me? I was more worried about this forced bonding. I just couldn't seem to get over my personal issues with anyone else touching me. I'd been better about it than I ever had before, but Brooke made it very clear what to expect as we got changed for our workout by grabbing my hands every few minutes. And then linking arms with me as we made our way outside. I began to relax when the same reaction didn't happen with Brooke.

At the back door, I'd paused. It was with reluctance that she let my arm slip through hers as we observed the guys already stretching on the lawn, I looked for my brother noting that he wasn't out here yet. The sight of all that exposed muscle was distracting and intimidating, especially since most of them weren't wearing shirts. I gulped as my eyes swept over them.

"It'll be fine," Brooke said after it became clear I wasn't going to move on my own.

All of them turned toward us when they heard her voice and I wanted to shrivel up and die right on the spot. I'd never been the type of girl to pant after a guy, let alone five at once. Evan was a temporary loss of my sanity; one I got over quickly before swearing guys off indefinitely.

Vian came out as Brooke led me blindly over to where they were. Liam immediately went into instructor mode, taking us through several stretches, most of which my high school gym teacher had never taken me through.

"Kitten, pay attention," Liam barked.

My head snapped in his direction as I blushed, knowing he'd just caught me staring at Ben's abs as he stretched his arms in the air.

"Sorry," I muttered.

"It's fine," he said, smirking at me. Oh yeah, he definitely caught me staring. Fucking kill me. "As I was saying, once you learn how to control your body with the right alignments and enough will, you can do pretty much anything you can imagine. Our potential is always expanding."

Nodding, I continued stretching. Liam was beside

me, showing me the best way to loosen up my muscles as he explained the theory. I made more effort to listen to his words, but I was starting to get a bit distracted by the muscles in his arm. Especially when he raked a hand through his blonde hair. He caught sight of my face and reached forward to tap my chin. "You're doing that thing with your mouth again," he chuckled. "Do you have any idea what I've been talking about?"

My mouth smacked shut, unwilling to correct him about the expression on my face. If he wanted to think it was my confused face, I'd let him. He didn't need to know *what* I was confused about. He winked at me before he launched into another explanation.

What the fuck was wrong with me? I'd been fine this morning but now I couldn't seem to stop staring at them. It had nothing to do with their tight athletic wear or flashy muscles. Or the fact that I could clearly tell Flynn wasn't wearing underwear.

With an internal sigh, I ripped my eyes away from the man in question and cut Liam off. "Do I really need to know the theory to practice?"

Ben turned toward us, cocking his head in thought before answering. "Technically, no. It helps, but really you just need to think about what you want to happen and position yourself in a way that lets the energy flow. Any form would do, but we train so it becomes muscle memory." His eyelashes fluttered in the sunlight as he spoke, drawing all my attention to his face, but I found myself staring at his mouth. His bottom lip was fuller than the top, with a slight indent when he spoke.

Yep. My expression had nothing to do with him talking because I understood what he was saying. For the second time, I clamped my mouth shut. To my right, Flynn snorted and leaned into Lucien with a smug grin on his face. They whispered back and forth. Those fuckers. Those beautiful, sexy, shirtless…

No. Stop right there.

My tongue darted between my lips as I forced my attention back on Liam. "Let's just run through some forms then. I'm never going to be good at understanding this stuff if I don't do it for myself."

"Wait, so you're a tactile learner?" Ben asked, a thoughtful look on his face.

"Umm, yes, no, maybe, sure, why not?" I answered as I spread out on the grass and stretched my calves. Liam came around behind and put his hands in the middle of my back.

"Grab your toe," he said quietly, kneeling behind me before he applied pressure with his hands causing me to lean forward more.

With a huff, I easily grabbed my toe as I folded myself in half until my upper body was flush with my leg. I wasn't a nut about sports, but I was fit. If I hadn't been too busy trying to survive in high school, I might have found the 'give a damn' others seemed to have and gone for track. "This good?" I asked sharply, equal parts annoyed with him and distracted by Flynn and Lucien whispering again as they observed us.

"Yep. If you're that flexible, you should umm, you should—" he stuttered behind me. "You should, *fuck*, just push as far as your body will let you." His hands slid around to my waist before he dropped them to the grass and stood up. I turned my head to look at him but before our eyes could meet, he turned his away. "Okay, that should be enough stretching. Let's work with air today, guys," he called to the others. "Should be the easiest thing for her." He stepped away as I climbed to my feet.

Stretching, I could do, but once they started practicing forms, I faltered. No matter how many times I watched Liam or one of the others as they ran through the simple movements, I could not get it right. I was awkward and completely ungraceful, unlike Brooke who performed it perfectly and was rewarded with a small buffet of wind that kept distracting me.

"You look like a duck taking its first waddle," Flynn snorted as I lost my balance for the hundredth time. He strolled over and tapped one of my legs on the inner thigh. "Lean into this leg more and arch your back." I followed his instructions, trying not to think about his hand on my lower spine. "Good, now bring your arm up a bit more." His chest pressed against my back as he lunged behind me, shaping his body to mine, making my brain freeze. Only to be electrified as his arms came around me and one of his hands skimmed under my arm, bringing it up in an arc. "Perfect," he said against my hair. I trembled; he was so close, I could hardly think.

His arm dropped away as he stepped back and Liam crossed in front of me, checking my limbs. "Very good," he said, giving me a wide smile. "Take a quick look at Brooke and watch the lines of her body." I glanced over to the blonde in question. Her longer limbs were graceful as she focused on her center of gravity. There was no way I could ever look like that. "Do you see her shoulders, how they're squared, and her spine is perfectly aligned. That's to help the energy flow."

Something inside me snapped as I watched her spin on her front leg and another gust of wind rushed past me. My arms dropped to my sides and I brought myself up to my full height. "If you're just going to point out how inept I am, then you can fuck off," I bit out glaring at him. My eyes started to burn, and I closed them. They could walk me through the moves a million more times and talk about expanding capabilities until they were all blue in the face but I would never master it the way Brooke had.

"That's not what—" he started but I shook my head.

"Give me a second," I grit out. One breath. Then another. Letting my hurt wash through me but trying to not hold onto it. When I felt calm enough, I opened my eyes to see Liam standing in front of me still.

"It just takes practice," Liam said quietly. I cut my

eyes around, finding Flynn nowhere near us. He and the rest of the guys were taking a break while Liam used Brooke to show me what I should look like. Vian was the only one openly watching us with concern on his face. The rest of them were huddled in a quiet conversation. "Hey," Liam called softly, drawing my eyes back to him. "No one is judging you here, Kitten. If you got it right away, it would be a shock."

I shook my head at him. We'd been at this for what felt like hours and I was exhausted. I had a new respect for dancers, since what we were doing seemed closer to ballet than martial arts. At least for now when I had to go through the movements so slowly.

"Try one more time and then we'll break for the day," he said, giving me an encouraging smile that I couldn't return.

Blinking, I pushed everything else out of my mind and dropped my center of gravity, moving into the lunge and arching my spine. My right arm swept up in front of me as I put more weight onto my front leg and then swept my leg around me in a full pivot. The only thing I forgot was to focus on what I wanted to happen. Instead, all I thought about was how tired I was, that I wanted this torture to be over with. Something rushed through me, lighting up inside me and I let out a giddy laugh.

"Holy shit!" Lucien cried, heading toward me in a dead sprint just as I finished my spin.

Someone grabbed me from behind and hoisted me into the air, pulling me back. I squeaked in surprise and looked down only to see a perfect circle of dead grass. Lucien paused at the edge and stared up at me in shock.

I swatted at the arm holding me up. "Put me down!" My head turned only to meet Flynn's eyes over my shoulder. How the hell did he get over here so fast?

"Don't get shitty with me, Princess. You're the one killing the yard."

Liam appeared in my line of sight with a grim look as he stared at the grass. "You were tired and you… hell. Pushed her too hard." Then to me," How do you feel now?"

"Fine, I guess. I don't know." I smacked at Flynn's arm again until he reluctantly lowered me to the ground.

I spun around and put a finger in his face. "Minus ten points, Asshole. Do not grab me like that."

"How are you keeping track of that?" Ben asked. I looked at him over my shoulder. He was squatting by the circle of dead grass I wanted to ignore.

"I'll put a board up in the kitchen. Brooke can we get me a white board?" I asked her sweetly.

She grinned and rolled her eyes. "Fucking done. Just don't put me on there."

"Deal," I said. I lightly pushed Flynn away from me and inspected the grass. "I—can we fix it?" The idea of killing grass bothered me. What if I hadn't pulled from the grass? What if it had been a person? I shook my head to clear the thoughts from my head.

"Flynn can fix it later," Kieran said, offering me a smile. "Try it again but think about your intent this time. I was watching. You did the movements perfectly."

I blew a breath out between my teeth, hoping we could be done with practice for the day, but I could try once more. I waited for them to back up before dropping into my stance and focused on making a gust of wind. This time, something within me aligned. Instead of the giddy surge from before, something rushed through me as I spun. A brutal wind swept through the yard. Everyone stumbled back or fell over entirely except Kieran who looked like he'd braced himself. His grin was wide as he turned to steady Lucien.

I clapped my hands over my mouth as I straightened, both elated and horrified. "I'm so sorry!"

Ben was the first to recover, climbing quickly to his feet before he stalked toward me. I backed up, fear rising to the surface, but I didn't get far before he grabbed me around the middle and hoisted me up against him in a crushing hug.

"That was spectacular!" he exclaimed, pulling back to stare at me. "I can't wait to run some tests." His jewel-toned eyes lit up as he ran his gaze over my stunned expression.

"I can't believe it," I finally said as it sank in. I'd done it. Killing grass was one thing, but somehow this made it all real. More real than meeting a cat and having a full conversation with him. Ben let me down slowly and stepped back. As soon as my feet were on the ground I started bouncing on my toes. "I did magic!"

Liam groaned, burying his face in his hands. "It's not magic, Kitten."

"Shut up," I said, swatting at him. "Do not ruin this for me. I did magic. Wait, did I hurt anyone?" I scanned everyone from head to toe just to make sure no one was limping or bleeding, relieved when I found none.

"Come on, Doll. Help me make dinner tonight," Lucien said through a devilish smile as he grabbed me around the middle and hoisted me over his shoulder.

I smacked at his back with a screech. "Put me down, you caveman. I know how to walk."

"I know, but it's more fun to carry you," he said with a laugh that had his shoulder digging into my stomach as he marched toward the house.

I grunted as the blood rushed to my head. "You're making me dizzy," I complained, trying to lift myself upright, but dropping back down when we passed through the door. He didn't set me down until we were in the kitchen proper.

And by set down, I mean propped me on the counter and straightened, caging me between his arms. I backed away until the back of my head hit the overhead cabinets. "Hey," he breathed, his eyes catching mine. "Great job. Really, you did better than you think." He spoke quietly as the others trickled through the kitchen, heading for the stairs.

"Luc, bring her up in a minute," Flynn called from the bottom step. "I'll help you cook after."

"Oh right, I forgot," he said with a sheepish laugh.

"Forgot what?" I mumbled, completely transfixed by the light in his eyes.

"Your surprise," he replied before rubbing his thumb against my chin.

I blinked at him before I remembered. He'd mentioned it at breakfast and lunch, but with everything going on I hadn't the energy to try weaseling details out of him.

"Do you prefer Lucien or Luc?" I asked suddenly. I'd been calling him Lucien this whole time, but Flynn's comment and my earlier rant about nicknames had alerted me to the possibilities of other names.

He smiled at me again, flashing me with his dazzling teeth. "Luc, but whatever you want to call me is fine."

I snorted at him. "Luc it is, then. What do the others prefer to be called?"

He edged away from me and collected bottles of water from the refrigerator. "Honestly, don't worry about that." He handed me one after cracking it open.

I rolled my eyes. Jesus, I could handle opening a bottle on my own. I snatched it from his hand and downed half of it in one go. "Fine. I won't worry about it. Except Asshole. I'm never changing that."

Lucien threw his head back and laughed. "Trust me, love, it doesn't bother him at all."

"Oh." I muttered. "Damn, I'll have to think of something else he'll hate."

"I might have a way for you to mess with him…" he teased.

"Really?" I asked. "Tell me."

"It's gonna cost you," he replied in a sing-song voice that didn't match his expression. He was still in my space and the way he looked at me had my breath catching in my throat. We were being playful, flirting almost, but it didn't feel like a game.

"What's the cost," I asked softly,

"Just a favor." He smirked, tilting his head closer.

"A favor…" He was so close. All I would have to do is lean into him and his lips would be on mine. I wouldn't, but I wanted to. "I reserve the right to decline if I don't like the favor."

"You've got a deal. I'm sure we can find a favor to your liking." His eyes grew dark with mischief before he leaned in to whisper in my ear. His breath tickled against my skin as I listened. I tried to ignore how the brush of his lips made my insides clench. When he leaned away, I sat back on my hands with a slow smile.

"Really?"

"Oh yeah," he said with a dark chuckle.

My lips split into a huge grin.

CHAPTER 19

Lucien led me up the stairs and through the upper floor with a secret smile on his lips. It was a bit infectious, but I couldn't for the life of me figure out what the others had in store for me. Every few seconds, his eyes would meet mine and I'd have to look away, reminding myself that if things were different, if I were still in school, I would have stayed far away from him. I knew I shouldn't be entertaining crushes, there were so many other problems taking up space in my head. But Luc was a handsome guy, all sharp lines and perfect angles. Paired with his features, it was his personality that drew me in the most. He was sweet, flirty, like a ray of warmth from the sun.

I couldn't take it any longer, both his beautiful face and the excitement of figuring out the surprise. "What are you guys doing?" I asked.

"You'll see, Doll. Come on before you combust with curiosity," he said, grinning.

We turned a corner at the end of the hall and headed in a direction of the house I hadn't been back to since the night I woke up here. We bypassed Flynn's closed door and paused at a door at the very end of the hall. He rapped on the wood lightly. Inside, I could hear muffled voices before someone cracked the door open. One of Kieran's blue eyes peered out before crinkling with what I thought might be a smile. "Cover her eyes first."

I froze as Lucien stepped around me and put both hands over my eyes. His body—still shirtless, I might add—pressed against my back, sending a shiver up my spine. He smelled like lemons and something crisp that I couldn't identify right away.

"Is this really necessary?" I said, trying for a bored tone even though I was anything but and knew I failed. I sounded breathy. My body was coiled tight with Luc's heat wrapped around me.

"Patience is a virtue," Kieran stated with a laugh. I heard the door scrape against carpet as it opened.

"A doctrine I've never subscribed to," I muttered. Lucien pressed into me and someone took my hands, leading me forward. I was led several steps in before being turned around. A few seconds passed and I let out a nervous laugh. "Is this where you guys murder me…" My sentence drifted off as my eyes were uncovered and I blinked several times before they adjusted to the sudden light.

It was a bedroom—more specifically, one painted in my favorite color, mint green with a darker olive green to accent the room. Slowly, I spun in a circle on the beige carpet, luxuriating in the soft feel of it between my toes. The first thing to draw my eye was the enormous four poster bed that took up most of the space. It had gauzy black curtains that hung down and were pulled back to reveal the white bedding and cushioned headboard. As I turned, I took in a set of French doors with heavy blinds and a mahogany desk, already set up with a laptop and stereo system. Along another wall were two doors, one of which was open. Inside was a walk-in closet, already filled with the things Brooke and Lucien had purchased for me the other day.

"When…I…" I spun again, taking in more details. "This is…"

"All yours," Lucien said as I came face to face with his wide smile.

"Does that mean you like it?" Ben asked. Glancing in his direction, I saw an openly nervous look on his face as he chewed the corner of his index finger.

"It's…" I couldn't seem to articulate how I felt in that moment. The room was beautiful. I was having trouble believing my eyes.

"I think she's speechless," Flynn drawled.

I moved to the bed, pressing down on the mattress before flopping onto my back, letting out a small squeal at how soft it was. Later, when no one was around, I was going to lay on it and kick my feet into the air. "I love it," I finally said, fighting the urge to cry. I barely got those words out before my throat closed down. I wanted to thank them, but I knew if I did, I'd break down. Tears were not something I wanted when I was so happy.

"Good," Liam said as he crossed the room, making himself comfortable on the bed before he pressed a kiss to my forehead and then rolled back onto the mattress.

Propping my head up, I gazed around again. Let's be real, I was going to do that several times before it really sank in. This was my room. My own space. I'd never had that before. Ever. Vian and I had shared a room when we were little. We'd had a playroom that could have been a second room, but we'd never wanted that. It was obvious they had designed the room to fit my taste, and my gaze continually swept the room trying to memorize every detail, afraid that at any moment someone would say that this was just a joke and I didn't actually get to keep the room. As I looked around, I found one problem.

"Why aren't there any locks?"

"We don't need them. The bathroom locks from the inside, but the rest of the house doesn't have any," Liam said grinning up at me.

Lucien busted into a fit of laughter. As if it were funny that I'd be worried about locking my door. It wasn't, but then, they'd probably never prayed for a locked door to hold before. "I can't believe you didn't notice that before."

"What do you do when you have girls over?" I forced myself to ask, instead of focusing on my own need to have a lock. I didn't want to bring it up. Instead, I asked something equally stupid because it bothered me more than the missing locks. Sure, they were all about me now, but eventually, there would be girls. They were young, handsome. A sick feeling filled me at the thought, and I hated those nameless girls. "Bet that gets awkward... Unless you use the sock method, I suppose." I tried to chuckle, but it sounded much darker than the light tone I'd been aiming for.

Liam's smile slipped away, morphing into a guarded look. "That's not something you'll have to worry about," he answered lightly.

My head cocked to the side. Why wouldn't that be something to worry about? I swept a look over the four other guys in the room and I realized that Brooke and Vian weren't here. "Where are the lovers at?" I could have kicked myself for not seeing their absence before now. But then again, these guys were distracting. It was like they seemed to suck up all my attention when they were in the same room together.

"They got called away. They'll be back for dinner," Liam said quickly. Too quickly.

I narrowed my eyes at him. "What? Are they off having sex or something?" I cringed as I said it, but Flynn's face turned red as he fought not to laugh at me. Kieran's hand whipped out as he hit his brother with the back of his hand in the stomach, which left Flynn doubled over, wheezing. I flinched at the sudden display of violence and had to stop myself from yelling at Kieran. Flynn might not be my favorite person, but that didn't mean anyone had the right to hit him, no matter how much of a jackass he was being. There didn't seem to be any anger between them, which puzzled me more.

I opened my mouth to say something, but snapped it shut. I'd gone from happy to tense in a matter of seconds by that single act. Looking around the room, I noticed the others chuckling. Maybe I was reading the situation wrong?

Kieran threw me a wink. "Trust me, you did not want to hear what he would have said."

Liam rolled his eyes and turned his head toward me. "We got a summons from the council and they went to play nice. It's nothing to worry about."

Every time someone mentioned the council, I noticed a small change in them, especially Liam. They wanted me not to worry, but I could tell they were. And even if it wasn't worry, it was something that made them tense. "Are you lying to me?" I asked, glaring at him. I decided to be direct. I needed to know if my brother was there. Nothing bad could happen to him. It would kill me. His eyes widened as he sat up. I immediately regretted how accusatory I'd been. "I'm sorry," I said quickly, running a hand roughly through my curls.

"That's our cue to go make dinner," Lucien interjected before anyone could say something else. He walked over and popped a kiss to my cheek. "I'm glad you like the room," he whispered. Then he grabbed Flynn who was only just recovering and looked like he was already plotting revenge against his twin.

Ben shook his head at their retreating backs with a soft look that made me stare after them too. Flynn's broad shoulders swayed as he followed Luc. I looked out the French doors of my new room, wishing that Vian and Brooke would walk through them. What was so bad about the council that it made everyone worry?

I squealed when something tickled my side and smacked out blindly, connecting with Liam's bicep. Liam rolled away from me with a smirk on his face. "For the record, I hate being tickled. It's like forcing someone to laugh against their will." I tried to keep the sting out of my voice, having already been a royal bitch to him just moments ago, but it was a struggle. I hated being tickled that much.

"Sorry, Kitten. I was just trying to be playful."

I smiled weakly at him. I could appreciate the effort, if not the application. "I'm just…I feel this emptiness without Vian here," I admitted, realizing that was exactly it. My twin wasn't here to share this with me.

"It's nothing to worry about, Liv," Kieran said.

"They're just answering questions the council has. They're keeping a particularly good eye on our circle. We're being careful with the information we feed them," Ben said smoothly breaking into the conversation.

"I don't remember them leaving though. Luc and I were in the kitchen, we'd have seen them leaving," I argued.

"Hello," Liam said waving his hand from the end of my bed. "Bender of space and all that shit."

My eyes slammed shut with a wince. I'd forgotten that little tidbit. Well, not forgotten it, just…not thought about it. "Right," I said, sucking in a breath.

The bed dipped and warmth sank into my back as cedar and something flowering swept over me. My eyes popped open as I looked over my shoulder, coming face to face with Kieran as he draped an arm around my waist. He looked somewhat apologetic for it but didn't back off in the slightest. His nearness was making it harder for me to pretend I wasn't attracted to him. Him and his four friends.

"Liv," Ben started, cutting off my lustful thoughts before they took off running. "I meant to sit down and talk with you about the council before this but with everything that's been going on..." He sounded pained as he spoke which made me prickle inside. I didn't like the sound of where this conversation was headed. "You're really powerful. As in, off the charts normal for an Entwined. It's triple the access that Vian has. Demaric is a friend to our families so he didn't report that, but…"

With every word he spoke, my unease grew. "What does it matter how powerful I am?" Was I really going to just believe this? Everyone kept talking about how much power I had, but I didn't feel powerful. I was like a fish, flopping along the shore, trying to find the water again. I mean, yeah, a few weeks ago I wouldn't have believed that I could make wind, or read tarot cards, or have an out-of-body conversation with a freaking cat. Fuck.

Kieran pressed his face into my hair. "Because the most powerful Entwined usually become twisted. They don't have the same limitations the rest of us have. They—the council could make trouble for us. Try to study you. There have been instances in the past where—"

"I think that's enough for now," Liam cut him off quietly, not looking at any of us. He stared up at the gauze over my bed, his eyes far away from here.

"No," Kieran said firmly. "She should know what's ahead of her. Of us. I've said that since the beginning."

"I agree," Ben said. "But it isn't just up to us three. Everyone should have a say so we should shelve this conversation until later."

My head dropped back onto the bed as I tried to count to ten. "I don't think that's fair. To keep me in the dark just because all of you have to agree. What about what I have to say?"

Liam rolled over, looking me in the eye. "That's not what this is about. It's not about keeping secrets from you. We're trying to not color your opinions. This whole thing is a very delicate topic." I turned away from the earnest look in his eye, but he just grabbed me by the chin and brought my head back. His eyes closed for a moment; it was clear that he was struggling to control his expression. "Some things are just not that simple." He bent down until his forehead touched mine. "Just like you don't like talking about your abuse, we don't like talking about ours."

My heart pounded in my chest and I shifted uncomfortably. "Can you at least tell me why the council is keeping track of us?" I looked up at him, eyes wide open to show that I was trying and that I understood where he was coming from, but I needed to know what I was facing. He held my gaze and I saw his struggle there. It was almost enough to make me take back my question.

"Our history has shown us that Entwined who have too much power almost always go wrong," Kieran answered. Liam growled at him and rolled away again sitting up.

"Wrong?"

Ben coughed and I turned my head so I could look at him. Liam stalked out of the room behind him. His shoulders were rigid as he fled the room, I imagined it was to get away before he did or said something he would later regret. Kieran had been right; I really wasn't the only one who struggled with their past. The unease I'd felt before had now morphed into full out dread and regret of my own.

The two remaining guys said nothing to answer my question, leaving me to make my own conclusions.

I had to admit, their silence on the matter made it worse for me and I wished I'd listened. Wrong could mean so many things.

"Would they take me away?" I asked quietly. Fine, they didn't want to answer my other questions, but this I needed. I turned sharp eyes on Kieran.

The amount of remorse I found in his eyes had me holding my breath for his answer. "Yes," he finally said.

"I think I need a shower," I said softly, holding my hands out for Ben. He smiled and reached over to lift me up but as our eyes met, I could feel the scrutiny in his gaze as he searched my face. The smile on his lips slowly turned downward at whatever he saw in my eyes. I broke our connection and without a backward glance went to my closet to find some clothes.

As I stepped into the spray of the water my pulse pounded through my veins and a bubble of panic rose up as I thought about what Kieran had confirmed. Separated again from my twin. From the guys. Brooke. I'd already lost Emma. I had no idea how I would ever bridge things with Payton and the thought of being ripped away from this family, one that wanted me in it, made my stomach twist into knots.

And that word. Wrong. It wouldn't go away. How much more could go wrong with me? Wasn't it bad enough I could detect danger but not avoid it? Didn't I pay in blood for needing my brother? And my heart, God… what I had left of that was so broken, I doubted it would ever be whole again. Life had been nothing but a disappointment. Maybe that's what they meant by wrong. Would it get worse? How wasn't it already?

And I couldn't forget how frustrated I was with myself. I'd all but admitted to myself that I was crushing after five guys who lived with me. I could try keeping it as platonic as possible, but I wasn't sure I'd be able to pull it off. We were supposed to be a Circle, a family and my stupid hormones were getting in the way of that.

I had to keep it to myself. Whatever the hell was going on with me, I wouldn't let anything happen. With any of them. They were only touching me, being nice to me, because of this stupid bond that we had to forge. The feelings those touches evoked were all on me.

A familiar sense of peace wrapped around me, trying to strangle the surge of emotions. It was something I was starting to associate with my guardian, and I knew he was here with me.

"You better know what you're doing," I said into the spray of the shower. "I can't lose what I have here. I can't." I took a deep breath trying to rein in my thoughts. If it did get to that point, I'd leave, before I could ruin this for my brother. It would be hard, but I would do it if I had to. Vian was happy here. He had Brooke. Brothers. A real life, with a real future...

CHAPTER 20

After dinner, I spent the evening in my new room, still a bit dazed by the fact that they'd gone to so much effort to put this together for me. I wanted the time to myself to decompress from the day. Dinner had been nice, relaxing even, except for the frequent exchanges of energy that left me blushing more than once. I'd also tried to thank them all for everything they'd done for me but that had blown up in my face.

"I don't want you to thank me, Princess," Flynn had stated, looking murderous. He hadn't looked at me, but I still shivered from the intensity behind his words.

The moment had been softened by Ben who leaned into me. "No one should have to be thankful to have a space to call their own. We know what it means for you, but it pains us to hear it." He'd followed it by planting a sweet kiss on my cheek. I'd fled the table as soon as humanly possible after that.

I noticed new additions to my belongings on my bedside table as soon as I entered. A cell phone, which I tucked into the waistband of my leggings immediately without looking through it, and a deck of tarot cards that called to me like a siren song. There was an itch on the palm of my hands that begged me to pick them up. I ended up sitting in the middle of my bed, knees drawn up with the side of my face turned in their direction.

The others had wanted me to join them for a movie, but Ben had notions of watching *Mary Poppins* which I was so not into. I liked music and some musicals, just not *those* sorts of musicals. The ones that were all happy smiles made me want to claw my eyes out. Maybe I could get him to watch *The Genetic Opera* instead some time.

"What's so funny?" Flynn asked, startling me so bad I screamed.

Hand on my heart, I glared up at him. He just smirked down at me before dramatically falling over on the bed. His weight displaced mine and I went rolling onto my side with my hair spilling in my face.

"Asshole," I muttered as I pushed myself up.

"You need new material," he chuckled, earning him a hard roll of my eyes.

I settled back, putting a foot of space between us. "What do you want, Flynn?" I tried to look at him, but my eyes slid past him to the deck of cards as the urge to pick them up hit me again. *Fucking cards.* A panicked thought settled into my brain.

"I was wondering if—"

"Can Arts be addictive?" I interrupted him, my eyes locking with his.

His smirk disappeared as he gave me a quizzical look. "Umm, maybe? Ben would—"

I waved off his answer and smirked in return when he glared at me. I knew I was being mean, but the cards kept prickling at me. It was irritating the fuck out of me. My gaze slowly turned from his face to them again. He tracked my line of sight and sighed. Loudly.

"Guardian," he muttered, grabbing the deck, frowning as he did so and held them out to me. "It's not going to go away. Liam probably gave these to you since you and Vian are precogs."

"Wonderful. So, I have to carry these around or something so I can tell people's fortunes?" I asked, snatching the cards from his hands. As soon as I touched them, the feeling faded. "Jesus. That's weird."

"Just shuffle them and get it over with," he said with a wave of his hands.

"Is it stupid to admit I don't want to know the future?" I asked quietly. Part of me really didn't. I'd never liked that part of me. To me, it brought nothing but pain. Sure, this morning, it had seemed cool, exciting even, but I'd had a long day to think about it and I just...didn't want it.

"Hey," he said, scooting closer to me, "what's wrong?"

"I don't want to know," I said back. "Knowing what's to come feels like I should be able to do something about it and I can't. I never have."

He pierced me with a heavy look, one very different than any other I'd seen on his face so far. Instead of the intense glare he usually wore, this one seemed to see right through me. "Sometimes, I get woken up in the middle of the night." His voice was soft as he spoke, keeping his indigo eyes on me. "I'll have to get out of bed and head into the woods, sometimes for miles, just to heal something. Just last week, I had to go fix a tree that got hit by lightning."

"That's insane. Your... ability makes you do that?"

He smiled. "No, Princess. Our guardians. Yours is trying to tell you something."

"So, why doesn't he just come out and say it?" I asked, looking around, almost half expecting my cat to appear. He didn't.

"Because, sometimes, they can't. They have their own lives. We're their job. Our job is to keep the balance." He laid down, putting his head right beside mine. I almost leaned into him to smell his dark hair. Almost. Doing so would show him I craved him. Even when he was an asshole, but even more so when he was being sweet.

"What balance?" I needed to distract myself.

"Of everything. Life, death. The endless cycles. We keep this orb we live on going," he replied.

I thought it over for a few seconds. "Seems like such a huge job. Does that mean not all Entwined live here then?"

"All of us have a home here. But no, most don't live here full time. We're out saving the world."

I laughed then. As in completely lost it, laughed. "Saving the world? From what? You make it sound like we're superheroes or something."

"Maybe we are. Did you think about that?" he asked seriously. "Consider everything that happens in this world. How people fuck it up all the time. Pollution, senseless violence, corruption. We keep it all from going completely out of whack."

"How can we possibly prevent war and violence?"

"The things our Circle are capable of are only a few of the gifts that Entwined have. There are empaths, like my mother. There are others with the gift of persuasion. We have people in every government across the world who work hard to deescalate tough situations."

"That's sort of incredible," I said, a bit in awe. "I feel like I need a second brain just to remember all of this. Sometimes, it seems so big that I can barely wrap my head around it."

He chuckled. "You'll get there. You've known about all this for maybe two weeks. Give yourself time to adjust."

"Can you go back to being an asshole?" I asked. "I sort of like you better that way." I was joking and smiled to let him know before he really thought I wanted that.

"Wow. You're a piece of work, woman," he said playfully. "Anyway, shuffle your cards and then get dressed. You and I are going for a walk."

I groaned and rolled into his shoulder. "I changed my mind. Stay nice," I joked.

He laughed into my hair and rolled off the bed. "Up, Princess. If you're a good girl, I'll give you a treat later."

My blood heated at his comment even though I knew he probably didn't mean it to sound so flirtatious. I buried my head in my pillows until I was sure my face wasn't blushing. When I lifted it, he was gone. "Fuck me," I whispered. Keeping shit to myself was going to be terrible if I blushed like that all the time.

The cards were still clutched in my hand and while Flynn had distracted me for a few minutes, the insane itch to read them returned. I grimaced at them before placing them on the bedside table. I'd read them after our walk if it was still there later. No way, no how, was I going to let it control me.

I MET Flynn on the front porch. Everyone was still in the living room watching movies. Luc had given me a curious look when I paused in the doorway looking for Flynn, but Kieran had nodded toward the front door, so I just gave them a parting wave and headed outside, checking to make sure I had my new phone still tucked into my waistband. It wasn't the best place for it, but something so expensive and easily lost would stay as close to me as possible.

The man in question stood at the railing looking out at the forest, wearing a long-sleeved henley and a pair of dark jeans with sturdy boots. I stopped for only a second, admiring the way his shoulders looked in such a tight shirt. The waning light cast him in shadows, looking more handsome. My breath caught in my throat as he turned toward me.

He looked me over from head to toe, making me shift uncomfortably. I glanced down nervously, thinking I'd buttoned my flannel shirt wrong, but everything looked fine. Paired with my gray leggings and sneakers, I sort of thought I looked adorable.

"Gonna be warm enough in that?" he asked.

I nodded, still feeling nervous. Ugg, why was I so nervous? It was just a walk. Nothing crazy. Still, part of me wanted to go grab Brooke and make her go with us.

"Let's go, Princess." He kicked off the rail and led the way down the front steps and set off down the dirt road.

I hurried to catch up with him, only glancing back at the house once. "Where are we walking to exactly?"

He kicked his feet in the dirt as he went, bring up plumes of dust and shrugged. "Nowhere in particular.

Just figured you probably needed some air. You've been in the house a lot."

"So have you." In truth, I felt a bit guilty about that. They'd made it clear everyone was sticking around the house to be around me and help me adjust.

He nodded, glancing at me. "Lately. We usually spend a lot of time outdoors. Camping and such."

"Camping?" I asked. I loved camping. I remembered doing it a lot with my parents. When Emma had learned this, she purposefully planned camping excursions. Mostly we stuck close to the house. There'd been a small lake only a mile or two away and we'd spend entire weekends hanging out there. Our foster parents didn't care as long as we checked in. With no money, except for what Payton made part time, it made sense for us to be within walking distance if we ran out of food or the weather turned sour.

"Yeah. Once things settle down, we'll probably plan a big trip somewhere," he answered.

"Cool." Oh my God, could I be any lamer? Cool? *Cool!* We walked for several minutes in silence while I mentally kicked my own ass. Without the others as a buffer, I felt incredibly awkward.

If Flynn noticed my internal struggle, he didn't say anything. At least until he reached out to grab my hand. When I gave him a confused and probably frightened look, he shrugged, saying, "Bond." My brain short circuited after that. His hand was warm in mine and I could feel that slight tingle Luc had told me to look for. At least he didn't shove his energy at me like Luc had done.

"Did you read the cards?" he asked suddenly.

I looked up, caught off guard. "No," I answered. "I…uh. I didn't want to give it power over me."

He pulled on my arm, leading me down a smaller track of dirt off the main road. Glancing around, I realized I had no idea where we were, and I was letting a guy I barely knew lead me off into the woods. Not that I thought he would do anything to hurt me but the situation sort of smacked me in the face with a whole lot of *you are stupid.*

"You shouldn't ignore it. I know you don't like it, but I don't think it's a good idea. Guardians are there for a reason." It was getting darker now, whether because the sun was finally setting or because the trees were getting thicker, I wasn't sure.

I grimaced at his admonishment but didn't reply. He shook my arm lightly. "Are you okay?"

I nodded quickly, even though I wasn't. My head felt too full. Entwined. Witches. Flynn. My brother. Everyone. Just… I wanted it to stop. I blinked several times and clenched my fists, trying to collect myself but nothing helped. Flynn's hand tightened around mine, returning the pressure in a reassuring way.

The first random thought that entered my brain flew out of my mouth. "So, Ben's a Disney addict."

Flynn tipped his head back and laughed as we walked. "Yeah, he's a secret Prince Charming," he quipped. "Which makes you…never mind." He raked a hand through his hair and walked a bit faster.

That was stupid. So stupid, Livvy.

Flynn pulled me into his side wrapping an arm around my shoulder as the sound of rushing water invaded my ears. I was so obsessed with clearing my head that I hadn't registered the sound at first. "Welcome to my favorite spot," he said, still giving me a one-armed hug that I almost wished would end. We were approaching what appeared to be a small brook. He pointed upstream and I saw a waterfall. We veered in that direction as the rush of water grew louder until we were standing at the edge of a moderately sized pond that fed into the brook. The pool couldn't have been more than thirty feet wide. Water fell from a cliff above, making it ripple. I had to admit, it was very pretty, especially in the low light.

Flynn shifted around behind me and pulled me backward into his chest, which made it impossible to ignore that he was there. He leaned down to talk loudly in my ear. "The water's high right now because of the warm weather, but once it cools off, the water slows to a trickle."

I turned my head, trying to imagine what this place would look like in winter with snow and ice everywhere. "Have you lived here your whole life?"

He nodded against the side of my face. "Kieran and I grew up with Ben, Brooke, Emma and Ella." He pointed back the way we came. "My parents live just a few miles down the road from us. Only reason you haven't met them yet is because they're giving you time to settle in."

"Are twins really that common here?" I asked, perplexed about how that worked. No one had given me a straight answer before.

His lips brushed against my ear, his breath against my neck as he answered. "Single births are rare for our people." My insides coiled, my breathing hitched, and I struggled not to squirm, either away or toward his mouth. I couldn't decide. Why was this so fucking hard? "Every set of twins born in the world are sensitive to the Arts, but we have people in place who screen twins born to human couples for their potential as well. Not all of them are gifted, but occasionally, we find full blooded Entwined. There have been more cases of Entwined disappearing in the last hundred years, only for their line to reemerge thanks to scientific advancement."

I turned my head, shocked to hear these people were so involved and froze when his lips grazed my own. It felt soft, gentle, like butterfly wings. Both of us tensed for a second. Flynn unfroze before me and nuzzled my nose with his own, staring into my eyes. Then he closed the small distance and pressed his lips against mine. My reaction was instantaneous as heat raked over me and my fingers clenched into his shirt. When his hands came up to my hair to deepen our kiss, I wrenched myself away and took off running.

CHAPTER 21

"Olivia!" Flynn yelled behind me, but I didn't wait. Why did I kiss him? Or let him kiss me? Or kiss him back? Ugh, I was so stupid.

I had no idea where I was going as I tore between the trees, pushing myself as hard as I could. I needed distance. One thing I knew was that while I was fast, he could catch me in no time. He had longer legs and years of training, whereas I only ever ran when I had to.

Sure enough, after a few minutes, I recognized the sounds of pursuit behind me, and I opened my pace even more. I did not want him to catch me. If he did, we'd talk about it, or he'd say something scathing. Everything was complicated enough as it was.

Fear tore at me, growing stronger with every second, every thud of my feet on the forest floor. I didn't check over my shoulder, just kept my eyes in front of me, making sure I wouldn't trip over anything. It didn't help me in the slightest when a figure stepped out in front of me.

I ran full tilt into them, hard enough that we went rolling through the brush until we hit a tree with a heavy thud. Pain, white hot, seared up my back, making me scream. The person was half on top of me, but they clamped a hand over my mouth, cutting off my yell.

"Shut the fuck up, bitch," Evan hissed down at me.

My head spun as his voice registered and then I was fighting him with everything I had. Nails raked against his skin. I bucked as hard as I could. I screamed when his hand slipped as he fought me for control. "Get the fuck off me, you psycho!"

The ground dug into my back as we struggled against one another. A wild fear gripped me as I fought him with everything I had. My body was covered in sweat, making it hard for him to hold onto my wrists. I slapped at him whenever I could, using my short nails to do as much damage as possible. We struggled for what felt like hours but was probably only minutes until I was panting, and he finally managed to pin my hands in the dirt above my head. Not once did I stop trying to dislodge his considerable size or cease screaming. I had no idea what I was screaming but I prayed Flynn would hear me. Once my hands were secure, he fisted my hair in his hands and slammed my head backward into the ground, making me see stars.

"You thought you could just run away from me? That I'd let you? You're fucking mine, you whore!" His spit hit my face as the world spun around me.

"Get off," I tried to shout but my voice was slurred. "I will never be yours."

"No," he growled, shaking my head with his hand. The motion sent a searing pain through my head and I screamed. Through the painfilled haze, I saw him grin down at me, as if he was enjoying himself. He probably was, the sick fuck. The thought was horrifying. "I've been all over this fucking island trying to find you. Lucky for me, you ditched your boyfriend."

He released my hair and started tearing at my shirt. A new panic filled me when I heard the buttons rip and I managed to get one of my hands free. I palmed his face, trying to dig my fingers into his eye. He howled, rearing back, giving me enough space to get one of my legs up between us. I pushed as hard as I could before he crashed down on top of me, forcing the air out of my lungs as my body was contorted in a painful position.

He snarled in my face. "Don't be so fucking difficult," he hissed. "If you'd stayed like a good little bitch, I wouldn't have to punish you now." He snaked a hand down between us, pushing my leg down. He fumbled with something at my waist as he tried to jerk down my pants. I could barely breathe. No, no, no this couldn't be happening. I could not be losing my virginity this way. My brain scrambled and my stomach heaved. I didn't know what else I could do to escape him. I was frozen as the top of my leggings ripped. "I'm going to show you you're fucking mine to do with what I wan—"

He jerked sideways with a scream as something heavy connected with the back of his head. He fell off of me. I scrambled up, crab walking as fast as I could away from him and whoever had attacked him.

"Livvy, no," Payton called, dropping the branch in her hands. Evan was slumped on the ground, barely moving, save for breathing. "I'm not here to hurt you. I followed him. I knew he was looking for you." She stepped forward cautiously, but I scrambled further away until my back hit a tree. Through the tattered remains of my shirt I could feel the bark grate against my spine. I hissed at the pain.

A growl sounded through the trees and Payton's eyes widened in fright as two large figures appeared on either side of me. Shimmering ghostly wolves bared their teeth at her. Their pale fur was nearly translucent with gray thick strands that practically stood on end. I had to blink several times before I could believe they were real. I brought a trembling hand up to my mouth to choke back a sob. My brain was finally catching up with what had almost happened. The wolves flanked me on either side as Payton stared at us.

"I'm not here to hurt her," she said softly before glancing over at Evan's still form as he groaned.

Please don't let him get up. Let him stay down. Payton stooped to the ground and collected her branch again before stepping closer to me. The wolves growled at her, but she turned her back, putting herself between me and Evan. "Are these your guardians?" she asked over her shoulder.

"I… what?" I said, still trying to make sense of the situation. "How do you know about that?"

"Liv, I've been your friend for two years. And I know a lot about Entwined from Emma. More than my coven does." Her voice shook. If I hadn't been terrified out of my mind, I might have admired her fearlessness.

"He...wha…fuck. He wasn't supposed… I can't think," I finally forced out. Evan groaned again and shifted on the ground. One of the wolves paced forward, stepping in front of Payton.

She backed away until she was right at my feet before spinning to eye the other wolf. It seemed to be in guard position, but it wasn't looking at her as it growled softly. It stared beadily at Evan. Satisfied she wasn't about to be mauled, she stooped. "Are you hurt anywhere? You might have a concussion. I'm sorry it took me so long to get him off of you. I had to find something to use. No spells on me. So stupid. What witch goes somewhere without ingredients?" She rambled on as she checked me over. "I'm so sorry, Livvy. I don't think you're bleeding anywhere but you have a nasty bump on the back of your head."

"How did you find me?" I asked wincing as her fingers trailed over a tender spot.

She snorted and offered me a weak smile that didn't reach her silver-grey eyes. "I knew where you were the whole time. It just took Evan a bit longer to figure it out. I've been keeping an eye on him, but I think he found some of my spelled ink that has yours and Emma's blood in it. Don't worry, I destroyed the rest after marking myself. He won't be able to do it again."

"You're not making sense," I muttered, resting my head in my hands.

"Olivia!" I heard as footfalls thudded through the trees. Flynn crashed by but skidded to a halt as he saw the wolves. "Good girls," he panted. The wolves growled louder as Evan groaned again. His eyes followed the sound until they settled on my attacker and then raked over me. He grabbed the wolf by the scruff of the neck. "Get him off this island before I murder him," he spat. He let go and moved to me, pushing Payton aside with barely a glance. His stare caught mine as he bent over, trying to catch his breath. He pointed between the wolves as they surrounded Evan. "Nymphs. All over in these woods. I asked for their help."

I stared at him, overcome with the bizarre need to hit him. "I hate you," I hissed before eyeing the wolf-nymphs. "Fucking nymphs? Like real nymphs?"

He smirked at me for a second before he pulled something out of his pocket. "Grab onto my neck and think of the house," he instructed and then to Payton, "I suggest if you don't want to be mauled, you grab my arm."

It was the only warning we got before he cracked something in his hand and the world jerked sideways. My body slammed into his. I briefly recognized the thorn jungle before we were moving and then spilled out onto the kitchen floor.

Payton stared around her in shock and fell over before she promptly vomited everywhere. The commotion brought a stampede of footsteps before Ben, Lucien, and Liam appeared in the doorway.

"Holy fuck, what happened?" Liam shouted. He bent to help Payton stand. As soon as he had her upright, his face flickered with recognition. "You brought a witch here? Are you insane?"

Flynn shrugged him away, already lifting me onto the counter and raking over me with his eyes. They were wide, almost fearful, as if he didn't know where to start. In the harsh light of the kitchen, every scrape I had was on display. Lucien and Ben bypassed Payton and Liam to come stand on either side of Flynn. Ben reached forward and pulled my shirt closed but when it wouldn't stay shut, he quickly took his own shirt off and pulled it down over me. His hands slid down my waist and then settled on my thighs.

"Is she okay? What happened to her?" Lucien demanded, his brown eyes round. His hand found my hair as he pushed it away from my face. It had fallen out of its braid during my struggle with Evan.

"He tried to rape her," Payton bit out, finally recovered from Slipping. My stomach rolled as she told them, but I shoved my discomfort away. I was rattled, but I reminded myself that Evan hadn't succeeded.

"I'm okay," I said quickly.

Flynn growled, startling me. The last thing I needed right now was an aggressive man growling at me. I pleaded at him with my eyes. I needed him not to make a bigger deal out of this. I knew it was bad, what had almost happened, but if he kept looking at me like a victim, I would lose my mind. Maybe I wasn't okay, but I would be. His eyes softened and I slumped in relief on the counter.

I looked over at Payton. Liam had her arm in a vice-like grip. He wore a haggard expression, but it didn't look like he was hurting her. Payton looked paler than she had before. I catalogued her features, matching them with how she normally looked. Thinner face washed in grief and desperation, and no small amount of anger. My heart broke for her even though I was still mad. There were so many lies between us. Did I even know her anymore? But she'd also stopped Evan so maybe our friendship wasn't entirely lost.

My vision tunneled for a moment. Emma's face flashed in front of my eyes. Ashes swirled. Then Evan's horrible expression as he pressed me into the ground. For a moment, I was drowning in fear. But it wasn't right. I couldn't smell him. Ben's scent wrapped around me, mixed with Flynn's. With effort, I pushed the visions away, digging my nails into my palms. I used the pain like a beacon to come back to myself.

I was safe.

My guys were with me. Everything was okay. I couldn't let this break me.

Sometimes bad shit happens to good people. I heard Brooke's words replayed for me. Everything in me would use this to make me stronger.

Only a few seconds had passed, but it was long enough that every eye in the room was turned in my direction. I forced myself to sit up straight and met their stares. If my breathing was heavier, let them think it was from anger.

"He who?" Liam asked in a deadly quiet tone. Internally, I sighed with relief.

"Evan." My tone was steady, despite the tension in the air. The room was thick with it, nearly suffocating and I knew I was partly to blame for it. If I hadn't run off…

Liam's gaze turned darker. His brown eyes were almost black. His fingers flexed around Payton's arm, turning white as he glared at her. "Start talking, Witch.

"I followed him here, you idiot," Payton snapped, tugging her arm out of his grip. She pushed him away from her and turned, trying to head in my direction but he stepped in her way.

"Fuck you if you think I'll let you anywhere near her." I could feel the rage pouring off Liam in waves as he glared down at Payton. His eyes begging her to make a move. Even I was afraid of what he might do if she did.

She squared up to Liam, only being a few inches shorter than he was. "If I wanted to hurt your Lehnu, I would have done it already. Now back off so I can check on my friend." The guys looked from her to me for a second and then back. I wasn't sure what they were looking for. Permission? It didn't make sense why they would start asking me what I wanted. No one ever did.

"It's fine," Flynn finally said to Liam's back. "She got there before I did."

"Why was she alone in the first place?" Ben asked quietly. His eyes were hard as he stared at Flynn and I realized this was the first time I'd seen him even marginally upset. He was always so… not relaxed, but mellow. His long fingers flexed on my thigh, like it was an effort for him not to squeeze them.

"I ran," I said softly. I was so stupid. So, so, so stupid. I'd been given one directive by my guardian and I hadn't listened. None of this would have happened if I'd listened. And fuck… those damn cards. That cat knew somehow that this would happen and tried to warn me. I couldn't take all the blame for it. Evan's weird obsession with me was most of it, but it didn't alleviate my guilt. "I…" My gaze swept over the five of them who were crowded around me. I settled my tired gaze on Payton. "Thank you. I…"

Her eyes softened and looked away. "I don't expect you to trust me ever again. Evan… this wasn't supposed to happen."

"What wasn't supposed to happen?" Lucien finally spoke. His voice was low, barely above a whisper. He didn't sound angry like the others. Just tired. "If your people had just left her alone, we could have…" He stopped himself abruptly and spun away from us to pace around the kitchen.

"We thought she was alone. My Mom caught wind of her file and we thought we were saving her from other covens. We weren't the only ones who knew about her," Payton said pleadingly. She was speaking to Lucien, but her eyes were on me. She wanted to explain it for me.

"Fucking witches," Flynn bit out. "You made a deal for her, didn't you?"

"No," Payton said, shaking her head. "There was no deal. We just made sure she was near our community and, yes, I admit that we wanted to draw her into the coven, but we weren't going to force her."

"How do you explain your fucking boy then?" Flynn shouted, flinging his hands around. Ben walked over, placing a hand on Flynn's shoulder. "How do you explain the fucking spells we found on her?"

Payton paled, opening her mouth to speak but

Flynn cut her off as he brushed Ben's hand off and stalked toward her. "You can't. You thought you were protecting her, but you weren't. You just put her closer to some psycho who wants to use her until she's fried."

"No, that isn't true," Payton said, anger coloring her tone. "Emma found out about the spells at a doctor's appointment. Evan never touched her after that first time. We made sure of it. It was his uncle who put those on her during what should have been just a routine exam. And get off your fucking high horse. Everyone knows what your kind does to spares. You think we don't know how fucking sick your council is? I wanted to keep Livvy from that fate." She was up in his face by the time she was done shouting.

I sat there shocked, but something nagged at me. "What do you mean spares?"

"The ones without their twin. They use them, study them. Emma was a fucking science project for years before being sent to help you. And only because she should have belonged to your little family. They didn't love her," Payton spat.

"That's not true—" Lucien said as he charged across the room and shook Payton by the arms. "We loved her. Get the fuck out of our house." He was seething as he shoved her toward the doorway. She stumbled but managed to catch herself on the frame.

"Do you want me to go?" she asked, locking eyes with me, as if someone hadn't just shoved her. Carefully, I surveyed the others, reading their anger and trying to reconcile myself between the girl who cared about Payton and the woman I was trying to be. Did I want her to leave? No… not really, but it wasn't up to me. Not after what she said about Emma. I walked around the house every day and saw the shadow of grief on my Circle's faces. How devastated they were. They pushed it aside when I was around, but it was still there.

I looked down at my legs. There was a tear in my leggings I hadn't noticed, and the exposed skin was scratched to shit. "I think that…we should talk when everyone's calmed down, but for now you should go. Text my brother a number I can reach you at."

Her only response was a single nod. She reached into the pocket of her jeans, pulling out a thin silver chain and tossed it. The piece of jewelry slid across the counter until it hit my thigh. I recognized it instantly. My mother's bracelet. I looked up, lip trembling as Liam escorted her from the room.

CHAPTER 22

After a scalding hot shower, a tense meeting with everyone who'd been away, and the attack still on my mind, I'd laid for hours in the oppressive darkness of my room. My only comfort was the sound of breathing, spread out either on the bed or on another mattress. Flynn had taken it from his own bed and deposited it on the floor of my room. I'd watched in equal parts fascination and discomfort when he'd pinned me with his eyes and all but dared me to challenge him.

All my fight had fled me after I had put on the bracelet. I was never letting it off my wrist after almost losing it forever. As for the others, I was too tired to push them all away. Moreover, I didn't want to. It had taken a long time for my hands to stop trembling. And that was only because Kieran did his magic and healed me. Physical shock had a lot to do with it.

When sleep did come, it was fitful. I woke several times with a scream dying on my lips, covered in sweat, and soft reassurances that I was safe. Finally, Kieran demanded we keep a light on. After that, things were easier on everyone.

I woke in the morning to quiet conversation around me. I drifted with their voices for a few moments before I started to listen.

"I don't understand why they want her so bad and not Vian," Lucien questioned.

"You've seen the file the council doctors sent back. She's powerful. Anyone even remotely sensitive would be drawn to her," Flynn muttered.

"They still haven't made a counter move," Ben said. "Eventually, they're going to want to see her in action. If they even think she's one of the Vanished, they'll take her."

"There's absolutely no proof in our mother's records that she was carrying triplets," Vian replied heatedly. "I still haven't talked to her about our parents yet. Every time we think we're going to get a break, something else happens and it never feels like the right time."

"Shh, you're going to wake her," Brooke said as my hair was smoothed from my face. I recognized her touch instantly and tried not to tense up.

A heavy masculine sigh sounded and shifted in the sheets. "What I want to know is why she was alone in the first place. You never answered that, Flynn," Liam said in a dark tone.

There was silence as the tension in the room ramped up, but I only had to wonder for a second whether Flynn would answer. "I fucking kissed her, okay?" Flynn admitted.

Everyone groaned quietly. I heard rustling before Kieran spoke up, "Where are you going, Luc?"

"Away from him before I deck him," he replied. I heard the door open and shut.

"If you screw this up, Flynn, so help me, I will kick your ass," Liam said darkly. "We have a plan."

"Your plan is complete shit," Brooke scoffed. The bed dipped and I imagined her crawling to the edge and getting up as well. "The five of you should have been upfront from the start."

"It's not your decision," Ben said quietly. "She's not ready for that sort of thing. She barely trusts us as it is."

I decided then to stir, having heard enough. Why they decided my bedroom was the best place to have secret meetings about me—with me in the room, no less—was beyond me. Anything I wanted to know later, I was going to ask Brooke or my brother about.

When I opened my eyes, I saw everyone had either climbed to their feet or was already leaving the room. Well, everyone except Liam and Flynn. Asshole himself sat at the end of the bed, giving me a death glare while Liam leaned against my dresser, not looking at me but staring daggers at Flynn.

"You are in so much trouble, Princess," Flynn said, his eyes dark with promise.

Kieran turned at the doorway and marched back across the room. "Don't fucking start with her."

"You can't be serious," Flynn said as his twin glowered down at him. "She should know what she did."

"I do know," I said quickly. His words probably should have angered me, but they didn't. I completely understood it. "I shouldn't have run. It was reckless." I sat up and brushed my curls out of my face, only to notice the bruises on my arms. Kieran had healed the cuts and the shock, but the bruises must not have shown up last night. They were glaring at me against the pallor of my skin. I could ask him to take care of them, but I wanted to keep them. Not only as proof to my own foolishness, but also because it proved I'd fought. Knowing that was important to me. I looked at Kieran. "No matter how upset I was last night, I knew better than to be alone out there."

Flynn sat back with a smug smile and looked up at his brother who'd crossed his arms to lean against the post of my bed. "I'm glad you're able to be mature about it. But he doesn't have shit to be proud of here." With that said, Kieran grab his brother by the arm and dragged him out of the room.

With a covert glance, I looked to the last man standing. Liam still leaned against the dresser, not looking at me.

"Are you mad too?" I asked quietly as I picked my way out of the sheets and pillows that were scattered around me.

"Not at you," he said after a long minute. "You should get ready for the day. We're going to train."

"Okay," I replied, letting out a breath.

"Why didn't you use what you knew?" he asked.

I stopped short and sat back on the bed. "I…" Why hadn't I used any powers to help me? "I wasn't thinking," I finally said.

He nodded. "Get dressed, Kitten. Today is going to kill. Have Kier take care of those bruises." With that, he marched out of the room, not even sparing me a parting glance. A heavy feeling settled in my chest as I thought about what Kieran had said the other day about Liam and Lucien's past.

THE DAY DID KILL, just as Liam promised. By the end of it, I was physically exhausted. So much so that I managed to blacken a quarter of the yard which irritated Flynn beyond belief. He'd been surly all day, either barking orders at me or getting into heated debates with the others.

It finally came to a head shortly before dinner when I'd had enough. I watched as everyone headed inside, still stretching out my tired and sore limbs as Flynn repaired the damage I'd done to the grass.

The sliding glass door was barely closed before Flynn hoisted me up and set me in his lap with my back against his front before speaking quietly into my ear. "I know you have things you're working on in that brain of yours. Trust being the major one. But you cannot run from me ever again, no matter how pissed off you are. If you stopped to observe beyond yourself for one minute, you'd realize we're trying to help you."

"I…" I never got to finish what I wanted to say. One second, I was sitting on his lap and in the next I was sprawled across it before his hand smacked down on my ass, knocking the breath from my lungs. Then he smoothed his hand over the now stinging area, eliciting tingles that spread throughout my body like wildfire. Heat pooled between my legs. I lay there stunned for a second before I realized what had happened.

A feral scream left my throat as I tore out of his arms and sprawled backward on the lawn. "Don't you ever fucking hit me again!" I choked out as he smirked at me. Tears burned in my eyes as confusion barreled through me. Slowly, his arrogance dripped away as he realized he'd done something wrong, that he'd hurt me.

"Liv, I—"

"Go inside, Olivia," Liam barked as he charged toward Flynn. I didn't need to be told twice as I scrambled up and headed for the door, determined not to cry about this. I knew I deserved to be lectured about what happened the night before but not what he'd done.

I heard the yelling before I made it to the door, but I didn't turn around. "If you ever put your hands on her again like that without her permission, I will ruin you," Liam snapped.

"I wasn't thinking," Flynn said back.

"You're damn right—"

The words muted as I slammed the door shut behind me, making the glass rattle in its frame, and charged through the dining room into the kitchen.

"Olive?"

I didn't pause to explain to any of them. With a hand, I waved toward the back door and raced from the room. By the sounds from behind me, I knew at least one or two of them were following me, but more feet thundered toward the back. I couldn't get into my room fast enough.

Once there, I slammed the door shut in Lucien and Brooke's shocked faces. With a glare and a wave of my arm, the stereo flared to life. Music blared from the speakers, drowning out the knocking that started on my door. It was a fitting song, one that spoke of pain and heartbreak. I broke down then, wracked with sobs. I ended up on the far side of my bed with my butt on the floor as I hugged myself. Time drifted, music changed, the knocking stopped. Sunlight slipped away and the room grew dark. I cried on and off. Broke apart and went about picking up the pieces and trying to fit them back together again.

I questioned my reaction to what he'd done. Yes, he'd hit me, and it had hurt, but for a moment, I'd liked it. More than liked it. But afterward, when all that shame came crashing in, I'd wanted to die. I hated myself for liking it. Was I so twisted in the head that any sort of affection would do?

No. I shrugged those thoughts aside. Not even a day ago, I'd been brutally attacked and nothing but terror had filled me. So, what made it different? Was it because it was Flynn and I expected him to be an asshole? Why was it that I was more affected by a guy spanking me than someone trying to force themselves on me? I had to be fucked in the head.

Eventually, my legs grew stiff and my hunger started to gnaw at me. A gentle stillness had surrounded me, but my body protested to being in one position too long. Slowly, I climbed to my feet to check the clock. With a scream, I fell back when I saw the shadowed figure of someone sitting on the other side of my bed.

The light clicked on to reveal Lucien. "Sorry, Doll. Didn't mean to scare you," he said quietly.

I clutched at my chest, waiting for my heart to start beating normally again. "I didn't hear you come in."

He offered me a sad smile. "It was some time during the *Halsey* portion of your playlist. I'm sorry for the intrusion. I know you wanted to be alone but no one… The Clone's mother suggested you shouldn't be totally on your own right now."

My eyes widened. "Who?" A small amount of mortification filtered through me.

"Mrs. Chadwick, my adopted mom, Kieran and…" he eyed me as he trailed off. I got the impression he didn't want to mention Flynn. "They live down the road. There was a pretty big altercation earlier and we needed a mediator."

"By altercation, you mean?"

"Liam and Flynn got into a fist fight. Kieran broke them up, but he was pretty close to finishing the job once we heard why they were fighting. Ameris—Mrs. Chadwick—works as a counselor, both here and off the island. Anyway, that's not important. She just has experience with abused—fuck!" He dropped his head into his hands. "I'm not saying any of this right."

"She was worried I'd try to hurt myself," I finished for him, unsurprised. "No, I wouldn't ever consider that. I may be a bit fucked in the head, but I couldn't do that to my brother." When he looked up, his eyes shone with unshed tears that nearly broke me. The pain he felt was so evident that I climbed over the bed and wrapped my arms around him. "I'm sorry," I said quickly. "I'm so sorry I scared you. I just needed time to process."

He held onto me for a few minutes while I ran a hand through his hair. When he pulled away, his eyes were clear, if a bit red. "Nothing to apologize for. Just… we were scared. Brooke had to drag Vian out of the house because he was so angry. They're staying at her parents for the night, maybe longer. This is the worst fight we've ever had," he said with a forced chuckle.

My heart clenched with guilt. I'd promised not to

cause them more problems. My lip trembled. Already, I was separating them. The words were on the tip of my tongue, to tell Luc I should leave, but I knew he'd fight me on it. If I had to do it, it would be without telling any of them. "I should call him. Let him know I'm okay," I said softly.

"Are you though?" He worried his bottom lip, waiting for my answer.

The question brought me up short. People asked all the time, but it always sounded like they were asking out of habit more than genuine care or concern. With Luc, I could see how much my answer meant to him. It was because of that look in his eyes that I took my time to consider it, to search for a real answer other than fine.

"No, not really," I admitted, pursing my lips. "But… I think I will be." I reached forward, grabbing his hand and giving it a squeeze. "Just give me time to figure it out."

He pulled on my arm as a small smile spread across his lips. I let him drag me into his lap where he buried his face in my hair. "Time's all I'm asking for," he breathed softly. So softly, I almost didn't hear it.

CHAPTER 23

"As much fun as it is to have you to myself," Lucien said, "we should probably go talk out our problems like adults. Plus, you haven't eaten since lunch and it's getting late."

I groaned, already rolling off the side of the bed. "I'm really not that hungry," I lied out of habit as we walked out of my room.

"That's because you killed half the yard. But stealing energy from the ground isn't a replacement for food," he lectured. "I have a theory. If you ate properly, you probably would have more control over that. You get tired because your body doesn't have enough calories to keep you going."

"You sound like Ben," I retorted, sticking out my tongue.

He pulled me to a halt at the top of the stairs and slowly pressed me up against the wall, crowding into my space. He regarded me for a moment, watching my reaction. My stomach flipped as his head bent toward me until his mouth was right next to my ear. "A small tip. Don't offer your tongue to a bunch of horny men." He pressed a chaste kiss to the skin just under my ear before he backed off and gave me a meaningful look that had my retort dying in my throat.

In that moment, I knew if he had kissed me, I would have kissed him back. Probably would have regretted it after, but I was finding it harder to ignore the facts around me. My body responded to him. It responded to all of them. And I was in huge trouble because of it.

My brain didn't start working again until we reached the living room. Liam and Kieran sat side by side, just staring off into space. Flynn had his forehead pressed into Ben's shoulder who absently ran his fingers through Flynn's hair. All of them looked as though they were taking comfort in each other, which isn't what I expected. Somehow, I'd pictured them still in some sort of standoff. It made me feel a bit better to see that despite their frustration with each other and me, it wasn't enough to keep them apart.

It took them a few minutes to notice us and only because Ben cleared his throat and nodded toward me. Flynn stood immediately and went to head toward me, but Liam blocked him and whispered something in his ear. He glanced at me, checking me from head to toe before he sat back down.

"Well, I'm happy to report that Liv is not suicidal," Lucien announced, as if it was something to rejoice about. It was highly embarrassing.

I sent him a dark look before moving further into the room and perching on the end of the couch. "Before…whatever this is about to be takes place, I'd like to call my brother and let him know I'm okay."

"Where's your phone?" Kieran asked.

"Umm…" I looked around me, trying to remember where I'd left it with a wince.

"Did you lose it in the woods?" Flynn asked.

I winced again, remembering that last time I'd seen it was just before our walk.

"I'm going to go get you some food," Lucien whispered in my ear. I smiled at him and mouthed thank you before he left.

"Use mine," Ben said, getting up from his seat. He sat down next to me and pulled me down into his lap, which was very unlike him. Out of everyone, he didn't typically touch me, except for on the hand. He pushed his phone into my grasp and pulled me against him before burying his nose in my hair.

My nose scrunched up as I texted Vian. "Are you sniffing me?" I asked absently.

Ben: Hey, it's Livvy. I'm good. ILY.

"Yes," Ben replied simply. "I was worried about you. A lot has happened in the last couple of days and …"

I turned slightly so I could look him in the eye. The action brought us nose to nose and my heartbeat quickened when I saw the unguarded look in his eye.

What was it with these guys? Why did they have to be so sweet? Didn't they know how confusing it might be for me to have all this attention centered around me?

"Don't worry about me," I said softly. "I may look small, but I'm a big girl."

He closed his eyes and nodded. "I can't stop thinking about what almost happened to you last night. We're your family and you…"

"Hush," I said quickly. The magnitude of what he felt reflected back on me, and it was too much for me to consider. I swallowed and leaned my forehead against his. "It didn't happen," I breathed, surprising even myself. The whole attack could have been so much worse than it was. I wouldn't dispute anyone's claim that it was traumatic, but when I thought about what could have been, I shuddered.

"Can I stay with you tonight?" he asked quietly, backing away so he could look me in the eye again.

He was so sweet. I nodded quickly before I could change my mind. Just then, Luc came back into the room with a bowl in his hand. He smiled down at Ben and I before throwing himself into the seat next to us and drawing my legs up into his lap. It was then that I realized everyone had been quietly watching Ben and me. I didn't know how much they overheard. None of it, I hoped, but knowing me, my luck wasn't that good. As I covertly checked in on them, I was relieved to see that none of them were upset.

Glancing down, I looked at the bowl in my hand and sighed. Lucien had given me a large portion of alfredo pasta. I glared at him. He smirked back and I begrudgingly took a bite. The taste of garlic lit up my tongue and I greedily spent the next five minutes devouring the entire bowl. Someone flipped on the television where some sitcom played. It helped to break up the uncomfortable silence in the room. When I was done, I went to get up and go wash my bowl, but Flynn jumped up and took it from me.

"I can wash my own bowl," I called after him.

"He feels bad," Kieran grunted. "Let him atone." He grabbed the remote and muted the television. My lips pursed as the sound of running water started. I eyed Kieran, unhappy with how rigid he sat.

"I don't want him to atone," I said quietly. And I really didn't. I was upset with him, yes, but I seemed to be the only one who realized what I'd put him through. I thought back, remembering my disheveled visage just before I showered, before I let Kieran heal the scrapes. If I had found any of them looking like that, I didn't know what I would do but it wouldn't have been pretty. Hadn't I manhandled Brooke and Ben when they put themselves in danger over that hex? I completely understood Flynn's reaction and his need to show me his anger.

Liam sat back with a sigh and stared at me thoughtfully. "He shouldn't have hit you," he said tiredly.

"He—"

"We should wait for him," Kieran said, cutting me off.

We didn't have long to wait as the water shut off followed by Flynn entering the room a few seconds later. Instead of going back to his seat, he sat down on the floor right in front of Ben and I, leaning against the couch before he laid his head back and stared up at me. I didn't see the guy I spent the day with. The one who had lashed out every second, glaring his way through our practice. Or the guy who felt so entitled that he could take me over his knee and spank me like a petulant child. Right then, I saw a man who deeply regretted his actions. The guy who held my hand through hours of medical tests when everyone else found better things to do. The one who less than twenty-four hours ago had pressed his lips to mine on a whim. Who I ran from because I was too busy caring about how I felt and couldn't be bothered to think about anyone else.

"I'm sorry I ran. That's what I was going to say earlier."

"I know," he whispered. He licked his lips and glanced away. "I—"

"No. I don't want an apology," I said, cutting him off. "Just please don't ever do that again. I understand why you were angry. How badly I scared you. Everyone," I tacked on. "It could have been so much worse than it was. I realize that. I'm… not good with… people. Life actually." I let out a small laugh. "But I'm trying."

"Since we're airing things out, I'd just like to say I think we've been going about this all wrong," Kieran said, leaning forward to eye everyone individually. "She deserves to know everything."

"Everything?" I asked, confused. Part of me internally crumbled. What other secrets did they have that I didn't know? I was starting to see that I needed them to trust me just as much as I was trying to trust them.

"The council," Kieran amended. "When we brought you home, we told you it was safe here. We promised a family and a place to belong. And at the time, we thought that we could give all of that. But the truth is, we're about to have a shit-storm on our hands."

"Ooooookay," I said, dragging out the word. "Wait, does this have to do with my energy or whatever?"

"In part," Liam said. "It's... we have our problems as a community. Bigotry, ignorance, that sort of thing. But we didn't realize how bad it was until we got a chance to talk with Ameris. She said the council is pushing to formally meet you. Because of your parents."

"What about my parents?" I asked guardedly. I didn't think I was ready to discuss this subject yet. I'd conveniently locked away the information about them having been a part of this community in light of other recent developments.

"They used to live here," Flynn said softly. "Our parents were friends. But they left when your mother was pregnant with you and Vian. Both were spares with no Circle which was unusual to begin with, but it wasn't uncommon for people without a Circle to rely on each other."

"You're getting ahead," Kieran cut in. "She's going to get confused if you don't explain about the other thing first."

Flynn sighed and nodded before continuing. "What Payton said is true, in part. The council isn't kind to people who don't have a twin. The ones who are born without a twin are usually stronger, vastly stronger. They're labeled as the Vanished since it's believed they absorb their twin in the womb." Flynn shuddered, closing his eyes. "They also tend to disappear once they hit their majority at fourteen. Some of them come back, but they never talk about where they went."

"Then there are the spares, like Emma, who have to submit to monthly testing. She would be gone for days at a time. When we asked where she went, she said she couldn't tell us. We started to suspect things weren't right with her when she jumped at the chance to monitor you. She begged her parents to make it happen, even though she swore it wasn't to get away from us. The only plus was that it put her with you." He looked up at me with a small smile.

"We wanted to extract you right away, but the council refused to let it happen. The witches were an excuse. We could have gotten you with the snap of our fingers," Liam explained. "It didn't make much sense, but we compromised as long as Emma was allowed to go. She pushed for it so hard."

"So, how does this tie in with my parents or me?" I asked.

"Ameris believes you're one of the Vanished. That your mother was expecting triplets. They're considered rare and usually get labeled as quads. Whichever child is strongest becomes Vanished," Ben said. "There's no proof of that though. I've searched through every record available."

"If there's no proof, then why do they think that I absorbed at least one or two of my supposed siblings?" I asked, still confused.

"Because of how strong you are. Every channel you have is blown wide open. You may be a precog, but with your chakras, you can do anything, and I do mean anything. If they get proof that you're Vanished, they'll demand we hand you over, no matter if you're part of a circle or not," Ben explained patiently.

"Not to mention all the history," Liam said sourly. Flynn's head popped up and stared at him, shaking his head minutely. I reached out and twined my fingers in his dark hair and gently coaxed his head back.

"What history?" I asked. "It doesn't help us if I'm in the dark."

Flynn gritted his teeth. "About Vanished going insane. They lose their minds. Go hungry with power. Almost every single one has upset the balance in one way or another. So now the council steps in before that can happen."

I sat back, stunned. It was so much information to think over. My parents. The council. I'd already suspected the last part, about how powerful Entwined go insane. They'd mentioned it before. I also remembered the promise I made to myself. I would leave before I hurt these people with my problems. They were already going above and beyond what anyone else had ever done for me and I would be damned if I hurt them.

"We didn't tell you because we didn't want to worry you," Kieran said finally. His warm gaze met mine, and I fought a small smile that wanted to form on my lips. "No one wanted to add to the stress you're already going through." He stood up suddenly, his expression growing dark, and gripped his hair in frustration. "It keeps coming at you from all sides and we're all so…"

"No, I understand," I said, wanting to reassure him. I hadn't seen him like this since that first night. Kieran seemed like the cool and collected guy ninety-nine percent of the time, but he had his limits like everyone else. "We'll figure it out. Thank you for telling me."

CHAPTER 24

No one seemed to want to sleep, despite how long of a day it had been.

"What are you thinking about so hard over there?" Lucien asked.

I rolled my head, which had been set against Ben's shoulder. Instead of thinking, I'd been trying to work out why twins smelled similar. Ben smelled distinctly of lavender which reminded me of Brooke, but there was something else underneath it, woodsy and sharp. It made me wonder what I smelled like. I don't think I could handle it if I smelled like Old Spice.

"What do I smell like?"

"Uhh…" Lucien eyes cut around the room.

"Why is this important?" Flynn asked lazily, still on the floor at Ben's feet.

"Never mind, it's not important." I had lost my nerve. What if they said I smelled terrible? I might actually die.

"Apples," Ben mumbled. "And cinnamon, like Vian."

"Oh," My shoulders relaxed slightly. "That's not so bad. Like apple pie or oatmeal. Thank God. I can't stand his scent. It's so weird…I swear he bathes in whatever cologne he wears."

Kieran burst out laughing. Like full on, doubled over, laughter. After a few seconds, the rest of them started laughing.

"What?" I exclaimed, completely baffled. "Why is that funny?"

Ben's head came down on my shoulder as he fought his laughter. "That's… Okay so, twins of the opposite sex don't smell appealing to each other. Brooke and I can't stand each other's smell either, but it's also oddly comforting, right?"

"Are you for real?" I said, sitting up fully. "That's…huh. Okay, I guess that makes sense. Wait, does he know this?"

"He does," Flynn crowed. "Remember when he came back that first Christmas complaining about how he couldn't get her scent off his stuff? He bleached everything. Twice!"

"Is there any other stupid twin Entwined shit I should know?"

"Well…" Ben said evasively.

"Spit it out," I demanded.

"Jesus, woman, he'll bore us to sleep covering all of that right now," Flynn laughed.

I smacked lightly at his shoulder. "I happen to like learning. Especially when it's Ben." My mouth slammed shut. I hadn't meant to say that last part. Truth time? His voice just did something for me. When I'd first met Liam, his voice had sounded sexy, but it was nothing like Ben's. Don't get me wrong, Liam still had a voice that sometimes sent a shiver down my spine, but Ben was like listening to a gentle waterfall.

"Alright there, Princess?" Flynn asked jokingly. I blushed furiously and turned away from the knowing look in his eyes.

Lucien leaned forward, grabbing my attention. "I have an idea. I know you said you're not mad at him, but now would be the perfect time to do that thing we discussed." His eyes alighted with mischief.

I grinned back wickedly at him. "You know, that is a perfect idea. But not here. I think we should be responsible and try to get some sleep so let's go to bed. What do you guys think? Up for turning in with a movie?"

Liam and Kieran nodded, exchanging glances.

"Lucien," Flynn said cautiously. "What have you done?"

"Oh nothing, Brother. Nothing at all. Just, you know, helping Livvy here get into the swing of things. Assimilation and all that," Luc quipped. "Come on, let's go make some popcorn. We'll meet up in Ben's room since Liv has already agreed to spend the night there."

"Who said that? We could easily sleep in my room," I offered, hopefully.

"Yeah but you don't have a TV yet," Kieran said, climbing to his feet. "I'll meet you up there."

Luc pulled Flynn to his feet and they set off for the kitchen. I waited until I was sure they were out of earshot before leaning into Ben and whispering the movie into his ear. He almost choked on his own laughter when I told him. "You are evil, Liv. He's going to hate that."

"So, you approve?" I asked impishly.

"It's almost too easy, you know," he mused.

"I don't want to know," Liam said before heading upstairs after Kieran. "I know nothing about this. But I'll see how it plays out."

Twenty minutes later, I stood gaping from the doorway. After changing into my own pajamas, I followed the noise of the guys only to find them rushing around Ben's room, trying to clean it as fast as possible. It didn't matter though. No amount of speed would have made it much better. There were clothes literally everywhere. Whether they were dirty or clean, I had no idea. Just that I couldn't tell what color his floor was.

I cleared my throat when Flynn went to open the closet, making him jump. It was a bad move because the door swung open and junk came spilling out to pool around his legs. Everyone paused and followed Flynn's gaze, which was locked on me in my long tee-shirt. I had shorts on underneath, but the tee went almost to my knees.

"The sheets are clean," Liam rushed to say. "I literally just changed them."

"This is hopeless," Ben breathed, staring around him in panic.

"It's fine," I said. "I've lived in worse than this. If the bed's clean and it doesn't smell, I'm good." I picked my way across the floor, careful not to touch anything I was uncertain of. "Though, in the future, we should make sure someone cleans up in here. I'm sure Ben just gets distracted."

"I usually do it," Lucien replied with a smile. "We've been a bit busy and he tends to just throw things on the floor whether they're clean or not."

I chuckled as I climbed up on the bed. "It's really okay. Like I said, this isn't that bad. It's not like I've never seen clothing before," I said, pointing to my shirt.

"Well, I'm not going to argue," Liam said cheerfully. "Let's get the movie started. Who knows when we'll ever get a night like this together again?"

I turned my head, looking at him with curiosity. "What are you—"

"Make room for me," Lucien jumped between us on the bed. "Start the movie, Ben!" I got the impression he was trying to hide something from me, but I couldn't figure out what it was and decided it was not the time to push the issue.

The rest of the guys piled onto the bed and got comfortable as Ben pushed play on the DVD player.

Flynn climbed in on the other side of Ben, but grabbed my legs, making me squeal. He maneuvered me until my legs were slung across Ben's torso, forcing me to drop my head onto Luc's chest. Once I was settled, he started kneading my feet with his fingers. It was a struggle not to moan as the three of them pushed small amounts of energy into me.

One on one, the exchanges were almost unnoticeable, but together like that it left me a bit euphoric. Once I adjusted to it, I found myself peeking at Flynn from the corner of my eye. He smirked at me, and I fought a guilty smile as the opening scene started, panning past a tree to reveal a poster. Flynn dropped my feet almost instantly and turned toward me. "You picked Tangled?" His face twisted in disgust as he stared at me.

I shared a quick glance with Luc before I lost all composure, giggling like a fool. "What's the matter, Flynn? One would think you'd be right at home with this. Snarky rogue who falls for the damsel? Oh, but that's right… I'm not to your tastes." Everyone burst out laughing at the shocked expression on Flynn's face. Luc held up a hand to high five me, which only made me laugh harder.

"Both of you will suffer for this," Flynn promised, a ghost of a smile on his lips. "Let the pranks begin."

"We both know you'll never beat me," Luc challenged.

"We'll see, Luc. We'll see."

"Okay, let's dial down the testosterone and just watch the movie," I chuckled, getting myself more comfortable between Luc and Ben. Flynn glowered at me for a few seconds before shifting his eyes to the screen.

This looks cozy, a voice said in my mind as I became aware. I stood at the end of the bed, staring down at my body tucked underneath the sheets. Luc lay on one side of me, his head nestled into the base of my neck. I scanned their faces as they slept, peacefully unaware.

I realized where I was. Inside the Thorns with my guardian.

"Where's Ben and Flynn?" I asked, scanning the rest of the room, as if it would reveal them.

Having a long-needed discussion. But don't worry about them. We have work to do, the Lynx said at my side. He sat on the floor staring at the bed, looking very un-cat-like with his head tilted to the side, as if he were measuring us.

"What work?"

I found the girl. Grab hold. I'll take you to her. My nerves spiked and I watched as my body sucked in a breath. It was disturbing to see my own physical reaction to stress while in this state. The Lynx nudged me, purring loudly, before slipping his head under one of my hands until it rested on the base of his neck. His fur tickled my thighs as he pressed into my side. Gently, I twined my fingers through his fur and gripped the skin around his neck. Unlike his topcoat which was coarse to the touch, his undercoat was soft, like a kitten. *See, you're not so stupid after all.*

I snorted just before the world tipped sideways, taking on a green sheen as we moved. Or rather, the Thorns moved around us. They picked at my skin, almost unpleasantly. It was a peculiar feeling. Almost like a tickle, but with a bite. My fingers flexed as something tugged harder on me. Instinctually I knew that if I let go of my guardian, something very bad would happen to me.

"What's your name?" I asked, to distract myself from the sensation.

Piddles, the cat deadpanned as we came to a stop that made my head spin.

"Are you fucking with me?" I asked. "That cannot be your name." Looking around, I realized I knew where we were, even though there were no trees. Just thickly woven vines covered in sharp thorns that glistened with a purple light. Through a small break in them, I could see a tall water tower, dulled from its normal bright blue to a dull gray. If we walked through the break, we'd come to a road. *The* road. Where Emma had died.

My name isn't all that important. Let's go. I'd rather do this quickly before we draw attention from something else. The cat padded forward on silent feet, stepping cautiously through the break. I tentatively followed. The smell hit me first as the road came into view, something cloying, yet a bit sweet. Like rot. It was strange to see the world from the Thorns, things looked the same and yet completely different, I noticed spots around the area where light was just floating. I watched one for a moment as the light moved. People, they were people.

You see them. Good. You're advancing after only a few days. They're watching the area, but they won't see us.

"What's that?" I asked pointing toward the road. There was another bright patch that swirled around. As soon as I pointed to it, it started to move frantically in a large circle. Then I felt it… the panic, the agony as it slammed into me. I started running. The lynx surged ahead of me, swinging its head from side to side, as if he were keeping watch.

She can feel you. It's a spelled circle. The whole place reeks of witches. At least four different ones. She's trapped. That's why we couldn't find her before.

"How do I get her out?" I asked, on the cusp of tears that couldn't seem to fall. Emma's helplessness pressed in on me, making me stagger.

With enough will, you can walk through that circle. All you'll need to do once you're over is call to her. He pointed with a front paw toward a thin black line on the ground. It was barely visible but for the sickly smoke that wafted up from it.

"So, I just think it hard enough and that's it?" It was too easy. If I could feel my heartbeat, I had no doubt it would be beating out of my chest. I edged closer to the line, repulsed by it, but unable to turn away. It was sickening, both the feel of Emma's energy and the spell that held her there. Who does that to another being?

Stop stalling, girl. I can only mask you for so long and eventually they'll find a way to harvest her when she grows weak enough.

"You better be right about this or I'll figure out how to make you into a rug," I gritted out, then swallowed thickly, glancing at my guardian. I closed my eyes for a moment, drawing on whatever mental strength I had. I focused my will, like Liam had taught me. When they opened again, I thought about how I wanted into the circle.

I lifted one foot and edged it toward the line, then over. There was resistance, but once half my foot was through, something started to sizzle. A silver blast of light flared up, blinding me for a second before it died down.

The mass of light that had been trapped slammed into me and settled in my limbs. The familiar sense of Emma wrapped around me. Relief. Grief. Love. Peace. It all fell over me, making me sag under the onslaught.

I felt a mental sigh in my head. *A perfect Entwinement*, the cat purred at me. *Grab hold. Those witches are on their way and while they can't catch you, they'll try*. I glanced over the cat's head and sure enough the other lights I'd seen were now moving towards us.

The world slipped again as soon as my fingers twined in his fur and we were moving. "What's Entwinement?" I asked.

The merging of energy. You're a natural for someone who has no clue what they're doing.

"Everyone keeps saying that," I said, fighting against a particularly hard tug that tried to grab ahold of me. "I think…"

Yes. There are beings here that have festered and lost their purpose, he said, answering my unspoken thoughts. *And yes, you are a natural, as all Entwined are meant to be.*

"Half of what you say doesn't make sense, you know that right?" I replied tartly.

We all have our roles to play. You've been a long time coming. We just have to keep you sane. Now stop fighting so we can get out of here. You're slowing us down using your energy to speak.

I slammed my mouth shut and tried to relax without letting go of my cat. My chest had an uncomfortable weight to it that I'd been able to ignore by distracting myself. But the lynx was right. As soon as I stopped trying to talk, we moved faster. It wasn't long before we came to a halt back in the bedroom where I'd fallen asleep with the guys.

I'll be back for the ceremony. Stay out of trouble, the cat said.

CHAPTER 25

I sat up, gasping for breath. Someone yelped beside me and knocked into my shoulder as they followed me. A hand grasped my chin, turning my head until my eyes met Ben's blue-green ones. There was just enough light from the television on the wall to make out his features.

"Are you alright? Did you have a nightmare?" he asked as his gaze raked over me, assessing and concerned.

"I don't know," I answered quietly. "The cat, he… said his name was Piddles and we went—I don't quite feel right." Blinking several times, I tried to make out what was wrong with me. I broke off abruptly as my chest tightened. Emotions warred inside me, like bubbles, jostling one another to make room.

"Holy shit," Flynn said, leaning over Ben's shoulder. "Do you feel that?"

"I do," Kieran said quietly from across the bed. "Emma."

My head spun, still struggling to make sense of the situation. Everything I normally felt was there and then some.

"Cat took me to find her. He said she was trapped and shielded or something," I rushed to say. "I broke some sort of spell and she just…"

"That explains why we couldn't find her that night," Liam muttered from somewhere behind me. I turned to see him flop backward onto the bed on the other side of Lucien. The latter was quiet, thoughtful, as he looked at me.

Feelings of warmth and comfort swirled around me as I took in the guys. It was similar to what I felt whenever I saw Vian. Family, love. But it was different too because I knew it wasn't me feeling those things, at least not so extremely. My feelings for the guys were strong, I could admit that, but what Emma felt was almost blinding.

"This is so confusing," I said, closing my eyes, willing the foreign emotions away. It took tremendous effort and I sagged slightly before someone wrapped their arms around me. The scent of citrus and clean linen invaded my nose and I sighed into it.

"Probably just a bit drunk on energy," Kieran replied.

My eyes popped open. "Can that happen?"

"If you take on a lot at once, yes," Ben answered. "If she was trapped, she didn't have a chance to expel any excess she had, so in essence, you're carrying around the life energy of an entire person plus whatever she managed as an Entwined. When we die, the excess releases naturally and over time our 'spirit' - as humans would call it - lingers."

"Are you saying that there are actually ghosts?" I asked in disbelief.

"More or less, but usually it's other things that get credit for hauntings. People tend to be pretty weak-willed after death," Flynn said with a small smirk.

I stared at them with an open mouth. "Other things. Like demons? Wait, no. Shelve that answer. I don't want to know right now," I said. There was enough to worry about. I could look into ghosts and hauntings later. "So, what happens now, how do we…" I didn't know how to say it. They'd confirmed that I hadn't dreamed up my experience with Cat—no way in hell would I use Piddles—and now I wasn't sure what happened.

"It's customary in our society to have a Sending when a loved one dies," Luc said into my ear, his breath tickling my neck. "We would have had one sooner, but we didn't want to have the ceremony until we knew for sure we couldn't physically send her on. Now we can."

"Our families will want to be there," Kieran said, sliding off the bed. "I'll call Mom and we should let Brooke and Vian know. And Emma's parents," he finished quietly.

My heart pounded in my chest. I hadn't even

thought about her parents. But then again, I'd always thought she was an orphan like me. I didn't want to meet them, I decided. It would be awkward and painful. Not just for me but for them as well. I swallowed hard, trying not to think about the foreign emotions residing inside my heart and head. It felt wrong to push Emma aside like that, but it was hard enough dealing with my own emotions, let alone feeling someone else's.

"You won't be practicing Arts until the ceremony," Liam said into the void of conversation. "With you still in training, they could go very wrong or you could end up burning her out instead of yourself."

I nodded before unlatching Luc's arms from around my waist and sliding off the bed. I needed a moment alone, to not hear anyone's voice but my own. Every time one of them spoke, Emma pressed on me, smothering me with her emotions to the point I could hardly tell what was me and what was her.

No one asked me where I was going as I waded through the clothes on Ben's floor and out the door. On hurried feet, I slipped into my own room and then straight into the bathroom. At the mirror, I stared at my reflection. In just a week, I already had more weight on my frame. My skin had more color than ever before, but there was a weariness in my features. Deep shadows under my eyes made them appear brighter, but more haunted. I barely recognized the girl I was two weeks ago. Sure, she'd been tired, but not like this.

"Listen babe," I said to Emma, using my own gaze to look inward. I could feel her in there, even if I couldn't see her. I paused, unsure of what I wanted to say. There was so much, days' worth of words, but they failed me. The skin around my eyes grew red as tears threatened to fall. Wiping at them in frustration, I tried again. "I love you, you complete idiot. But you're going to have to work with me here. I can be strong for you and carry you wherever it is you need to go." My voice broke and tears really did fall then. I was speaking the very last words I ever would say to my first real friend in the world. They needed to be perfect. This was such an incredible gift the universe was giving me. A chance to make peace with it all. With her. I wiped at my face again and took a few deep breaths. "I will do whatever it is that needs to be done for you. I just need you to not confuse me so much. I can feel your happiness and how much you love everyone. Just try to tone it down and we'll get through this. Okay?"

The words weren't perfect, but they were the best I had. I waited for several moments, searching inward for some sort of response from her, but it didn't come. Maybe that was her way of doing as I asked. My eyes closed, the last of my tears fell. "I love you so much, babe," I whispered one last time.

I left the bathroom without looking back. The idea of rejoining the guys passed through my thoughts for a few seconds before I ultimately decided to crawl into my own bed. It was just after two in the morning and I was exhausted. I hadn't been sure if I'd be able to sleep again, but I started drifting off within a few minutes.

I stirred once when the bed dipped, and someone crawled under the covers with me. Whoever it was carefully draped a heavy arm around my waist, and I was out again. In the morning, I woke up with my face pressed into Luc's neck, one of my legs between both of his and his arms surrounding me.

For a few minutes, I listened to him breathe deeply. His normally kempt hair brushed my cheek. I pulled my head back to look at him. He mumbled something, tightening his arms to keep me in place. He looked so peaceful. I'm not sure how long I lay there, watching him. Long enough for the sun to slip across the wall, lightening the room as it went.

His eyes opened slowly, blinking at me before I stirred fully. A soft smile crossed his lips and I found my own returning one.

"Morning, Doll," he mumbled.

"Morning yourself," I said, somewhat shyly. There was something intimate about the moment that made me feel self-conscious. I struggled to find something to make it less awkward before asking something random. "Why do you call me that?"

"What, Doll?" He chuckled. "You're just so tiny. Beautiful, like a china doll." My skin heated at being called beautiful which made him smile wider. "How are you feeling?"

"Better," I answered honestly, somewhat grateful

that he didn't further my embarrassment. "I think I've got it—Emma—under control."

"Oh?" he asked curiously. "How'd you manage that?"

"We sort of…talked. I don't know, honestly."

He looked thoughtful for a moment. "If it becomes a problem, will you tell me or one of the others? Liam and I specifically, we have some experience with… this."

"With taking your dead friends' energy into yourself?" I asked jokingly. A dark look crossed his features, smoothing out his sinful smile into a firm straight line.

"Something like that," he said, looking away.

"What is it?" I found myself asking. I didn't normally pry into other people's problems or really want to know things about them in general, but the more I was around Luc, the more I did want to know. He was usually so carefree and flirty. Anything that hurt him, I wanted to take away.

"It's not something… fuck," he muttered. He pulled away from me, rolling onto his back, taking his warmth with him. His eyes searched the canopy over my bed for a few moments before he laced his fingers with mine and pulled me against him. "Liam and I didn't—weren't born in the community. If we had parents, we never knew them. We were brought up as slaves in a coven of witches in the Midwest. Of course, we didn't know it was slavery then. Only that our lives were miserable." I nuzzled into his chest, trying to sooth him without interrupting. His free hand ghosted through my hair and a small sigh escaped my lips.

"It was one of the more sickening covens. They used Entwined in experiments, forced us to steal energy from others. Except we didn't know that we were murdering them. I think near the end, we were starting to understand, but not for sure. It wasn't until they were raided and Ameris took us in that we realized the gravity of what we'd been doing." He paused, his breath stuttering. "So, yes," he breathed, "I know what it means to take someone into yourself."

I was horrified by his story. For so long, I'd lived my own version of hell that any other kind was inconceivable. But this was so much worse than what I'd experienced. What sort of evil forced children to murder? I couldn't even wrap my mind around it.

Without saying a word, I pulled myself up and threw my arms around his neck. For a minute he just laid there shocked at my sudden display but then wrapped himself around me, clutching me to him. His lips pressed against my throat, sparking a trail of electricity, making me moan softly. It so wasn't the time to respond in such a way, but Luc didn't seem to think so because he did it again, grazing my neck with his teeth. I shuddered and started to pull away, wanting to get some distance from the heat between my legs and his body.

"Sorry," he mumbled, letting me go easily.

"It's fine," I lied.

"Is it?" he asked, not buying it at all.

I swallowed hard, sitting back on the bed with at least a foot or two between us. How did he see through me so easily? "I don't know. Everything is confusing."

"That's what I figured," he said with a soft laugh before turning serious again. "You like us, you know."

I scoffed and rolled my eyes. "Maybe," I admitted.

"Oh no, I know you do," he replied smugly as he sat up and rolled out of the bed. "It's just you who won't accept it." He threw a meaningful look at me as he sauntered toward my bedroom door. The ghosts he'd just relived were nowhere in sight. His brown eyes were bright and playful again. "I'm going to shower, Doll. I'll see you at breakfast." With that, he left me with my growing dilemma, which was quickly climbing the list of problems I needed to solve.

CHAPTER 26

"The council is questioning Brooke again," Ben said, entering the kitchen with his phone in his hand. He frowned down at it; his brow furrowed.

Flynn was at the counter, drizzling icing over sweet rolls. His shoulders tensed as he looked up at me and then at Ben. "What's their reasoning now?" he asked in a light voice that didn't match his body language.

"They're not even trying to hide their interest in Olivia anymore," Ben replied, offering me a weak smile.

"Why don't we just let them get a good look at me and be done with it?" I asked. I understood why they didn't want to do that, but if this council was pushing so hard, it seemed silly to hide. Was I terrified of them and what could happen? Yes, but I was tired of hiding.

Mentally, I tallied my mounting issues. Evan was at the top, first because of what he did to Emma and second for his psychotic obsession with me. He felt like my biggest threat. After that was figuring out how to control my Arts and what made me so powerful. It wasn't precognition. Of that I was certain. I didn't have dreams like Vian and based on what I saw from the others, our powers should reflect our twin's. There was also the bond our entire circle needed to cement. Cat made that seem like it was life or death for us. Oh, and just for fun, let's tack on crushing after five guys, even if that was more of a personal problem. It was enough to make anyone's head spin. Yeah, we had enough to deal with. If we could get the council off our backs for a bit, I was all for it.

Silence stretched as Ben poured himself something to drink and rounded the counter to claim the stool next to me. Flynn resumed icing, wearing a thoughtful expression before he answered me. "Because the only basis they have is curiosity. And it isn't the full council pushing for this, just a few. If we were extended a formal request, we'd comply. They think because we're young, we're malleable, and I for one am willing to let them think that." He started plating breakfast. His dark hair fell forward over his eyes, giving him a roguish look. A flash of me pushing that hair out of his face entered my mind and I swallowed hard.

"Why do you want them to think that?" I asked in a thick voice.

"Because, Princess, if they don't see us as a threat, they won't be prepared for us to fight back. It's strategy. One I intend to win."

"But they already know how strong we are, right? With all those tests and…"

Ben leaned into me as my words failed. "They do know these things, but they have to prove that you're dangerous to everyone else before they could cause us trouble. You're also forgetting that Renee and Demaric didn't tell them everything. Such as how weak our bond is or that your chakras are blown wide open."

I sighed heavily. "They're already causing us trouble, though. Over me." Guilt licked through me, making my chest tighten.

"No," Flynn said, setting a plate in front of me. "This isn't your fault. It's theirs for keeping you from us in the first place. If they'd let us bond years ago, they'd have a much easier time trying to get to you. They put our suspicions here by keeping you from us and their actions now only confirm those suspicions." I looked down at my plate. Meeting his eyes was harder when he was being nice to me. He wouldn't let me though. His hand reached forward and pulled my chin up. Whatever he saw in my eyes kept him from speaking. His mouth opened and closed a few times before he released my chin. "Go hang out with Ben. The others and I need to head into town to get groceries and other items for the Sending tomorrow."

"Why can't we all do that?" I asked. I didn't want

them out on their own. Wasn't it bad enough that Vian and Brooke weren't here?

"Because, the less chance we give them to corner you, the better. But don't worry, the house is protected"

I frowned at him. "That's what Luc said about the island, yet, Evan and Payton still found a way onto it."

He rolled his eyes at me. "The house is different. It's a sanctuary only we can enter. No one can get on the property without us bringing them here."

Ben put his hand on my shoulder before I could bite back at Flynn. "Come on Liv, bring your food, we can eat in my room."

I threw Flynn a dirty look, which he smirked at, his eyes twinkling. I wasn't sure if I wanted to scream at him or throw myself at him, maybe both. I turned away, leaving my breakfast on the counter in a show of defiance.

"He does it on purpose, you know?" Ben said as we climbed the stairs.

"Does what?" I asked, not really paying attention. My mind was still back in the kitchen warring with myself.

"Flynn. He likes to fight with you."

"What? Why?" Who the hell enjoyed arguing? It was stupid.

We turned into his room, still a mess. I stood in the doorway while he walked around collecting books and a machine I recognized from the council's lab. I shuddered and let out a groan. He glanced up and smirked at me.

"Don't worry. I just want to get some readings. Nothing insane," he said, brandishing the electrometer at me with a wink. I grimaced at him but didn't say anything. "Come on, we can do this outside by the pool then go for a swim afterwards."

"I don't have a suit," I replied quickly, thinking about my scars. Knowing Brooke, I probably did have one, but I didn't like wearing bathing suits.

"You do. It's in the top middle drawer of your dresser," he said.

"How do you know that?"

"Because I helped put your clothes away," he said brightly. My cheeks filled with heat. Had he seen the ridiculous underwear that Brooke got for me? There had been all sorts of lacy lingerie stuffed into the top three drawers of my dresser that I'd been forced to wear. Nothing she bought was practical.

Mentally, I pushed down the urge to throttle her next time I saw her. "When will they be back?" I asked with effort.

"Probably around lunchtime. Brooke and Vian have plans to visit other family to let them know we're having a ceremony for Emma."

"Oh." Since my private conversation with her, I hadn't felt much from Emma. Small twinges of emotion that weren't mine, but otherwise, nothing.

"Go get changed. It's a gorgeous day out. Vian said you liked the outdoors so…"

I smiled to myself, because Ben remembered I liked it outside despite the idea of throwing on a swimsuit. The truth was that I missed the freedom of the forest. Emma and I were always outside, hiking, or swimming at a local lake when the weather was nice enough for it.

"Okay," I said softly before padding down the hall to my room.

As I entered my room, I wondered if the others had already left yet. The house was eerily quiet, and I was only just now noticing. Or maybe it was just the tension I felt at being alone in the house with Ben. Even when I was alone in my room, I knew there was a buffer because there was always someone else in the house.

Closing my door, I quickly stripped out of my sleep shirt and shorts and went to inspect my options in the dresser. True to his word, there were at least four different swimsuits to choose from. Three of them were string bikinis I would never be caught in, but the fourth was a one piece. I pulled it out, inspecting the corded green material and grimaced. Despite being a one piece, it had thin straps that tied around on a low back.

I slipped out of my underwear and pulled it on, turning slightly in the mirror that was over my dresser. The back dipped low on my spine, leaving the entirety of my scars revealed. I quickly tied it, adjusting it so it was tight across my small chest. Then I searched through another drawer, looking for a light shirt to throw on over it. I was rewarded with an off the shoulder white top that fell to my thighs. It was slightly see-through, but it made me feel less self-conscious.

My door popped open just as I reached for the knob, revealing Liam and Lucien standing there. Liam kept his eyes on my face and smiled at me, but Luc had no issue running his eyes up my legs first with a smirk on his lips. Anyone else would find it predatory, but Luc never made me feel that way.

"You look hot as hell," he said, leaning into the door frame. "I almost didn't believe Ben when he said you guys were going swimming."

I narrowed my eyes at him, trying to ignore the flutter of heat that passed through me after he called me hot. "Why wouldn't I?"

Liam smacked his brother's arm. "Ignore him. You look pretty, Kitten." I felt myself blush at his compliment and suddenly wished I'd picked out some shorts too. "Anyway, just wanted to say goodbye before we left." He shuffled in the doorway, looking awkward and not meeting my eyes anymore.

What was going on there?

"Umm," I said nervously. I had no idea what to say. I turned a panicked look toward Luc. He smirked for a few seconds before stepping forward and kissing me lightly on the forehead.

"We'll see you at lunch, Doll." With that, he grabbed his brother and steered him down the hall. I stood for a moment letting my pulse go back to normal. Liam's comment about how pretty I was floated through my mind as I made my way downstairs. These guys were going to be the death of me.

I stepped out the backdoor, hiding in the shade of the porch for a moment as I watched Ben. He sat in one of the lounge chairs in a pair of blue boardshorts. His blonde hair glinted in the sun; his head bent toward the book he held in his hands. He was shirtless, revealing his slim frame, corded with lean and tanned muscles. As if he could sense me, he glanced up and smiled.

"Are you going to stand there or are you going to come enjoy the day with me?"

I made my way across the patio and went to take the chair next to him. Before I could put my weight on it, he scooped me up and deposited me on his lap. He'd been doing that more often lately, touching me. I had to remind myself he did it because of the bond we were supposed to be forging, but it felt far too intimate. His face was inches from mine, over my shoulder.

"Hi," I said in a small voice before mentally kicking myself. Who the hell says 'hi' like that when they're sitting on a dude's lap?

"Hi yourself," he breathed. My own breath hitched. If he noticed, he didn't react. Instead, he lifted the book in his free hand and brought it across my lap. "I figured we could do some reading since you can't use Arts. Lucien suggested learning about chakras and nutrition since you have trouble maintaining your levels. Plus, Flynn would really like to stop healing the grass. It makes him grumpier."

At the word 'nutrition,' I realized I hadn't eaten breakfast. I'd left my plate at the counter and if I knew much about Luc by now, I knew he'd probably be upset about it. I'd noticed myself putting on a bit of healthy weight in the last few days. "I should have just eaten the food instead of using it to needle at Flynn. Did Luc see it?"

Ben laughed lightly in my ear. "Don't worry. They're all nags. I forget to eat sometimes. It's something we can work on together." He lifted the book as my head settled back on his shoulder. He started reading aloud. "Chakras are natural ports in the body that allow energy to flow, starting from the base of the spine to the crown of a person's head…"

I listened to the cadence of his voice, letting myself get lost in the words, somewhat surprised that I was able to pay attention while my thoughts drifted a bit. His breath tickled my ear while his body heat soaked into my back. My eyes closed of their own volition and I started to nod off. When he chuckled in my ear, I snapped awake.

"Sorry," I muttered. "I'm paying attention."

"No, you're falling asleep."

"I am not!" I protested, turning my head to look at him. "A healthy diet of clean organic foods helps Entwined focus their energy flow so they can pull from around them without damaging the earth. I've been using the energy around me to sustain myself unnaturally, which is why I get drained so quickly and have to use the energy in the ground to keep myself from burning out. Correct?"

His eyes grew surprised for a second before he hit with me a blazing smile. "Yes. Essentially." I smiled back, somewhat shocked myself that I'd gotten it right. His eyes dipped to my lips and back up. The pupils in his jeweled eyes contracted before he cleared his throat. "Let's go for a swim. It's getting a bit hot."

I couldn't get out of his lap fast enough, sure that if I stayed there, he was going to do something stupid, like kiss me. After the last time I'd been kissed, I knew I wouldn't run, but it would make things awkward. Without thinking, I tore off my cover-up, throwing it aside and jumped into the pool.

The world quieted as I submerged myself in the water, letting myself sink to the bottom, enjoying the peace it brought me. It was only a few seconds later when I heard a muffled splash. I opened my eyes underwater to see Ben sinking down next to me. He grabbed my wrists and pulled me up toward the surface.

He pulled me into the circle of his arms as I tread water to keep myself afloat. I swept the water and hair from my face, annoyed that I'd forgotten to braid it. Ben moved us easily until my feet touched the bottom of the pool, then guided me toward the wall until my back was against the stone edge. I thought he would back off then, but he stayed in front of me, caging me in on either side until I was forced to look up at him.

I'd hoped that by jumping in the pool, he would forget about the moment between us, but I was wrong. If anything, he looked more determined than ever to continue it. His front pressed against me, filling my body with heat along every inch of our skin that touched. He hoisted me up onto the edge of the pool and stepped between my legs so that we were eye level. My breaths came out shallow and my hands came up to grip his shoulders to keep myself upright. When he inclined toward me, I thought he would kiss me, but he didn't. Instead his arms wrapped around my waist and he pressed his face into my neck, breathing deeply.

The pit of my stomach bottomed out, whether in disappointment or relief, I wasn't sure. My arms slipped around his shoulders until I was hugging him back. Softly, his hands skimmed over my exposed back, eliciting tingles along my spine. Between my legs, I could feel his arousal, but he didn't press into me like most guys would. He just stood there, holding me to him.

"I thought we were swimming," I asked, just to say something.

"This is much better," he mumbled against my neck. He wasn't wrong. It was…nice. I turned my own head into his neck and nuzzled against him.

Jesus, what was I doing? I had no idea. I didn't want this. Or maybe I did. Just a few days ago, I'd kissed Flynn and now I wanted to kiss Ben. And Luc. With perfect honesty, I admitted it. It wasn't just those three either. I wanted Liam and Kieran too. Fuck… what was I doing?

I clung to Ben tighter and stayed there for as long as he was willing to hold me.

CHAPTER 27

The others came back shortly after Ben and I decided to head inside. He'd noticed I was starting to turn red—*thanks genetics*—and suggested we find a movie to watch until the others got back. I was just heading up the stairs when the guys popped into existence in the kitchen, making me jump, clutching at my heart and dropping my glass of water. It shattered, glass covering my feet and opening a few cuts on my toes.

I yelped, trying to get out of the way of the shards only to step on a few smaller pieces. Flynn charged around the corner and came to a stop when he saw me. He assessed me for a second in my swimsuit before he realized I was standing in glass. He reached up the few steps and plucked me from them like I weighed nothing and carried me into the kitchen, despite my protests to be put down.

My butt landed on the cold countertop, making

me flinch as he dropped down to inspect my feet. The others crowded around us.

"What did you do?" Liam asked in concern.

"Is that glass?" Kieran's voice was thunderous as he stalked forward, pushing the others out of the way.

"Don't heal her yet, we've got to get the glass out," Flynn commanded.

My eyes met Luc's, open wide with embarrassment. *Help*, I mouthed to him. He smiled at me, somewhat regretfully. "Sorry, Doll. You broke a rule."

"What?" I sputtered, wincing as Flynn picked a piece of glass from my foot and threw it onto the counter. "I didn't do anything. I was just going upstairs!"

"You hurt yourself," Luc replied with a laugh, hoisting himself up next to me and throwing an arm over my shoulder. "The Clones hate it when we injure ourselves. It makes them cranky."

"What's going on?" Ben asked from the dining room door. He'd just come in from outside. His gaze swept over the room before landing on me and the dark-haired Neanderthals prodding at my feet.

"They scared me when they arrived, and I dropped my glass. It's all over the stairs."

"On it," Liam said, looking relieved to have something to do. He went to a door on the other side of the kitchen that I hadn't explored and came back with a broom before heading toward the stairs.

"Ouch," I snapped when another piece of glass hit the counter. Luc squeezed my shoulder.

"Princess, stop healing yourself!" Flynn snapped.

"I'm not," I spit back. I didn't know how, and he knew that.

Kieran stood up and looked at me. "I don't think she's doing it on purpose." He grabbed my hands, and a flood of electricity zipped through me. It reminded me of the time Vian had talked me into putting my hand inside a lamp when it was plugged in without a bulb. He'd turned it on and wanted to see what would happen.

My body shook for a moment, freezing me in place, just like when I'd electrocuted myself, but it didn't hurt. I just couldn't move. The sensation was actually sort of pleasant and if I could have, I would have snapped my legs together to keep myself from getting so turned on. Jesus.

"Uhh, I wouldn'..." Luc started to say but it was too late. The pressure built in a familiar way and even though I couldn't move, I panicked. *No. Please no...* My body skyrocketed with pleasure, on the brink of release when Kieran dropped my hands.

"I'm so sorry, I didn't even think about it," he said quickly, trying not to look at my pebbled nipples that were popping through my bathing suit.

"I got the glass," Flynn said, standing. He was probably the only one who didn't realize what had almost happened and I sat there still frozen, for an entirely different reason. My breathing was labored as heat rushed through me for the thousandth time that day. Flynn took me in with one sweep of his eyes before he burst out laughing. "You look like a lobster, Princess."

"I hate you," I breathed, not really meaning it. "Can I leave, please?"

No one answered me so I shrugged out from under Luc's arm and raced out of the kitchen. Passing Liam on the stairs, he called out to me, asking me what was wrong, but I ignored him, instead sprinting for my room. I couldn't lock the door, so I threw myself into the bathroom, bolting that door behind me and started a shower, leaving it cold.

These men were going to kill me, I thought as I stepped under the spray, still wearing my suit. I stayed there for at least thirty minutes before I started washing my hair so I could braid it to dry.

When I left the bathroom, wrapped in a towel, I found Kieran and Liam lounging on my bed. I blinked at them for a second, completely unprepared to deal with any of them after the scene in the kitchen.

"Livvy, I'm so sorry," Kieran said, sitting up quickly. "I didn't mean for that to happen. It's such a rare reaction and I didn't even think about it."

"Can we not talk about it?" I begged. I really didn't want to even think about it. Ever again. I went to my closet and stepped inside, closing the door firmly before turning on the light to find something to wear.

"I told you not to bring it up, dude," I heard Liam say. "She's got enough shit on her plate."

"That's easy for you to say. You didn't practically rape someone with your energy," Kieran responded with heat.

Is that what he was thinking? I took a deep breath and pulled down a shirt and some dark jeans. I didn't have any underwear in here, but I wasn't going out there in my towel to get some.

"You know that isn't how an exchange works," Liam tried to placate. "It has to be mutual or else it wouldn't—"

"She doesn't know that!" Kieran snapped. It was always a shock for me when he got angry, he was always so quiet and steady.

Buttoning my jeans, I opened the door and stalked toward the bed and summoned my courage. "It's fine Kieran. You didn't hurt me. It just..." I struggled for a moment. "It surprised me is all and there were—Let's just forget about it, please?" I climbed up onto the bed and settled between them on the spread.

"How are your feet?" Liam asked after a few minutes of silence.

"They're fine now," I answered, wiggling my toes to emphasize my point. "So, is that something everyone can do? Heal themselves?"

"No. Healing is one of the harder skills," Kieran said. He collected one of my hands in his. "But I'm starting to think we might have your affinity pegged wrong. You and Vian should share the same skill, but he can't heal like that."

"Then what am I?" I asked, confused. I was

relieved that someone else had noticed the issue with my Arts. I didn't know enough to dispute their claims.

"I don't know, but Ben's been researching it."

"Why didn't anyone say anything before if this was a concern?"

"We're as lost as you are, in some regards," Liam answered honestly, turning into my side. He placed his head on my shoulder, his blonde hair tickling my chin. I turned my head slightly, trying to covertly smell his hair. He smelled like citrus and brine, a strange combination, but still alluring. All the guys smelled good, but something about his intrigued me.

We lay there in silence and my eyes drifted closed. With Liam's scent heavy in my nose and Kieran's warmth on my other side, I feel asleep. I woke much later to a soft sensation against my neck that spread warm tingles through my body. Someone trailed their lips back and forth across the exposed skin. It was feather light, raising goosebumps. I moaned softly, arching into whoever it was. From the scents in the air, it had to be either Liam or Kieran. Dimly, I thought I should know the difference between them—the two were so different from one another—but I was too wrapped up in the warmth their touch brought me. I could feel the energy exchange between us which only muddled my head where they were concerned.

The single noise that rippled from my throat was all they needed before they pressed against me, kissing my throat. He leaned into me from behind, suckling on my neck before nipping at me with his teeth. His pelvis ground against me, letting me feel how aroused he was. One of his hands snaked under my shirt and came to rest on my ribcage, just under my breasts, crushing me back against him.

"Fuck," I heard someone whisper. I opened my eyes to see Kieran up on one elbow, watching me with heated eyes. I hadn't felt him move to sit up, but his front was against mine as my chest heaved. From behind me, Liam bit down again on my neck, just underneath my ear, making me moan again.

The fire inside me grew hotter, pooling at the apex of my thighs. My body bucked forward, rubbing against Kieran. He leaned forward, capturing my lips with his, sweeping his tongue inside my mouth as I gasped.

He swallowed my passion, expertly tangling our tongues together. His hand came up to cradle my face, angling my head so he could deepen our kiss.

"You're so beautiful," Liam whispered in my ear as he ground against me. His hands skimmed up and down my stomach, teasing me, never going higher or lower, to the places that ached to be touched.

My head swam with the sensations that rippled through me. I was on overload, unable to make coherent thoughts. Every time my brain would form one, it would slip away. Kieran's lips left mine to trail down my chin to my neck. I turned to give him better access, only for Liam's hand to skim the edge of my jeans. My body begged him to go further, but I didn't know how to ask. Another hand moved up my waist, over my shirt to gently caress my breasts. I turned more, seeking Liam's lips with a whimper of need.

"She's so responsive," Kieran groaned against my neck. "We should probably stop though." Several kisses covered my collar bone. I arched into him, not wanting him to stop. "Fucking hell," he muttered.

I'd never been so turned on in my life. If we stopped now, I would combust.

Liam leaned in to kiss me, devouring my mouth with his own. Where Kieran had kissed me with languid motions, Liam was more needy, kissing me so hard, our teeth practically clashed, working me over with a new frenzy.

"Liv," Kieran groaned. I could feel how erect he was against my front, but I couldn't seem to angle myself while kissing Liam to build up any friction between us. A hand was on my hip, keeping distance between us.

"Shit," Liam said against my lips before kissing me hard one last time.

When he pulled away, I was gasping. My limbs trembled with the spike of adrenaline and arousal. The absence of Liam's body against mine woke me up fully and with it came horror.

"Oh God," I groaned, pulling away from Kieran as I scrambled off my bed.

Kieran followed me, trying to stop me, but I wrenched away from him. "Liv, it's fine. Don't—"

"Shut up, Kieran!" I screeched. I spun in a circle on the carpet, trying to find a place where I could curl up and die from embarrassment. It was my room, but I didn't even think to make them leave.

A door crashed open in the hall before pounding feet sounded and my own door burst open. Luc stood in the doorway, light flooding in behind him. Kieran kneeled on the edge of the bed, a devastated look on his face. It was too much for me to deal with right now. I didn't want to hurt him, any of them, but that's what I was doing. Hurting them. And myself. There was no way I could be with all of them.

I shoved past Luc and fled, stumbling as I went and slammed into Flynn. I looked up at him in horror. His eyes met mine for a second. "What the fuck is going on?" he asked quietly. I started shaking my head, begging him not to ask.

"Nothing," Luc said, coming up behind us. "I've got it. Go back to bed. We'll talk later."

"No, we'll talk now," Flynn said heatedly. I stared at his chest, unable to meet his eyes. "She looks like she's about to cry. What the fuck did you idiots do?"

"You know what?" Luc barked, completely unlike himself. "Fuck this. Go deal with your brother. I've got her. You're probably freaking her out more."

"What's wrong with Kieran?" he demanded as Luc threw an arm around me and guided me down the hall. Two doors down, he opened his door and guided me inside without turning on the lights. I'd never been in here before, but his familiar scent all over the place started to calm me. Luc knew that I liked all of them. He wouldn't judge me.

Yelling started up, sounding like it came from my room. I clamped my hands over my ears, trying to block it all out while Luc guided me to his bed. He left me momentarily and music started up. It helped drown out the sound of arguing. The bed dipped for a second, followed by a cold rush of air before Luc pulled me down next to him and wrapped his arms around me.

"I'm sorry," I said, teeth chattering. "I don't know how it happened."

"There's nothing to be sorry for," he said. "Is this okay? Do you want your brother? We can call him." I shook my head no. No, definitely not after this.

"Don't let them fight over me," I said quickly. "I... It's not okay."

"Let them deal with it. This isn't on you, Doll. Just try to relax."

I didn't. I couldn't. Eventually the shouting did die down, but guilt ate at me. The illuminated clock on Luc's bedside table told me it was barely midnight when we came in. By two am, I was still wide awake. I was certain Luc had fallen asleep so when I tried to slip out of his arms to find something to do, I was caught by surprise when his arms locked around me and he spoke.

"Our first and only priority is always going to be our family. That includes you. Have no delusions about this. Everyone in this house has one goal in mind and that is keeping our family alive. Not even you could destroy it. You need to trust us to own up to our own mistakes and to fix them without making it about you." The anger in his voice stunned me. "Now, please get some sleep or I'll have Flynn put you into another coma. I'm sick of seeing the bags under your eyes."

I swallowed hard and lay back in his arms, saying nothing. Despite his threat I didn't fall asleep. It was impossible. But I did rest, even though I slept most of yesterday, and waited for the sun to come up.

CHAPTER 28

Sometime around dawn, I pulled myself carefully out of Luc's bed and ambled downstairs. I was tired after spending the entire night lost in my own thoughts.

I felt a bit stupid about my actions the last few days though not unjustified. But Luc wasn't wrong, and neither were the rest of them. They'd been telling me over and over to trust them and at every turn, when push came to shove, I thought of only how all of this was impacting me. While I did have guilt over how the guys would react to me liking all of them, the real underlying issue was that I was scared I would ruin what I had going here. Support, stability, love. They were such precious ideas that I'd let go of years ago. I was alive for the first time in years and it was tied to them.

After so long with having so little, I had finally started to get everything back. A family or the beginnings of one. People I could trust, vouched for by my brother and loved by Emma. Something I knew she didn't—hadn't—done well either.

I moved about the kitchen, searching through the cabinets for something to make for breakfast. Luc and Flynn always did the cooking, and while I didn't cook well, I could at least try.

That's really what I needed to do. Try. In everything. In a few short weeks, these people had done nothing but try for me. And I returned it all with attitude and distrust. That was going to change today. It took Luc's anger, the most playful of my new family, to jump start my brain. If this had been Emma, I never would have treated her this way.

I settled on scrambled eggs and toast since it was easy. Flynn walked into the kitchen as I was mixing the eggs and smiled at me sleepily. His hair was mussed, with his shorts slung low on his hips and without a shirt. I paused, drinking him in as he moved to the coffee pot.

"Morning, Princess. What are you doing?"

"Breakfast,' I muttered, turning away to hide my blush.

"Thanks," he said. "Do you want coffee?" I thought about it for a second and shook my head, setting the bowl down to add salt and pepper. The fridge opened behind me as Flynn rooted around inside. He came out with a bag of shredded cheese. "Add a cup of this. They'll love it."

I grinned at him, taking the bag. It dawned on me

how domestic and normal this was. Probably the most normal thing I'd done in weeks. I stared down at the beaten eggs, smiling to myself, lost in the feeling.

Arms snaked around my waist, pulling me back into a hard chest. Lips landed on my neck as Flynn's scent wrapped around me. "Seriously, Olivia, thank you for this." My heart skipped a beat as warmth spread through my chest. He let me go, leaving me bereft for a moment.

My hands trembled as I added cheese to the mixture and moved to the heating stove. Sound trickled down as the others roused, getting ready to start their day. Every few minutes, I peeked glances at Flynn who pretended not to notice.

Something sparked inside me, an intrusion that tugged at my mind. It was followed by a sense of dread that I was all too familiar with. His head snapped up suddenly, his cup of coffee frozen in front of his face.

"Flynn," I whispered. "I think someone's here."

"I know." He set his cup down then threw a hand into the air. Four balls of silver-blue fire sparked into existence and streaked out of the room.

"Who is it?" I asked, hoping he would know as I watched the unnatural fire leave the room. I wanted to learn how to do that.

"No one good. Stay by me," he demanded, pulling me into his side as we left the kitchen and moved to the front door. He peeked out the glass window at the top that I couldn't reach. I hated being so damn short. "There are four of them." He cocked his head to the side. "No, five. There's someone further back in the trees."

Footsteps pounded down the stairs moments before Luc and Ben joined us. I blinked at Luc for a moment, he was wearing only his boxer briefs, my mouth went dry and I tore my eyes away.

Flynn ran a hand roughly through his dark hair. "What are they waiting for? They're just standing there…"

More heavy footsteps signaled the arrival of Liam and Kieran. I glanced at them and did a double take. Liam had a pair of swords in each hand while Kieran hefted a crossbow. I'd never seen either of them with weapons before. Didn't even know we had weapons.

"What do you feel?" Luc asked, directing his question to Kieran.

Kieran sidled up to his brother to look out the window and cocked his head to the side. "Two elementals and three witches." Liam stiffened, his brown eyes growing dark as he glared at the door. Kieran's face took on a look of horror as he continued. "Blood magic. They've got someone's blood." He turned to me and grabbed my chin. "Close your eyes and find the line. Ben, check on Brooke."

"The what?" I asked, confused, reaching up to grasp his wrists.

"He means your tether to Vian," Luc explained. "Through the tether you can tell whether he's okay or not. In time, you'll be able to communicate through it."

"Fuck," Liam muttered. "We should have taught her that first instead of going directly into Arts."

My heart was already clenched in fear at the idea of my brother being hurt. I clutched at Kieran's hands on my face. "What am I looking for exactly?"

"Just close your eyes and think of him. Put your will behind it."

Immediately, I closed my eyes and pulled up a mental image of Octavian. Something purred in the back of my mind and wrapped around me. "Cat, help me," I whispered. He leapt forward grabbing the reigns of my will and showed me what I was looking for. In my head, a bright gold line appeared.

He is fine. Do not let the witches take you. Above all else.

Cat's awareness slipped away, and I opened my eyes. "Vian's fine," I told them firmly.

"So is Brooke," Ben said.

My guys let out a collective breath. An arm snaked around my waist as someone pressed their face into my neck. "We need a plan," Luc said, his words muffled in my hair.

"I don't see them just leaving. And I don't think they can get inside the house with us here," Flynn said.

"What if we Slipped out. They can't follow us," Ben suggested.

"Hell no," Liam replied angrily. "There are witches on our property and two of our own. I say we confront them. With Liv's raw power and our training, they'll be overwhelmed.

Flynn glared at him. "We don't want them to know how powerful she is! The whole point of hiding out was to control what the council knows."

Kieran put a hand on his brother's shoulder. "They're going to know eventually Flynn. We can't keep her hidden forever. Valek thinks they already know."

Who the hell was Valek? I wanted to ask, but it was so not the time. "Why don't you ask me what I want?" I said quietly. "Don't you think I should have a say?"

"That's not how this works, Doll. We all have to agree."

"Well no one ever asked me," I pointed out, trying to keep the heat out of my voice.

Ben sighed, hanging his head. "She's right. We didn't."

Flynn threw him a dark look. "No," he gritted out, turning his glare in my direction.

"Enough," Liam barked. "You can't control her and make her do what you want. It hasn't worked up until now and it's not going to."

I met Flynn's gaze and leveled him with one of my own. With my best effort, I smoothed my anger and tried to appeal to him. "If we run now, we're proving their point for them." He stared at me, his anger slowly changing to one of agony that ripped at my heart. He was afraid. I stepped into him and lowered my voice. The others could still hear us, but I had to believe them, that whatever this was between me and them wouldn't break our family. "I don't want to be afraid anymore. I've been afraid for so long. If we run now, I'm scared I won't ever stop."

His eyes closed. His forehead met mine, mingling our breath. His lips moved in silent words that I could feel against my own, like he was saying a prayer. When he pulled back and opened his eyes, they slipped over my shoulder, staring at each of the guys in turn.

"Fuck yes," Liam said, a scary amount of glee in his tone.

"We go out together," Kieran said. "Ben, did you tell Brooke?"

"Already done. She went to wake our families. They should be here soon."

"Then let's go out and make our stand," Luc said softly. He stepped forward, linking hands with me. Flynn grabbed the other one, looking down at me before he pulled open the door and we stepped onto the porch.

Four cloaked men—at least I thought they were men judging by their frames—stood in a line against the trees in the deeply shaded morning light. Someone flipped on the porch bulb, so that it illuminated their faces. It revealed the fifth person who was bound and gagged. Payton's eyes glittered with unshed tears. I gasped taking in her ragged appearance. I tore my eyes off her scanning the other faces and my vision tunneled on Evan standing in between two men. My ears started to ring.

Dimly, I realized that someone was speaking, but words didn't reach me. A rage so heavy settled over me, amplifying my own at the disgusting smirk that sat on his face. He was here for me and he thought he had me. But he didn't know – likely none of them did – that I wasn't alone. Emma's hatred and grief swirled within me at the sight of her murderer.

"Livvy," someone called, breaking through the haze, but we ignored them. The air around us grew thick, practically crackling. We pulled on it, filling us with power. With barely a flick of my wrist, the ropes binding Payton disintegrated. She slumped toward the ground, pulling off her gag. My wrist flicked again, and she rippled out of existence, sending her home. Satisfied she would be safe, my other hand came up, clenched into a fist. Something invisible was within my grasp and I yanked it back toward myself. Evan fell forward and slid against the ground, coming to rest just a few feet from me.

"You think I would let you touch her. After everything you did," the words came from me except it wasn't my voice and I wasn't the one controlling my mouth. In fact, it had been several confusing seconds before I realized that my actions weren't entirely my own. Emma's will pressed against mine, taking control from me. I fought with her, pushing back. I didn't know what she was going to do, but I could feel how angry she was, how much she wanted him to die.

Emma shoved back at me before she crouched down, placing her hands on the grass and started to draw energy from the earth. The ground beneath our feet rumbled with the speed in which she gathered it. My own anger was replaced with fear as everything around us turned black. A chasm opened before us, the earth sounding dry and brittle as it ripped apart from itself. The men in front of us tumbled to the dead grass as the earth shook. "None of you will ever touch another soul again," Emma screamed.

With her rage, fire leapt into existence from nothing. The ground started to crumble. Trees burned, reduced to ash in seconds, blown away by a fierce wind that ripped at our skin.

Emma, please, I begged her, trying again to exert my control. It was my body, my mind but she had all the power.

Someone growled and I felt Cat prowling somewhere close by. Mentally, I reached for him. What little ground I'd regained in my body fell away. In front of me, the ground opened wider and Evan sank between the cracks, screaming. There was blood on his mouth. His face was twisted in agony. I almost felt bad for him. *Almost.*

I was powerless to stop Emma.

Cat, I pleaded. I needed his help, but I couldn't quite reach him. Emma's anger morphed into elation, deranged and lustful for Evan's blood. So unlike the girl I knew. The Emma I loved was never cruel. Fierce? Yes. Protective? Always. But never crazed. It took everything in me not to give in, to not disappear underneath her.

The ground heaved again as the cracks in it shifted. I realized just as there was a sickening crunch what Emma meant to do. Evan screamed again, his eyes practically bugging out of his head as he was crushed by the earth.

Grab hold. The whole place is unstable, Cat growled to me. I reached for him with my mind again, desperate to escape the scene in front of me. I wanted to be sick or at the very least, close my eyes. I couldn't understand how Evan was even still alive. The men who had come with him fled, leaving him sticking part way out of the ground like a macabre lawn ornament.

Something grabbed hold of me, like a lasso, pulling me into the Thorns. The boil of emotions dripped away quickly, and I was in control of myself again. Underneath the surface, Emma's raw agony needled at me and I sobbed, both in relief and horror.

Release her, quickly! Cat said to me.

"Olivia," Flynn yelled, appearing at my side. He latched onto my arm and pulled me into him. The others appeared around us. Liam stared in disbelief at the lynx who paced in front of us, his tail whipping around in agitation.

Don't just stare, you stupid boys. Help her before it's too late.

"Is that…" Ben breathed.

I sagged in Flynn's arms, feeling stripped from the

inside out. "I can't help her," I sobbed. "I don't know how."

Cat darted forward, weaving around my legs and Flynn's. *Just let go,* he purred. *Relax and let her go.*

I tried to calm myself, but I couldn't seem to catch my breath. Not when all I could feel was how tortured she was. How twisted she'd become in a matter of moments.

Kieran stepped into me, wrapping his arms around me and his brother. One of his hands looped around to cling to my neck, stinging me with that all too familiar electricity that came with his healing. Except instead of refilling me, he was drawing from me.

No. Emma surged forward again. She tried to tear away from him, but he held us firmly in place with the help of Flynn. She fought harder, determined not to let this happen. Internally I screamed, ferally clawing at her will. I had to stop her. She would hurt them. I couldn't let that happen. She jerked in their arms, distracted by me. I lunged forward and pushed her back before I resurfaced.

Distance. I needed distance from them. I thrashed as much as I could. Another body pressed into my back, effectively pinning me against Flynn's front.

"Let me go!" I screamed, tears streaming down my face.

"Guys," Luc shouted in my ear. "We need help. She's fighting it."

"Kitten, let her go!"

"I'm try—" I choked on my own screams. Something cracked inside of me and we listed sideways. We crashed into the ground and rolled. The impact sent me sprawling. A body landed on top of mine and my head smacked into the earth, filling my vision with stars. Great, gasping breaths heaved in and out of me. I blinked a few times, trying to see past the pain in my head.

It took me a few seconds, listening to the groans of my guys all around me. Luc pushed himself up off me and stared down. "Doll?" His brown eyes scanned my face. "Are you alright?"

No. No I wasn't… Emma was gone. I was empty as the only thing that rolled around inside me was myself. I stared up, past his head at the green sky above us.

"Umm, guys. We have a problem." Kieran appeared overhead, also looking up at the sky where not one, but two suns were brightly shining.

*Oh shit…*was all I could manage to think before everything went black.

EPILOGUE

FLYNN

"Anyone have any idea where we are?" Kieran asked. He sat with Olivia in his lap. Instead of the jealousy I normally felt whenever one of them touched her, there was nothing except gratefulness. When she'd passed out, most of us lost our shit, completely forgetting everything else. It was scary how pale she looked. Normally, she was all cream and roses. I could see the blue veins in her neck, pulsing too hard, putting strain on her heart.

I wasn't sure what happened in the yard. One minute, she'd been next to me and in the next, she was destroying everything around her, pulling the life out of everything she could reach, even us. We'd just barely managed to shield ourselves before the house collapsed.

And now, she was unconscious. Kieran was doing his best to refill her spent energy, but it would take hours to get her back to normal. We'd exhausted ourselves in the Thorns.

I chewed on the inside of my lip, waiting for someone to start making suggestions. Me? I had no clue where we were. It certainly wasn't the Thorns, but it wasn't our earth either. That much was clear. This place looked sickly. We were in some sort of meadow of tall yellowed grass. In the distance, I could see trees, but they were gnarled and twisted. My natural art begged to help, but I couldn't give into it. This wasn't our world. There was no telling what domino effect could happen if we used our powers here, upsetting its balance.

"I don't think that's going to be our biggest problem," Luc said quietly, his eyes downcast.

Liam snorted, throwing a rare glare in his brother's direction. "Really? Because I'm pretty sure this takes priority."

Luc took a steadying breath, a fist clenched at his side. I knew what he was going to say before he said it. "You didn't see her face. How devastated she was."

I nodded. Yep. I'd seen it, in the Thorns. Olivia had brought us here, out of desperation and there was no doubt in my mind that we needed her to get back. There was no telling what state she would be in when she woke up. She'd looked utterly destroyed.

I snorted. All the progress she'd made in the last few weeks. Pushing past her own fears. Taking every hit the universe threw at her. It was ruined in just a few minutes. She'd looked like she had when she arrived, covered in scrapes and ash, practically emaciated, screaming in agony after what she'd witnessed. It was enough to chill my own blood and I'd barely known her then. What would she be like now? It would kill her to know Emma's fate after tapping into her energy. Hell, I got high off the exchanges between us and they were tiny in comparison. Olivia was strong in a lot of ways, several she didn't even realize, but she was weak in others. Her trust in people was hard earned. She feared what they could do to her. But what she hated most? Hurting others.

"You think it's funny?" Ben asked, giving me an incredulous look.

"No, I don't," I replied. "I'm pissed off, actually. We never should have let the council control us. We're adults in every way, yet we stupidly let them dictate what to do with our own circle." I pushed off the ground and started pacing. The more I thought about it, the angrier I got. "We allowed her to suffer. Her and Emma, based on flimsy reasons from the council. Even though we knew it was wrong. We hurt our fucking family—" I broke off, too frustrated to continue.

Liam stood up and stopped me with a hand. "It wasn't just you, man. We all went along with it."

I shoved his hand away, not wanting his comfort. Angry tears gathered in the corners of my eyes. "What if our mother had left you and Luc where she found you? Huh? Would that have been okay?" He shook his head at me, trying to cut me off. I shoved at him before he could speak. "No. Really think about it! That's what we did to them both. If we'd done it how we wanted, Emma would be alive. Olivia would have been safe. We could have made it work."

"Stop," Ben said, stepping between us. "Stop torturing yourself."

"How?" I asked, tugging at my hair. I needed the pain. Deserved it. It was the only thing keeping me sane.

Ignoring my question, he wrapped his arms around me, crushing me to him. Quietly, he spoke in my ear. "We all did this. And we'll all fix it. Don't take this on yourself. I know you keep saying 'we', but we all know you mean you."

"If my father were still here, he would have done the right thing. He would ha—"

"But he's not and we did the best we could with the options we had."

Olivia made a small sound which drew all our attention. In seconds, I was next to her in Kieran's arms as her eyes opened, revealing the green pools that always drew my attention whenever she was near. So quickly, she'd become everything to us. And I hated her for it. But I loved her for it too.

She stared up at me blankly, and finally I could breathe deeply again. Her eyes were vacant, but the torture I'd seen in them before was gone. My heart sparked with hope as I smiled down at her. It didn't matter how broken she was. I—we—would always be there to help put her back together.

To be continued...

AFTERWORD

Thank you so much for reading my book. I hope you enjoyed it and that you do not kill me for that cliffhanger. I tried to soften it as much as I could. I promise that Olivia and her harem will not leave you hanging for long. In fact, I'm pretty sure my beta team is already preparing a prison to lock me in. They're just as upset about the ending as you probably are. That said, would you please consider leaving a review? It would really help tell other potential readers if this book is for them.

NOTE FROM THE AUTHOR

As always, there are so many people to thank. An endless list, really. But I'll settle for the most important ones.

To my Husband, Alex - Your support and understanding
while writing this mean the world to me. Thank you for reminding me to eat, letting me complain about issues that came up, and for just being everything I could hope for in a partner. You're the best Snorkface that's ever existed. Yep. I said Snorkface.

To my Sharks – You're the best cheerleaders a person could ask for. From long days of writing, to building up my spirits, and most importantly, keeping me laughing.

To M – Woman… this book would not be half of

what it is without you. Thank you for fighting so hard for every word, phrase, and idea. You helped Olivia come alive in more ways than I expected. You revamped my excitement, brought out my fight, and didn't let me give up. I'm so thankful and grateful. I went into this looking for a content editor and walked away with someone I consider a wonderful friend that I'm never letting go of.

To Lee – Thanks for the life experience, you jerk. I love you. Even if you did electrocute me when we were kids.

To my betas – Fuck ladies. Your feedback warms my heart. To watch you all fall head over heels in love with these characters was such a joy. Thank you for being honest, looking past the typos, and for using your free time to make this the best book it could possibly be.

To B – Yeah, you made the list. Of course, you did. It was cute how you kept freaking out about giving me advice, but seriously, thank you. It's not every day that someone offers it so freely. But getting to sit with you in skype as you read, listening to you laugh out loud, or grow quiet. It was everything. It helped me swell with confidence. But also, thank you for believing in my story enough to tell others. Now, let's go drown readers in tears, yeah?

To Britt – Yep, you get to proof your own thank you. But you knew that already. Thank you for your patience while waiting to get your hands on this book. I hope you found it worth the wait. Now hurry up and tell me what you think of it, dammit!

To my readers – Again, thank you. Thank you. Thank you. I will never be able to say it enough. Thank you for reading my words. For reviews. For letting me distract you. Entertain you. I write for me, but getting to share it with you, that's the real gift.

ABOUT THE AUTHOR

Chrissy Jaye is an author freshly returned from Narnia. She rides on a white steed as she battles monsters and finds new love in fantasy lands (don't tell her husband).

On the rare occasions she spends time in reality, she raises her brood, stalks other authors and consumes copious amounts of coffee.

Links and Social Media
Website: https://www.chrissyjayeauthor.com/
Facebook: https://www.facebook.com/Chrissy.Jaye.us
Reader Group: https://www.facebook.com/groups/376865549524306/
Amazon: https://www.amazon.com/Chrissy-Jaye/e/B07HFKXZZ6
Bookbub: https://www.bookbub.com/authors/chrissy-jaye
Goodreads: https://www.goodreads.com/ChrissyJaye

ALSO BY CHRISSY JAYE

Hungry for More: A Harem of Recipes

Shades Beneath

Printed in Great Britain
by Amazon

22129733R00179